For a Few Pennies More

Trevor Norton

Copyright © Trevor Norton 2021

All rights reserved.

Trevor Norton has asserted his right under the Copyright, Designs and Patent Act, 1988 to be identified as the author of this work.

In order to protect the many colourful characters portrayed in this intriguing true story, all names, including place names, wherever possible, have been changed.

Dedication

I would like to dedicate this book to the memory of my good friend Alan Brunsdon who was always very supportive, rest in peace mate.

Acknowledgements

Thanks go to Paul Greenslade, a golfing buddy, who was my early spell checker, and most savage critic.

Thanks also go to all the colourful characters portrayed in this book, because without them the book wouldn't exist.

Prologue

From the high, mythical ivory tower to the sad and lonely scrapheap of life, Charles Henry's elder brother, businessman Albert Henry, well-known locally for being a spiteful, arrogant bully, had reached the age of 92. Having lost his faithful wife, Jess, of 70 years, he was now on his own. He was no longer able to drive his car or look after himself or his luxurious home.

Incontinent and full of remorse, he was sat slumped in a wheelchair of the last chance saloon. The exclusive residential nursing home catered solely for the very wealthy members of society, who had given way to dementia, Alzheimer's, or who had just simply succumbed to the frailty of old age.

It was the latter for Albert Henry, for his strong mind, firmly entrenched in the past, was still very active. But instead of blissfully reminiscing a long and happy lifetime, he was in utter torment; his own mind being the tormenter!

Thinking it was high time they paid him a visit, Charles and his wife made the long trek up from Dorset to see him. After signing in at the reception desk, they were both granted access through the sturdy locked doors of the secure nursing home. From there, they were escorted down the long corridor and into the bright and airy last chance saloon [communal lounge], where they saw some of the not-so-bright and airy inmates slumped in wheelchairs, their eyes glazed over, and their mouths open and dribbling.

'Age shall not weary them, nor the years condemn,' whispered Charles under his breath, while looking around for Albert.

'There he is, asleep, over by the window,' said the care worker, pointing him out.

'Thanks,' said Charles walking over. He gently tapped him on the arm to stir him.

'I'll have tea please, Miss,' said Albert in a low feeble whisper, thinking that Charles was the carer dishing out the morning refreshments.

'Sorry, Burt. You missed tea this morning,' replied Charles cheerfully, pulling his leg. Albert focused his sad weary eyes, and when he realised who was stood before him, a tear welled up and his bottom lip began to tremble.

'Hey, come on, Burt. Enough of that, mate. We've come to cheer you up. How are you, you old bugger?'

He cleared the throat that had once roared with menace, and his voice shook, as he fought back the tears that were now dripping off his chin.

'This is not me, Chas,' he sobbed. 'I had it all once, but look at me now. Who'd ever have thought I'd end up in a place like this, pissing and shitting my pants every five minutes? What's it all about, eh? You strive to work and worry all your bloody life. And for what?'

Knowing they wanted some privacy, one of the nursing staff directed them into a small room, whereby Albert broke down completely and began to pour his troubled heart out.

'I've had enough, Chas. I really have. The world has changed and it's not a nice place anymore. Nothing is the same. I just want to die,' he blubbered. 'I've even contemplated taking a one-way holiday to Switzerland.'

'And?' said Charley.

Albert groaned and wiped away his tears.

'It's the bloody taxman,' he grumbled.

'The taxman?' joked Charley, trying to lift his spirits. 'You're not thinking about taking him along as well, are you?'

Albert gave a weary smile. 'No. I'd only take him if he'd have the first injection. Not satisfied with robbing me all my life, the bastard wants to do it when I die as well. The thought of him taking half my money when I go is enough to make me want to live forever.'

'Nothing changes, Burt, does it? Don't let money rule you, mate. Take the holiday if you really want to. Your kids are more than capable. Let them worry about the taxman when you've fallen off the perch. Count your blessings: you've got plenty of money and you're well looked after here, so just sit back and enjoy life.'

'Enjoy? Bloody enjoy? It's all right for you to talk, Chas. You're 17 years younger than me. All I do is sit here day after day, alongside all these brain-dead people – this bloody nappy wrapped around me arse – looking back over me life. And I don't like what I see. What a bloody terrible bastard I was to everybody. If only I could turn the clock back. Look at the appalling way I treated my Jess. It was unforgivable, totally bloody unforgivable. Every time I close my eyes, I can see her poor sad face looking back at me. I'd give every penny I have just to spend one more hour with her.'

'And if that were possible, Burt, what would you do with that hour?' asked Charley.

'I'd scoop her up and hold her tight in my arms and tell her how very sorry I am,' he snivelled. 'She was a lovely lady, and I didn't deserve her. How she ever put up with me all those years I'll never know.'

Truly repentant, Albert was deeply disturbed by his painful memories. It was like his brain was switched to self-destruct because it was continuously playing back vivid recordings of the way he had conducted himself through his life. It was as though

Judgement Day had arrived for the big man, and, ironically, he was his own judge and jury!

'Unfortunately,' said Charley, listening to Albert's sincere heartfelt confessions, 'we don't get a dummy run at it, mate. Life is for real, and we can't go back and change it. If we could, everybody would be going back each week to change their lottery ticket.'

There was no hiding the fact that dominance and money had been Albert's driving force. In business, he was known as "Mr Angry". To his siblings, he was called "Happy", all of them having fallen out with him on many occasions over the years. The plain fact is, there weren't many people out there who had a good word to say about him other than that he had worked very hard in order to build his successful business. The trouble was, he trod on so many people along the way. For when Albert Henry was the king of the castle, everyone else was considered the dirty rascal.

However, Charley was so moved by Albert's tearful end-of-life revelations that he took a long hard look in the mirror and began to contemplate his own life, which started in 1944, when Adolf Hitler unleashed his new frightening terror weapon, the doodlebug, on the UK. The pilotless V-1 flying bombs rained down indiscriminately over London, England, destroying buildings and killing many people.

From humble beginnings, born to working-class parents, Charles Henry drew his first breath alongside the River Thames in London to the sound of air-raid sirens wailing, the deep sinister drone of the doodlebugs overhead, devastating earth-shattering explosions, fire engine bells, and Vera Lynn singing 'We'll Meet Again'.

Charles Henry was fourth in the pecking order of five siblings.

Chapter 1

※

1955

The ravages of the Second World War lay evident across the entire country. Many people were still suffering hardships, making do with clothes from jumble sales or wearing hand-me-downs.

News events of that year:

The Right Honourable Sir Winston Churchill was superseded as the UK Prime Minister by Sir Anthony Eden. Albert Einstein died. Bill Haley was rabble-rousing and rocking around the clock. Teddy Boys were rebelling the system. And Charles Henry failed his 11+ exam!

And so it came to pass that Charley's basic education was doomed to that of East Street, a lively, tough, overcrowded boy's secondary modern state school in South East London. Forget the pencil cases, satchels and the like: a gum-shield, clenched fist and a thick magazine was the kit best befitting that school.

'What about the schoolteachers?' cried Charley's younger brother, knowing that he was soon to follow in his footsteps.

'I was talkin about the teachers,' replied Charley, devilishly winding Alan up.

'Yeah yeah, ha ha. Very funny. Look at me. I can't stop laughing,' said Alan, forcing a grin, recalling all the wild exaggerated tales of intimation and bullying he'd heard from other lads fearful of going to that infamous school.

'Oh, you'll be all right, Al,' said Charley, passing on his survival tactics from brother Reggie, the next one up the pecking order. 'You only get picked on if they think you won't fight back. Swagger, curl your lip a bit. That should do it.'

Swallowing hard, Alan returned a lukewarm smile before questioning the need for the magazine.

'Hmm. Trust me, boy,' said Charley grimacing. 'You don't want to go to that school without one. You'll end up regretting it for the rest of your life,' he warned sternly.

'But why?' asked Alan, trying to understand so as to prepare himself properly.

'Why? Cos you need it to protect yourself against the old Bum Tickler.'

Alan gasped with horror. 'Bum Tickler?' he cried, with eyes bulging. 'Who the bloody hell's the Bum Tickler, then?'

Charley laughed. 'No, not *who*. It – the name all the kids call the huge gym slipper belonging to "Touch Your Toes Thomson", our old English teacher.'

Alan took a deep breath and sighed with relief. 'Shoo. I thought for a minute you were talking about some dirty old perv in a white mackintosh with a sticky bag of sweets.'

Charley frowned. 'White mackintosh?' he repeated. 'Well, as it so happens, Al, Thomson does wear a white raincoat. But then, in fairness, he's never offered me a sticky sweet before. That's not to say he won't offer you one, though.'

'I wouldn't take it if he did,' said Alan, looking as though he was about to throw up at the very thought. 'I'd tell him just where to stick it.'

'Hmm,' Charley frowned again. 'Stick it. I've seen lots of sweets stuck to the underside of desk lids!'

'Oh shit, have you?' said Alan, screwing his face up, imagining the raincoat and sticky sweets looming.

Like his slipper, Thomson was enormous, obese even, and he waddled around the classroom like a blubbery walrus on heat. His approach to the subject of English was to give the kids in his charge ten words to learn over the weekend, followed by a test on Monday morning. Seven or more spelling mistakes, and Thomson would flog his pupils mercilessly in front of the entire class.

Charley's first experience of Thomson's Victorian teaching methods was seeing the evil grin creep across his glum-looking face, moments before pulling the old Bum Tickler [the size 12 slipper] from the bottom drawer of his desk.

Gasps of astonishment filled every corner of the classroom.

'Right. As your names are called,' growled Thomson in a deep stern voice of authority, 'make your way out here, and prepare yourselves.'

Swallowing hard, Charley, together with eight of his young classmates, got up and filed out front, as ordered. Whilst they all stood there fretting, Thomson casually walked round to the front of his desk and began to swipe hard and fast at the air with the slipper.

The spine-chilling whooshing passing so quickly through the air was a step too far for one lad.

'Fuck this for a game of soldiers,' he cried, making a desperate dash for the door. Thomson tried to stop him, of course, but the lad was too fast for the big man. By the time he got to the door, the lad was already zipping quickly through the school gates, screaming his head off.

'Hmm, the one that got away,' muttered Thomson under his breath, as he shuffled back to press on with the punishment. 'Firstly,' he said, flexing the slipper in torment, 'I would like you all to remove the dirty magazines from the seat of your pants, and then stack them nice and neatly on my desk.'

Heavy sighs and groans of protest followed, as the magazines began to pile up.

Chancing his arm, Joe, one of Charley's classmates, hollered from the safety of the back of the room. 'I say, Sir, are you going to read them later?'

Laughter, jeers, taunts, and even some breaking wind, were heard from other classmates anxious to remonstrate their thoughts on the matter.

'I didn't hear that, Green,' replied Thomson.

Standing up and bellowing through cupped hands, Joe repeated his cheeky remark.

Whenever the opportunity presented itself, most of the kids in Charley's class would try and push the boundaries. But then Thomson was a brutal old hand and used to dealing with kids who thought they knew it all.

'You sit down now, Green. Any more lip from you, and you'll be joining the others out here. As for the rest of you louts, you can all shut up as well.'

Turning to deal with the kids awaiting the beating, a loud raspberry of rebellion reverberated the room, which caused spontaneous belly laughter once again.

'Anymore of that and you'll all be on detention. Every night for a week.'

Stood alongside Charley in the line-up was his best mate, Benny Benson, a lad he'd known since he was five years old. Whispering nervously from the corner of his mouth, Benny asked Charley if he still had his magazine.

'Bloody right I have, Ben. You seen the size of that blinking slipper?'

'Yeah, that's why I still got mine, Chas,' said Benny, smiling apprehensively.

Charley was the first to be ordered to bend over and touch his toes. As he did so, an eerie hush came over the class. Charley became tense and held his breath, waiting for the first wallop. But then Thomson hesitated before circling Charley slowly, with his eyes fixed firmly on his bum. After a nerve-racking minute or two, Thomson tapped Charley on his shoulder with the slipper.

'Oh shit,' thought Charley, looking up. 'He's only going to offer me one of those sticky sweets to soften the blow!'

'Aren't you forgetting something, Henry?' asked Thomson, pointing his slipper towards his desk.

'Forgetting, Sir?' repeated Charley Henry, standing up and frowning his ignorance.

'Magazine!' barked Thomson.

'Oh, that,' replied Charley on a sharp intake of breath. 'I thought you asked for dirty ones only, Sir ... only, mine's not dirty. It's a gardening mag. Look,' he said, pulling it from the seat of his pants.

A group snigger echoed the classroom. Even Thomson himself gave a nauseating smile before saying, 'Dirty enough, Henry. You plant things in dirt, don't you? Go on. On my desk with the others.'

Before commencing with the punishment, Terrible Thomson took time out to casually sit on the corner of his desk and explain to the class how much more it was going to hurt him than those young lads awaiting the beating.

'Er, you wouldn't like to bet on that, Sir, would you?' asked Benny Benson politely, while wriggling to disguise his own magazine as a ruffled shirt tail.

'I don't bet, Benson,' said Thomson, pointing to the pile of magazines on his desk. 'I *know*. So, we'll have your one as well, shall we?'

As Benny reluctantly put his magazine on the pile, Jonesy bent over and farted thunderously. There were roars of laughter – they all knew it was a fart of protest.

Shouting over the furore, Thomson asked Jonesy if he needed the toilet.

'Er, yes, Sir. I think I do after that,' he replied, holding his bum, as he dashed from the room.

Another more nervous kid peed his pants the moment he bent over.

Every week Charley Henry was out there touching his toes. Only, instead of the magazine for protection, some of his mates had lent him their gym shorts to wear under his trousers. As time went on, Charley was offered more and more shorts from other kids in the class. One day, he waddled out wearing so many pairs of shorts that he could hardly do up his trousers.

'Hmm, you seem to have gained a lot of weight just recently, Henry,' said Thomson, casting a suspicious eye over Charley's enormous bum. 'Perhaps you need more exercise?'

'Er, yes, Sir,' replied Charley, 'I do. I'll start first thing tomorrow morning, Sir.'

Thomson smiled caustically. 'No, no. You'll start right here and now,' he said.

'What, like jogging on the spot, Sir?' asked Charley in preparation.

'No. You can start by taking off some of those gym shorts you're wearing.'

Nowadays, they call Charley's problem dyslexia; but all those years ago, there was no excuse to hide behind. You were just labelled a dummy and then referred to as illiterate, which, for Charley Henry, was not only shameful but deeply humiliating.

Four years later, in the run-up to Christmas 1959, the closing days of Charley's schooldays, his cane-happy form master, "Hold Your Hand Out Hobson", went through the motions that were designed to encourage and prepare the pupils in his charge for employment in the outside world.

'I suppose it's a silly question,' he said rolling his eyes and yawning, as though he was totally wasting his time, 'but I'm going to ask it anyway. Do any of you unteachable louts know what it is you're going to do for a living yet?'

'Yeah,' hollered big Frankie Morrison, confident that within a few short hours he would be free from school and, as he hoped, the entire system as well. 'I'm going to be a bank robber, Sir.' Laughter filled the classroom.

'That's just bloody typical of you, Morrison. God only knows what will happen to the country when you lot hit the job market,' he said, sighing. 'And as far as you're concerned, Henry,' he said, wagging his forefinger, 'you can't even spell your own name yet. You haven't got enough brain cells to become a road sweeper even.'

'And what's wrong with sweeping the roads, Sir?' asked Charley, in defiance.

'Nothing. In fact, it's a very important job,' said Hobson, 'but unfortunately you're too stupid to do it.'

Charley was incensed.

'HIM call ME stupid?' thought Charley. 'The chain-smoking manic depressive who hated kids? The one who would light up a king-size cigarette in the classroom and leave it smouldering in the ashtray whilst he turned his back on us, the pupils of Lower 4C, to write on the blackboard? More often than not, when he turned back to pick up his fag from the ashtray, he found only a tiny dog-end. It was almost as though he had a problem understanding why the cigarette had diminished so quickly. Anyone else would have questioned the smile on our faces, or the presence of so many smoke rings hovering above our heads.'

Charley Henry may have been a bit naïve that Christmas when he left school aged 15 years old, but he certainly wasn't stupid. He just couldn't write or spell properly. That was all.

Walking out through the school gates for the last time, Charley vowed to himself that nobody was ever going to beat him again, with a slipper, stick or anything else for that matter. However, when looking back through the eyes of wisdom, Charley did admit that he, and most of his classmates, deserved all they got from the teachers for the way they rebelled.

Though rebellious they may have been, like all the kids of Charley's generation – rich, poor, good, bad or indifferent – they all had a massive respect for those who had fought and died for their freedom during the Second World War, which was still very raw in people's hearts. Every kid bar none in that school, no matter how hard-up their family was, always bought, and proudly wore, a poppy in the weeks leading up to Remembrance Day.

As for getting a job, Charley had no immediate thoughts about that, because he was lucky enough to have a good solid roof over his head, a dry bed to sleep in, and there was always food on the table. Besides, he was far too busy enjoying his newfound freedom with his mates to worry about such things. But then Charley's father, a tough man, who came up the hard way, one who had survived two World Wars, was soon to jump on his case and point him in the right direction.

'You're a man now, Charley,' said his father, asserting his authority, 'and it's time for you to stand on your own two feet. From now on, you pay your own way in this world. Now, get out there and find yourself a job or you'll end up in the workhouse!'

'The workhouse?' repeated Charley, frowning respectfully so as not to challenge him. 'But the workhouse closed down when I was a young kid, Dad...'

'You know what I mean,' he hollered. 'Just get on your bike and find a job. Better still, find one that teaches you a trade ... before it's too late.'

Charley wasn't the only one getting grief from his parents. Most of his mates were as well. Some had even left home because of it. One or two were even slung out by their less-caring parents to fend for themselves – old Smithy for one. He had no choice but to live in

"Cardboard City", under a park bench. He spent most days siting on the pavement by shop doorways, with a dog on a bit of string, begging. Charley was soon to realise that without the continued support of his parents, he had no means of providing for himself. And so, with no wish to join old Smithy, he did what his dad suggested and found a job that gave him a two-week trial as a trainee motor mechanic, for which he was paid the paltry sum of £1/8s/6d a week. His father was pleased that Charley had taken responsibility and acted on his advice. As a reward, he bought Charley a huge pair of second-hand hobnail boots that he saw advertised on a card in the newsagent's window.

'There you are, boy,' said his old dad with a cheery smile of encouragement, holding the old-fashioned things aloft by the frayed string that had been used as laces. 'A good stout pair of boots to start off your working life.'

'You've got to be kidding me,' thought Charley, *cringing at the thought of actually wearing them.*

'Well, don't just thank me, boy,' said Charley's dad, still holding them out.

Reaching out and clasping hold of the string, Charley returned a cheesy grin of appreciation for the unwanted gift.

'You be sure to give 'em a good coat of Dubbin,' added his dad, thrusting the tin towards Charley, as though it were a magic formula, 'and they will last you a lifetime.'

'A lifetime? Shit!' thought Charley. *'My poor size 8 feet swallowed up by those humongous antiquated size 11 boots, with all the hallmarks of two or more generations of owners.'*

It was now the start of the swinging sixties, and Charley didn't want to be seen striding along the road in broad daylight wearing battle-weary First World War army boots bristling with metal studs. In the dark, yeah maybe, because any would-be attacker hearing the sound of those boots crunching on the ground would think it was a whole regiment on the move. What a dilemma he faced. How could he possibly reject them knowing that his old dad would have given all he had to own such a pair of strong boots when he left school in the 1920s.

'Look, Dad,' said Charley, trying to be diplomatic so as not to offend, 'I, er, I don't mean to sound ungrateful or anything, but as much as I like 'em and all that, I'll never be able to handle 'em, cos my toes only reach half way up the boot. Look.' He struggled to get his foot off the ground.

'Oh, don't you worry about that, boy,' replied his father, trying to reassure him. 'Once you start work, your feet will soon grow into 'em. But until then, you just stuff 'em with old newspaper until they fit. You can always take a bit out as your feet get bigger.'

'Ah yeah, but what about the momentum the boots would generate descending steep hills?' asked Charley trying to sound technical. 'How will I control that then?'

'You don't, boy,' replied his old dad, smiling. 'It's called free energy. Just go with it, and you'll get to work much quicker.'

'Ah yeah, but what about going uphill then?'

'That's all right,' his father retorted. 'It'll build your leg muscles up. After a couple of weeks, you'll have all the strength and stamina you require to run up the hills.'

Charley Henry had enormous respect for his father. He also knew he wasn't a man to argue with. "Make do and mend" were the words of his generation, and so Charley had to do the same – at least until he could afford to buy his own boots, that is.

Having completed his two-week trial period covered in smelly black car undersealing compound, Charley was called into the office and offered a full apprenticeship to qualify as a motor mechanic. They informed him that he would, as part of the apprenticeship, have to attend technical college one day a week. Charley broke out into a cold sweat. The thought of going back to school repulsed him. All that spelling and writing: he just couldn't hack it. And so he turned the apprenticeship down and left the job altogether.

Charley was left with two choices: find a bit of string and a scruffy dog and join Smithy in Cardboard City, or go to the Labour Exchange to see if they had any jobs going.

No contest: Charley opted for the latter. Only when he got there, he was surprised to find a long queue of people trailing right back out into the street.

'Bloody hell,' said Charley to a tough-looking character at the end of the queue, 'are they giving away free money or something?'

'You taking the fucking piss, boy?' the grubby unshaven chap scowled, as though Charley had implied he was a scrounger.

'Who, me? 'Nah', not me, mate,' replied Charley with a forced grin, trying to defuse things. 'This is my first time down 'ere and I wasn't expecting to see the place so busy, that's all.'

The scruffy fella grunted, coughed and spat on the ground in front of Charley. Although Charley was grossly offended, he thought it best not to show any emotion, so he just swallowed hard and thought what a horrible lowlife git the bloke was.

'If you must know, boy, it's payday, and we're all 'ere to collect our dole money – which we're entitled to, of course,' he added, raising his voice as if to justify taking the money each week.

'Now, if you want to get your hands on some of that lovely lolly you was gobbing about just now, tell 'em you ain't got no job, and they might even take pity on you and give you some money.'

When Charley finally got to the counter, he was confronted by a formidable stone-faced woman. She glared at him like a ferocious mad dog on heat.

'Because you left your previous employment of your own volition,' she barked, rattling the grill that separated them, 'you're not entitled to any dole money.'

'Oh, shit,' Charley said under his breath. *'That's all I need.'*

'What about a lame dog and a bit of string then?' he asked, trying to lighten her mood.

'Try the dogs' home,' she woofed heartlessly.

'A bit of string, maybe?' retorted Charley, raising his eyebrows and smiling.

'Next!' she hollered, telling him to clear off.

With his hopes dashed, Charley left that grim unforgiving place feeling very dejected; his pockets empty. As he dragged his antiquated boots, with his shoulders slumped and his head down, he bumped into Big Frankie, Butch, Buster, BJ and John, some of his old classmates. Unlike Charley, they were all in high spirits: their pockets were bulging with cash. As well as their new denim jeans and James Dean leather jackets, they were all wearing the new fashionable Doc Martin boots – "bovver boots", as they became known.

'Silent and lightweight,' said Butch, showing off their versatility by dancing on the spot like a ballerina.

'Don't forget deadly and easy to use,' added BJ, with an outlandish grin.

'Yeah, like Butch just said, Chas, they got us out of many a scrape,' said Big Frankie Morrison, standing tall and waving a few quid in Charley's face.

'Thirty bob a pair they cost us,' he bragged. 'Anyway, enough about our tasty boots, Chas, you look a bit drained, mate. Must be those humongous demolition wrecking balls on your feet sapping your strength.'

'What, these fine family heirlooms?' replied Charley flippantly, lifting a foot off the ground, as though he was proud to show his boots off. 'They've got real sentimental value these have, Frank, and no amount of money could ever force me to part with 'em either.'

'I'll give you five bob,' said John, flicking two half-crowns across to Charley, laughing.

Big Frankie smiled and offered Charley their total support.

'Well, if it ain't your boots, mate, tell us who's causing you all this grief and we'll go and sort 'em for you.'

'Yeah, come on, Chas,' said Buster, diving into his pocket and producing a brass knuckleduster. 'All of us mates have got to stick together, ain't we? All for one, and all that crap.'

'Thanks, boys. I really appreciate it. Nice to know I can call on friends in high places, but save your breath, cos there's nothing any of you lot can do.'

'Cut the crap, Chas. Just spill,' said Frankie, talking like a second-rate actor in a low-budget American gangster film.

'Look, Frank, I don't want any of you lot getting hurt on my behalf, all right.'

Frank sniffed, sneered and casually took the last drag of his fag before flicking the dog-end into the road. Then, with a curled lip, he said, 'We ain't afraid of no man, Chas. Just tell us and leave the rest to us, all right?'

Charley smiled. 'Well, that's just it, Frank. *She* is not a man. She's a woman. Well, at least I think she's a woman...'

'A woman?' Frank screwed up his face, holding his belly with uncontrollable laughter. The others joined in, too.

'Yeah, Frank, a woman,' Charley replied with a cold shiver, pointing towards the Labour Exchange. 'Get too close to her, mate, and she'd chew you up and spit you out along with the rest of 'em.'

Again, they all laughed.

'So, she's a bit of a dog then, Chas. Perhaps if you took her a nice big juicy marrowbone next time, she might even give you some dole money,' said Frankie.

'Walkies!' shouted Buster.

'Sit!' barked John.

'No. Bollocks to all that working, or dole, crap,' Frankie cried, boasting how he and the others had turned to crime to make what they thought was easy money.

'Yeah. Only fools work for it!' added Butch, encouraging the rest to flash their ill-gotten gains, without a care in the world.

'Look at old Hobson…'

'Who?' asked Charley, trying to think what the hell he was talking about.

'Hobson. You know – "Hold Your Hand Out Hobson".'

'Oh, him. What's he got to do with it, then?' asked Charley.

'He only slung himself off Beachy Head the other day, didn't he,' said Buster, wiping his nose on his cuff.

'He's right,' confirmed BJ, whistling and doing all the actions of falling down to the imaginary beach below.

'No way!' said Charley, hardly believing his ears. 'Bloody hell. Did he die, then?'

'Course he bloody died. That cliff's over 500ft high!'

'Blimey. What did he do that for, then?'

'I don't know. Work, I s'pose. You know how much he hated that.'

'See, I told you: that's what working for a living does for you, Chas,' said Frankie, lighting up another cigarette with a ten-bob note, as if he was made of money. 'If you don't want to end up like him, come and join us. There's plenty more where this came from.'

'Yeah, yeah, Frankie. I've heard it all before,' said Charley. 'I remember Al Capone said the same, just before they captured 'im. And then he spent the rest of his life on Alcatraz wondering where he went wrong.'

A week or so later, Charley was stunned to learn that BJ had been arrested and charged with the cold-blooded murder of his own father. Like a hardened gangster, and in front of many witnesses, BJ calmly walked into the packed dockside working man's club brandishing a 12-gauge sawn-off double-barrelled shotgun. His sole purpose was to find and execute his father.

To make his presence felt, BJ made straight for the middle of the dance floor, raised the gun and squeezed the trigger, discharging one of the barrels with the most violent ear-splitting boom into the ceiling, showering club-goers with dust and debris.

'Oh, shit!' cried the lead singer of the rock band, diving for cover under the stage whilst countless people ran screaming from the building in fear of their lives. Many dropped to the floor and tried to hide under the tables. Some even stood traumatised in submission with their hands in the air, trembling uncontrollably.

BJ was surprisingly calm throughout the ordeal and as he reloaded, dropping the spent cartridge to the floor, he told the remaining band members to carry on playing.

'W-W-What would you like us to play?' one of them asked, apprehensively.

Calm as a cucumber, BJ replied, '*The St Valentine's Day Massacre*, please.'

The band member grimaced. 'I, I, I think that was a film, Sir...'

'All right, then,' replied BJ. 'Play me *The Man who Shot Liberty Valance*.'

Almost hyperventilating, the distressed band member said, 'I'm ever so sorry, but I think that was a film as well.'

BJ looked him straight in the eye and raised the gun.

'Please, please, don't shoot me,' begged the band member, thinking he'd breathed his last. 'I've got a wife and two kids at home.'

The tension was enormous.

'Now, what makes you think I'm gonna shoot you?' replied BJ, discharging another shot into the ceiling. 'I've got no beef with you, mate. I like your band. So, play on.'

But the band member wasn't convinced and so as BJ broke the shotgun to reload, he took his chances and dived headlong off the stage to join his mate.

BJ then calmly walked backwards and stood in silence. Casually chewing gum, his eyes scanned the club for his father. As soon as their eyes met, his father leaped to his feet and began shouting at BJ, to trying to intimidate him. For a moment, it seemed to work, because BJ looked to be very afraid of him.

'Give me the gun, you little shit,' cried his father.

BJ began to breathe very erratically and shake with fear.

Everybody in the club held their breath.

'I won't fuckin' tell you again, boy. Give it to me!' yelled his father. And so BJ did. Both barrels in fact. Blasting him to death.

Whilst it was horrifying for the onlookers, it was total freedom for BJ, because his torment and fear were now over.

Having completed his objective, he dropped the shotgun to the floor, walked out from the club and gave himself up to the police, who had surrounded the building.

Nobody knew for certain, but it was rumoured that BJ's father had been beating and sexually abusing him all his life.

The murder sent shock waves throughout the entire neighbourhood, and Charley's father was back on his case with renewed vengeance. As a consequence, Charley found new employment with his elder brother Albert.

17 years his senior, and with a similar education, Albert was running his own very successful timber and portable building manufacturing company. He paid Charley £3 a week, and he didn't ask any writing or spelling of him.

Even though Albert had more than doubled Charley's wages, Charley still wasn't happy. Albert was a tyrant, a throwback to a very harsh Victorian employer. One who spent the whole of every day gnashing his teeth and ranting and raving at everybody; more so at Charley, he thought.

One cold, frosty winter morning, the air went extremely blue, as Albert tried to start the old diesel lorry. After five or so minutes, he ordered Charley to go over the road and get him a sixpenny bottle of ether from the chemist. By the time Charley returned, Albert had already lifted the engine cover inside the cab. Holding his breath so as not to become anaesthetised by the powerful vapour of the ether, Albert started to drip the contents of the bottle into the lorry's air filter while turning over the engine. Normally, the lorry would immediately roar into life and discharge a thick, smelly cloud of black smoke into the air. But on that perishing cold day, the lorry wouldn't have it, no matter how much ether Albert gave it.

After being exposed to the vapour in the confines of the cab, Albert was gasping for air; his eyes were glazed over. Thinking he was about to pass out, he leaped out from the lorry, just in the nick of time.

'Are you all right, Burt?' asked Charley with concern, watching him stagger around clutching his throat.

Coughing and spluttering, Albert steadied himself against the lorry and grumbled something utterly intelligible.

'Pardon, Burt?' Charley politely replied, almost too afraid to speak.

'I said, don't just bloody stand there gawping, boy! Go round to Wonkeye's and ask to borrow his bloody jump leads so we can get this sodding thing going. And be quick about it!' he roared, flames leaping from his mouth.

So as not to risk another bollocking, Charley ran all the way in his clod-hopping boots.

With thick, matted, shoulder-length hair, and weighing in at more than 20 stone, "Wonkeye" was a full 6ft 6in of very aggressive motor mechanic. And what's more, he had an extremely short fuse.

When Charley got to Wonkeye's yard, he found him down the back stood on the front bumper of a lorry, arse up and head down buried deep beneath the bonnet. Remembering how hostile he could be, Charley was a bit reluctant to disturb him at first. And so, he just stood there for a moment, noisily shuffling his feet and occasionally clearing his throat in the hope of gaining the big man's attention.

Charley deduced from the rising spiral of blue smoke that Wonkeye was puffing on a cigarette as he worked, and that he would soon need to surface to discard the dog-end. He thought it best to wait, and wait, and wait. Before long, Charley became conscious that his very irate brother may have recovered. In fact, it was seeing him in his mind's eye, pacing up and down, gnashing his teeth and bashing his knuckles that prompted Charley into action. He cleared his throat once again, only this time he made damn sure he did it loudly. Yet, still there was no response from Wonkeye. So, while standing respectfully to attention, Charley called out very courteously,

'Er, excuse me, Mr Wonkeye. Can we please borrow your jump leads?'

Instantly, Wonkeye removed his head from under the bonnet.

'Oh good,' thought Charley. 'I've now got the big man's full attention.'

But then, like a thing possessed, Wonkeye leapt full flight to the ground. Charley took a step back and noticed that the cigarette was now jammed firmly into the corner of his mouth, and that his face, red and angry-looking, was partially covered by his mass of greasy, straggly hair.

'What's that you just fucking called me, boy?' he snarled through clenched teeth.

Charley was stunned. His legs turned to jelly, his heart rate soared and his body shuddered under the huge adrenalin rush that followed. Never in his entire life had he seen such a giant of a man so angry. Wonkeye was almost spitting blood.

'What on earth could have set him off?' wondered Charley, holding his breath.

'I'm still fuckin' waitin', boy!' Wonkeye bellowed, puffing a big cloud of blue smoke into the air.

Charley swallowed hard and tried desperately to think what would appease him.

'Come on! Come on!' boomed Wonkeye, flailing his arms. 'I haven't got all fuckin' day!'

'I ... er ... I didn't call you anything,' replied Charley, anxiously trying to use the right words so as not to exacerbate the situation.

With one stroke of his massive hand, Wonkeye swished the hair away from his face and glared at Charley.

'What did you fuckin' well say then, boy? Eh? Eh?'

Wonkeye's voice was so thunderous, it seemed to shake the very ground beneath Charley's feet, but he was determined to show him no fear. With a deep breath, shoulders back and chest out, he looked Wonkeye straight in the eye.

'Oh shit, you bloody fool,' said Charley under his breath. *'What have you done? You're going to bloody die now!'*

For the few moments it took to gather his thoughts, everything seemed to go in slow motion: the dog-end Wonkeye spat from his mouth; his huge hands gesticulating. Even his gruff voice, aggressive as it was, sounded barely audible. Like a distant rumble. But then Wonkeye's actions quickened, and his penetrating roar came through louder than ever before.

'I won't fuckin' ask you again, boy!' he bellowed, leaping towards Charley like a wild hungry beast set on devouring him.

Fearful of getting a clump around the ear, or even worse, beaten to death, Charley started to speak nervously, albeit in riddles, in the hope of confusing Wonkeye.

'Er … er … all I said was, excuse me, Mr Burt and I would like to borrow your jump leads, please, Sir. If you would be so kind, that is.'

The cross-eyed giant stopped dead in his tracks. An eerie silence followed.

He began to tilt his head from side to side, as though he were deep in thought; his forehead rutted with deep frown lines. Although his face was pointing in Charley's direction, Charley couldn't be sure where Wonkey's eyes were focussed.

Before long, Wonkeye startled Charley with an almighty grunt, turned and fetched the jump leads and threw them at Charley's feet.

As Charley bent to pick them up, Wonkeye raised his powerful right arm and pointed a massive forefinger,

'Don't forget to fuckin' bring 'em back, either,' he yelled.

After that near-death experience, Charley Henry was very suspicious of unusual-sounding names. Never again, he vowed.

Chapter 2

Two years on, and Charley Henry still hadn't found his niche in life. He was, in fact, still working for Albert and still only earning £3 a week. Albert, however, had moved up a few rungs of the slippery social ladder. Yet, he was still, as Charley put it, a bit of an arsehole to work for.

'I s'pose he'll be joining the old Masons next,' said Charley's Brother Reggie, who also worked for Albert.

'More like the Moonies,' Charley grinned.

'What – the Moonies, as in flashing his old deaf and dumb, you mean?'

Charley laughed. 'Well, I didn't mean he's gone all religious, did I?'

But despite their speculation, Albert had, in fact, joined the Rotary Club.

'He's definitely changed since he's been a member of the old "Rotisserie Club",' said Reggie.

'How d'you mean?'

'Well, he's no longer a bit of an arsehole, is he?'

'You're right there, Reggie. He's a complete arsehole now. All 15 stone of 'im.'

Having saved up a couple of quid, Charley retired the old hobnail boots and bought himself a pair of Doc Martens; shortly after that, a leather jacket and the old AJS motorbike he'd always desired.

However, the teenage population of the country was at war. Bitterly divided between parkas, pork pie hats and scooters, and leather jackets and motorbikes, it became known as the Mods and Rockers era.

Hostile clashes were commonplace at weekends. The TV news reels, broadsheets and tabloids were full of the running battles taking place in the streets and on beaches such as Brighton, Margate, Southend and Clacton.

It was total madness: half the mates that Charley grew up with turned out to be Mods, and the other half, Rockers. Charley's philosophy was always to live and let live, but that wasn't always possible at the time. Charley even suggested calling himself a "Mocker", but as he wore a leather jacket and rode a 650cc AJS motorbike, he was perceived by both sides of the divide to be a Rocker, whether he liked it or not.

Charley had no real beef with the Mods, he just didn't like pork pie hats and scooters. His passion was for motorbikes and he enjoyed the company of "kindred spirit", who he often met up with in the bikers' cafés far and wide.

One scorching bank holiday Monday, Charley and a few of his mates – Micky, Roy, Peter and Roger – rode their bikes into Margate totally unaware that the town was packed to the rafters with high-spirited Mods enjoying a day out. The first they knew of Mods was, when cruising carefree in the sunshine along the promenade, the distinctive growl from their five motorbikes drew hundreds of screaming Mods from the beaches and the amusement areas. Before long, the sheer mass of them had totally closed off the road ahead with a very noisy, hostile human barricade.

With no wish for confrontation with so many Mods, Charley and his mates skidded their bikes to a halt to consider their options.

'Fuck this for a game of soldiers,' cried Micky, astride a brand-new Triumph Bonneville TC120. 'I haven't even paid the second instalment yet.'

'Sod your bloody bike, Micky,' yelled Charley, seeing the frenzy of screaming Mods closing in fast. 'I want to live to see me next birthday!'

'Me and all!' Roger agreed.

Roy quickly unzipped his leather jacket and pulled out a pair of sunglasses from the inside pocket.

'This ain't no time for sunbathing, Roy,' shouted Charley, thinking he'd cracked up under the strain.

'Who said anything about sunbathing?' replied Roy, fumbling to put them on. 'They won't hit a bloke with glasses, will they?'

'Won't they? I wouldn't bank on it,' Charley said, looking at the lynch mob of Mods getting ever closer.

'I think you'd be better off with a pork pie hat, Roy,' Peter shouted, revving his bike in readiness for a quick getaway.

'Why don't you go the whole hog and get yourself a fucking scooter instead?' Micky yelled, as they spun their bikes around and sped off under a heavy bombardment of bottles and drinks cans. But the boys were soon to realise that the Mods had closed that end off as well.

The Mods had entrapped Charley and his mates in the same way that the Native American Indians did to Colonel George Armstrong Custer and the 7th Cavalry in the epic Battle of the Little Bighorn, in June 1876, in the Eastern Territory of the USA – the outcome of which saw Custer and his men totally overpowered and brutally slaughtered.

Short of riding their bikes through the shops or Dreamland amusement park, they were effectively stuck in the middle – with no escape. One could almost hear "The March of the Mods" blaring out, as they closed in for the kill. But with no wish to join Custer and his men in the bone yard, Charley and his mates spun their bikes around once again before it was too late; only, this time, to look more significant, they were in a chevron formation.

They revved up their bikes, and rode back along the promenade through a barrage of bottles, drinks cans, wire rubbish containers, bins and deckchairs. They were banking on the nerve of the Mods in their direct path crumbling. But like madmen, the Mods stood fast, shouting, taunting and waving their fists at the trapped bikers' approach. The bikers couldn't afford to break off and have another run, because the distance between the two ends had diminished. Without warning, a long wall coping stone was tossed into their path, breaking up their chevron. For a moment, they looked to be doomed, but then Micky accelerated straight for the Mods' line. With no wish to be left to the mercy of the Mods, the rest of the bikers went with him.

Faced with a line of very noisy bikes charging down on them at speed, the Mods finally cracked. With seconds to spare, they began to run and dive for safety, leaving a hole in their ranks just big enough for Charley and his mates to escape through without so much as a scratch.

Five miles out of town, and with their hearts still pounding from the ordeal, they stopped and piled into a transport café to calm their nerves. Micky was the last to come in. Everyone else was slurping their tea and talking about their amazing escape.

'Good thinking, Micky,' said Charley, glad to still be alive. 'If you hadn't accelerated when you did, I dread to think what would have happened to us.'

'I had to do something, Chas. Cos I was about to shit my pants. I needed the bog. Where do you think I've been for the last 10 minutes, eh?'

Towards the end of that year, Charley successfully passed his car driving test in one of Albert's old vans. Albert had climbed a bit further up the greasy social pole and become even more opinionated. In fact, to quote Charley, Albert had become "an arsehole's arsehole" – a very arrogant, angry arsehole at that. Even to members of his own family, siblings especially, "scum-bows" was Albert's favoured word to describe people who he thought were beneath him. He seemed to hate everyone, even most of the customers that came into his yard.

'You can't park there and, no, you can't use our toilet either,' he'd say to all the old boys in dire need, with their prostate problems. It's a wonder any of them ever came back.

But there was a day when he was seen to back pedal and bite his lip.

Reggie beckoned to Charley.

'Here, look quick, Chas. There he goes again,' pointing at Albert charging across the yard like a madman waving his arms and yelling at somebody parking their van.

'Oh dear,' said Charley, catching a glimpse of the driver. 'You know who that is, don't you?'

'Oh shit,' said Reggie, raising an eyebrow. 'It's Ronnie Easton.'

'Yeah, this is going to be interesting,' Charley said, seeing Albert skid to a halt, as the Easton brothers and Monty Jarvis, fully tooled up with his wooded leg, climbed out the van.

'What's up, Burt? You got a problem with us parking here?' asked Ronnie, closing the van door.

'Er, no, no, no, Ronnie,' said Burt, very respectfully. 'I wasn't yelling at you, mate. You can park anywhere you like. It's that bloke who just drove out the yard I was yelling at. Look, he dropped this on the ground.'

As Albert bent over to pick up a piece of paper, Monty pinched his bum and whistled.

Albert sprang up immediately, looking very angry.

'Did you like that, Burt?' Monty smiled.

Albert swallowed hard and gave a silly laugh.

The Easton brothers were well respected in the neighbourhood. Coming from a tough, hard-working family, they took no shit from anybody. That said, they were fair and honest people to deal with. Monty Jarvis was another very tough man who took no shit. He was in the Royal Navy during the war. When his ship went down after being torpedoed, most of his right leg went with it. They say that he was adrift for days, clinging to a life raft, and that he was barely alive when they fished him out.

Christmas was fast approaching and Charley and Reggie were both looking forward to having a nice two days off, far away from the old "Moaner" [Happy]. Christmas Eve came, and everybody who worked for Albert went across to the pub at dinnertime for a quick drink. Albert's idea of time-keeping was that all his employees had to be back and at their bench working a good five minutes *before* time started. Anybody arriving *on* time got a severe bollocking for being late. For the first time ever, they all got back to the yard two minutes late. Albert went absolutely berserk. Jumping up and down, he said that he and Jess had planned to give everybody a mince pie during their 3pm tea break.

'But none of you bastards are bloody well going to get one now!'

He then stomped off, with Reggie following in his wake. Soon afterwards, Reggie returned with his P45 in his hand.

'I told him to stick 'is job, and his mince pies, and 'is arse,' he said.

'What a dickhead,' Charley replied, catching a few large snowflakes fluttering in the air like cotton wool. 'All that fuss over just two minutes on Christmas Eve. Takes some believing, don't it?'

'That's it,' cried Reggie, excitedly. 'Christmas Eve! Dickens!'

'Dickens? No, I called him a dickhead,' said Charley.

'Charles Dickens's tale of Ebenezer Scrooge. Spirits past and all that. With any luck, Albert Dickhead will have a little visitation as the clock strikes 12 tonight.'

'Yeah, wouldn't that be good,' said Charley. 'If we all get a turkey sent round on Christmas morning, we'll know he's been shown the error of his ways.'

'What if it's only a stale mince pie from the day before?'

'I don't care, just as long as he's been shown his own destiny.'

But sadly, the only spirit Albert saw that Christmas was in a bottle. If only he'd been shown! Wouldn't that have just saved Big Bad Albert all the heartache he was now suffering in the last chance saloon!

On Charley's return to work, the day after Boxing Day, he was to learn that Albert had won a lucrative contract to make and supply big sturdy packing cases for a large engineering conglomerate. They shipped heavy machine parts all over world. Albert wouldn't admit it, but his father was instrumental in getting him the contract. Having worked for the engineering company for more than 40 years, he was able to blow in the right ears. Being on a real good earner supplying those cases, Albert offered Charley the chance to make a few pennies more.

'Instead of your weekly wage of £3, I'll pay you piecework to make the cases. One shilling a side. Six bob for a complete case.'

'Okay,' said Charley. 'You're on. I'll take it.'

With the incentive to earn a few pennies more, Charley started work extra early each morning, took shorter dinner breaks, stayed on after hours and when he did, he earned a couple of pounds more a week. Albert then changed his mind, saying he was now losing money on the deal, and that Charley was to return to the £3 weekly wage. Albert, of course, demanded the same productivity. That's when Charley told him to shove his job up the same orifice as Reggie did before Christmas.

Having had that small taste of free enterprise, Charley became self-employed, with the idea that he could generate enough work to pay his way in the world. Unfortunately, he still looked very young and inexperienced, and so he didn't get much in the way of work.

Charley bumped into Bill Jackson, Ronnie Easton's brother-in-law. Bill carried out small building works.

'You can give me a hand if you like, Chas,' he said.

'I'll have to leave you on this job this morning, Chas,' said Bill, who had a site meeting elsewhere. 'You can grab a cup of tea and a sandwich at Fred's Café dinnertime.'

Old Fred did a lovely egg and bacon sandwich, and while Charley waited for it to be served up, he decided to have a go on the pinball machine in the corner of the caff. He was getting a pretty good score, as it happened; that is, until Bales, the big flash second-hand car dealer, swaggered in with all his entourage.

'You can get off that now, boy,' he snarled, 'cos I want a go.'

'You'll have to wait your turn,' Charley replied, refusing budge.

Being an arrogant impatient bully, Bales deliberately pushed and tilted the machine. As he did so, all his mates laughed at Charley. Charley's heart rate quickened because he was annoyed about being pushed around, but he didn't have any money left for another go and so he reluctantly vacated the machine. After mocking Charley in front of the whole caff, Bales chuckled and inserted his threepenny joey into the slot and started to play the machine. Charley was so livid that he couldn't contain himself. He lent forward and pushed hard, tilting the machine.

'That makes us even,' he said.

'You little shit!'

'And you!' Charley replied, with grit teeth.

The tension was rising. The café went quiet. People stopped eating and looked on. Staring daggers at Charley, Bales snarled, 'You don't want to fuck with me, boy!'

'Or what?'

In the nick of time Fred brought Charley's sandwich to him.

'Best not to mess with him, son,' whispered Fred. 'He's a nasty bit of work.'

As Charley sat down and started to eat, the whole café, including Fred, heard Bales threaten to have Charley worked over by his heavy mob. When Bill came back, Charley told him what had happened.

'Oh, did he now? I don't like that cocky bastard. The arrogant git thinks he's it, the way he poses with his big expensive power boat. I think he needs to be brought down to Earth with a bump. I'll get Ronnie and Ginge. They don't like him either. We'll pay him and his tough guys a little visit. Teach them all some manners. It won't be tonight, though, but I'll let you know as soon as I have spoken with the other two.'

'Thanks, Bill. I appreciate that, mate.'

With Bill and the Easton brothers on side, Charley was bursting with confidence. Before it wore off, he walked onto Bales' car lot late that afternoon.

'He's in the showroom,' said the lad cleaning the cars.

'Thanks, mate,' Charley replied, brazenly walking in.

'You've gotta a bloody nerve showing your face around here, Henry. Come to apologise, boy, have you?' he smirked.

'Er, no, not exactly, Mr Bales. I was rather hoping you'd do that.'

'Me apologise to you? Piss off, you little shit! I don't do things like that.'

'Okay then, Mr Bales, but just so you know, my mate Bill Jackson and the Easton brothers are going to meet me here tomorrow night. Just as you close up, in fact, so round up all your tough guys.'

Bales gasped. 'Look, look. I was only joking in the café dinnertime. When you get to my age, you don't want any agro. Tell you what, come into the café tomorrow and we'll have a little competition on the old pinball table. What do you say? I'll pay.'

Just seeing the fear in his eyes was good enough for Charley. Bill laughed when Charley told him.

Charley had itchy feet and was anxious to move on and learn how to build houses. So, when a mate told him of a large new housing development site that was taking on labour, he was keen to get there and secure a job.

Early the following morning he rode his motorbike to the building site, slipping and sliding through the snow and ice that lay heavily on the ground. When he got there, the site office was still closed. Rather than go back home, he waited patiently in the freezing cold. And it was, whilst pacing up and down slapping his hands together and stamping his feet, that Charley's attention was drawn to the sound of raucous laughter.

Investigating further, he found, tucked away behind a huge stack of bricks, a dilapidated old wooden mess hut, with smoke bellowing from a pipe projected through a hole in the roof. Charley tried knocking on the paint-starved door, but with all the frivolity going on inside nobody heard him. He took a deep breath and pushed open the door to reveal a gang of burly building workers laughing and drinking tea around a tall potbelly stove. Spitting sparks and flames, the fire looked very welcoming on such a cold day.

'Er, excuse me,' said Charley respectfully, almost too afraid to go in, 'but I'm looking for a job.'

'A job, is it?' repeated a grouchy old bricklayer. 'Well, you can go and find some more dry wood to put on this fire if you like.' He dogged out his cigarette on the floor of the hut.

'No, no. I mean I want a proper job,' Charley replied.

'That *is* a proper job, boy, cos if this fire goes out, we'll all bloody freeze to death in here.'

'No,' said Charley. 'I mean a job like building houses.'

'Oh, so you build houses then?' the old boy said, winding Charley up.

Charley took another deep breath and gave a prolonged sigh.

'Look, shall I go out and come in again?' he asked, hoping that he would stop making fun of him.

'No, no, you don't have to do that, son. Just answer this simple question. Have you ever worked on a building site before?'

He'd noticed Charley's lean, hungry frame.

'No, mate. I haven't.'

'Well, it's a bloody hard life, boy. Are you tough enough?' he asked, still taking the mickey.

'Don't you worry about me, mate,' replied Charley, standing his ground. 'I can look after meself all right.'

'Well, I sure hope you can, boy,' he said, reaching for a length of string to tie around his donkey jacket. 'If the job don't kill you, the bloody weather soon will. Freeze your bloody bollocks off in the winter, get burnt to death in the summer; the rest of the time, you walk around soaking wet.'

'Oh, take no notice of that whinging tosser, mate,' said Ed, one of the chippies that Charley was to eventually work with. 'It's a good life, really.'

'Watch out, boys. Ivor's here,' cried one of the other brickies, throwing the dregs of his tea out the window. 'I've just seen him go into the site office.'

As they all began to disperse, Charley called out after them.

'Ivor – would that be the governor's name?'

'Er ... yeah, that's right, son. Ivor is his name ... Ivor Badcock. You catch on fast,' said the old bricklayer.

While they all laughed, Charley frowned, thinking back to the last encounter he had with odd-sounding names.

'What's up, boy? Lost your tongue?'

'On your bike,' replied Charley, defensively. 'You can't kid me, mate. I ain't bloody stupid.'

'On my life, son,' said the old boy with conviction. 'His name is Badcock. I'm telling you. Look on the site board if you don't believe me.'

Charley returned a smile of disbelief before walking over to find the site manager, but before knocking on his door, he did look on the site board. To his surprise, he saw in very small letters, at the bottom, "Site Manager, I. Badcock".

'Bloody hell,' thought Charley, 'that old sod was right.' But Charley didn't dare address him as such, just in case.

'Okay, Charley,' said the site manager, extending his hand. 'You've got the job. Now when can you start?'

'Oh, thank you, Mr … er … Mr …'

'Ian. It's Ian Benjamin Badcock,' he said quickly. 'We only use first names here on site.'

'Oh, thanks, Ian,' Charley replied with relief. 'I can start tomorrow if that's okay with you.'

The following morning, Charley proudly joined the other boys as a building worker, in their daily ritual of tea and banter around the blazing fire, in readiness for the harsh winter day.

'So, Ivor took pity on you then, boy?' said the old bricklayer, reaching for his length of string. 'Gave you the job, did he?'

'Well, I'm here, ain't I? But his name's not Ivor. You got that wrong, cos when I called him Ivor, he began to grill me as to who told me his name.'

'What did you say then, boy?' he cried, with panic in his voice.

'I told him it was you.'

'Oh shit! You stupid bastard!' he growled, in fear of his job. 'Couldn't you see I was only having you on?'

'Just returning the compliment, mate. That's all.'

'What's that fuckin s'posed to mean, then?'

'Well, you work it out, mate,' Charley answered.

Ed laughed. 'Don't turn your back on him, Charley, cos he'll want revenge.'

But the old boy bore Charley no real malice. They got on well after that, although he did keep on telling Charley how he'd been working on building sites long before Charley was even a glint in his old man's eye.

'What? When the dinosaurs roamed the Earth?' Charley laughed.

'You cheeky little bastard. Show a bit of respect, will you.'

'Yeah, I'm sorry, mate. Most rude of me. But as I'll still be working on building sites long after you're dead and gone, I must learn to give, and take, it.'

As the old boy said, life was very tough on the building site, and if you didn't join in with the banter, you were a target – and you wouldn't survive it.

It was an accepted fact back in those days that when a building project came to an end, so too did the job. When that happened, Charley had enough experience under his belt to get another job as an erector for Kenoric PLC, a nationwide prefabricated building company. Within the first year, Charley was promoted to buildings supervisor. He was even given a brand-new car to get around with. But with the job came the piles and piles of paperwork, which Charley struggled with. At the many site meetings he attended, he would hide his deep shame by scribbling onto his notepad, only to go home and try to decipher his illegible spellings before sitting up half the night with a dictionary, rewriting his reports. He couldn't carry on like that and so he coerced his mate Benny Benson into enrolling on a course at night school with him, to try and improve their spelling. Unbeknown to them, they had been spotted, and were followed through the school gates by an old mischievous school friend of theirs. Taking their seat, the memories of the weekly beatings with the slipper came flooding back for Charley and Benny.

'I don't know that this is a good idea, Benny,' Charley said, wishing he wasn't there.

'How else we goin' to learn?' replied Benny, wishing he wasn't there either.

As the teacher began to address the class, Charley and Benny were distracted by a face pressed tightly up against the window.

'Oh shit,' whispered Benny. 'That's all we need – bloody Joey Green.'

'Watch out, Charley. The old Bum Tickler will get you in there!'

'Do you know that person out there, Mr Henry?' the teacher asked.

Before Charley had a chance to answer, Joey had pushed two lighted fireworks through the open fanlight.

'Quick! Time to escape, boys!'

Both Charley and Benny were asked to leave the class and not return.

'With friends like Joe, who needs enemies?' said Benny, as they walked out through the school gates for the last time.

Charley's Brother Alan had left school and got a job on a building site as an apprentice bricklayer. Because it was a large, strict union site, Alan had to wear steel toecap boots. One day Charley and Alan had a falling out; a disagreement in the garden, which ended up with Alan kicking Charley in the shinbones with the very same boots.

'You little shit!' Charley cried, picking himself up and chasing Alan from the garden, upstairs to his bedroom, where they scrapped.

'You said I must stand up to bullies!' Alan shouted, as they wrestled on the floor, tearing lumps out of each other.

'Yeah, but not me, you little shit! You nearly broke me bloody leg just now!'

Their father was always very considerate to the neighbours regarding the noise levels his kids created, especially on a Sunday. So, when he heard the racket that Charley and Alan were kicking up, he charged up from his shed at the bottom of the garden and into the house to separate them. By the time he started to climb the stairs, his anger had boiled over to such an extent that he had punched both panels out beneath the handrail.

'Oh shit!' hollered Charley, running across the landing and locking himself into the bathroom while Alan tried to hide under his bed.

After dragging Alan out and giving him a good bollocking, he started to pound on the bathroom door.

'Go away!' shouted Charley.

'If you don't open this bloody door,' yelled his father, 'I'll smash it down.'

Charley didn't, and so a few seconds later his father's fist came straight through the door, punching the top panel clean out. His anger now dissipated, he returned, mumbling under his breath, to his shed, at the bottom of the garden. Both Alan and Charley shook hands and vowed never to fall out again.

In 1965, Charley married his girlfriend Barbara. With no hope of ever getting a house to live in, council or otherwise, Charley sunk every penny he had into the purchase of a large tin of paint and a tatty old caravan on a residential site in the heart of Kent. Charley felt that his life was being ruined by paperwork, and he wanted to be free of it all. And so after he and Barbara had moved into their caravan, Charley handed in his notice and left the job, and all the paperwork, far behind him.

He became self-employed, forming a verbal partnership with his next-door neighbour, Butch Weston. Butch was a swarthy, fiery and colourful cockney character. Full of life, he had a wife called Jan, two children and one on the way to support. Barbara was also pregnant at the time.

It was madness to think they could ever start up in business together, because Butch couldn't write or spell either. They had no money or any suitable transport. They couldn't even afford a telephone between them. The only one they had access to was a public payphone in an old, leaking wooden kiosk in the middle of the caravan site. Fortunately for them, the tatty old kiosk had an outside bell.

'The company phone, Butch,' said Charley, eagerly pointing to the kiosk. 'Our new office!'

'Yeah, good thinking, Chas,' Butch replied, enthusiastically. 'All we want now is the bloody thing to ring.'

'Oh, we'll get it to ring all right, Butch. All we gotta to do is think big.'

'Yeah,' Butch yawned, 'and just how are we gonna do that, then? We haven't even got a sharp pencil.'

'We need to run a big promotional advertising campaign.'

'Oh yeah, and what we gonna use for the old spondulix, then?'

'Oh, come on, Butch, use your imagination. We cut that old cereal box up into postcard sizes, write on 'em, telling everybody out there what we do, and stick 'em up in shop windows. It'll cost peanuts.'

'Yeah, and we all know what you get for peanuts, don't we?'

'We gotta start somewhere, Butch, so unless you got any better ideas…?'

And so that was how they started to find work. Except, there was another budding entrepreneur on site: Jim Hale. Jim, thinking on the same lines, had advertised for work in the same shop windows, so it became a bit of race to answer the phone whenever it rang. Unfortunately for Jim, he was only a little guy, and stood no chance against Charley and Butch.

The first time the phone rang after placing the ads, all three of them dashed to answer it.

'You get the little squirt, Butch,' yelled Charley, 'and I'll grab the phone!'

Whilst Butch brought Jim down with a superb rugby tackle three feet from the kiosk, Charley hopped over them both, opened the door and lifted the receiver.

'Hello. H & W Building Contractors,' he said breathlessly. But then, with disappointment, Charley pushed the door back open.

'Get off him, Butch. It's for Jim.'

Looking as though he'd been mauled by a lion, Jim took the receiver from Charley and, in the most awful American drawl, started his laidback spiel.

'Hi. You're through to Quick Clean, the all-new revolutionary window cleaning company. How can we help you? Building contractors? No, no. This is not a building company,' he said, shamelessly. 'It must have been a crossed line, Sir. Happens all the time here. I'll have to get on to BT again.'

'Cheeky bastard. Hark at 'im – "crossed line",' said Butch, as they walked away. 'If he ain't careful, we'll start charging 'im to use our phone in future.'

By pooling their pennies [£5 in total], Butch and Charley purchased a red and black hand-painted 1949 Fordson 10cwt pick-up truck. The beat-up old truck only had one seat, and that was for the driver. The passenger had to sit on a small offcut of plywood balanced on top of a roll of damp course on the floor of the van, which, incidentally, was full of holes, which water funnelled up every time they drove through a puddle. They had to bump-start the motor most mornings because the battery was a bit naff. The tyres were a bit ropey. The fuel gauge didn't function. The cab leaked. There were no windscreen wipers or indicators, and the horn didn't work. But apart from that, it was a good all-round truck.

'We can't afford both tax and insurance,' Butch grimaced, with one foot on the front bumper while rolling his fag.

'Oh, that's a minor detail, Butch. We'll get the motor insured first. That's the most important thing to do. We'll then stick a little notice on the windscreen saying "Tax in the post".'

'Oh good,' replied Butch, pulling a face. 'I feel much better now. Are we also going to stick another notice in the window about the new 10-year MOT test ticket that is now required by law that we haven't got yet?'

'No. Don't be daft, Butch. It's only a small windscreen. We can't go sticking everything in there cos we won't be able to see out of it, will we?'

'Okay then. Best we just stick to the minor roads only, eh? That way we won't get a tug from the Old Bill.'

Their plan worked well until the day of the violent bank robbery at Wrotham.

They were chugging along blissfully through the lanes, totally unaware of the robbery. Unluckily for Butch, he fitted the description of one of the robbers. As they rounded a bend in the tiny lane near the village of Gun Hill, they came across the police roadblock.

'Oh shit,' Charley cried, thinking they were about to get nicked for no road fund licence. 'What are we gonna do now?'

Butch stretched his neck and peered over the top of the dashboard.

'Shit!' he yelled. 'Spin the motor around quick! Let's get out of here!'

'You must be bloody joking, Butch,' Charley replied, with his foot hard on the brakes, trying to stop them crashing into the roadblock. 'The lane's much too narrow for that. It'll take at least a 20-point turn to get this blinking thing around.'

They eventually came to a standstill about 15 foot short of the blockade, whereby Butch slumped on the floor to think. Seeing Butch's head disappear, the police became suspicious and charged mob-handed towards their van.

'Oh shit! Leave the talking to me!' Charley cried, confident that he could handle this on his own.

They were totally surrounded. Thinking they had captured the robbers, the burly police officers drew their truncheons, ready for conflict.

Charley took a deep breath and slowly lowered his window.

'Hello, officers,' he said politely. 'And what can we do for you on this fine morning?'

A huge sergeant stooped and poked his head through the open window of their motor.

'And why are you hiding down there, Sir?' he asked, taking a keen interest in Butch.

'I'm not hiding,' Butch replied. 'I'm just sitting here nice and peacefully, minding my own business. There's no law against that, is there?'

An uneasy silence followed, in which time Charley noticed the sergeant's eyes wandering around the cab for something in particular. Stern-faced and without saying another word, the big man slowly withdrew his head and began signalling with his eyes, drawing attention to Charley's battered old briefcase. Confident that his men were in a position to overpower Charley and Butch, the sergeant quickly thrust his hand into their vehicle and grabbed the ignition keys.

'Hey, what's goin' on?' Charley asked, thinking they were about to get dragged from the van and roughed up.

'The briefcase, Sir,' the sergeant pointed. 'Now what would two likely lads such as yourselves be doing with a briefcase?'

'That's our business!' Butch cried.

The sergeant took a deep breath and gave a long sigh.

'Now, don't make this any harder than it need be,' he said, reaching for the door handle. 'If you've got nothing to hide, then you've got nothing to worry about, have you? We just want a quick peek inside the case. It'll only take a minute and then you can have it back, and, perhaps, we can all get on our way.'

Butch was a bit stubborn at the best of times but he certainly wasn't going to co-operate under pressure.

'With respect, officer, my old man fought in the war to beat fascism.'

'Oh yeah? And so what's that got to do with the price of bread, then?'

Butch frowned, thinking of what to say next. His brain cell was working overtime.

'Er, er … it means this is a free country and what you're asking is tantamount to an invasion of our privacy,' he said, smugly.

Charley turned to Butch. '"Tantamount"?' he whispered. 'What the bloody hell are you talking about, tantamount?'

'Trust me, Chas. I know what I'm doing. You just watch and learn.'

Butch continued to insult their intelligence.

'Before we say anymore, we want our solicitor present.'

'*Bloody steady on, Butch,*' thought Charley. '*We haven't even got the price of the bus fare home, let alone a solicitor.*'

The sergeant looked at Charley, tutted and rubbed his chin.

'Hmm, I, er, I see your road tax is in the post, Sir. And where are your windscreen wipers? Fallen off, have they?'

Charley took his comments as a threat and swallowed hard. Butch then unwittingly chucked fuel on the fire by muttering under his breath.

'Why don't they fuckin' go and chase some bank robbers instead of harassing poor innocent motorists like us!'

'I heard that, Sir,' said the sergeant with a broad grin, knowing that that's what they were doing.

Charley smiled politely and tried to dismiss the comment.

'Out of interest, Sergeant, why are you so interested in our briefcase?'

Anxious to redress Butch's disparaging remarks, a wry smile spread across the sergeant's leathery, weather-beaten face.

'Well, as it so happens, Sir,' he said, giving Butch a big toothy grin, 'there was a violent robbery earlier this morning at Wrotham, and oddly enough, a briefcase identical to yours, containing a large amount of money, was snatched from outside of the bank in the High Street. And what's even more astonishing, one of the men involved in the robbery was described by a number of witnesses as being Italian-looking…'

'Oh shit!' said Charley, totally flabbergasted. 'And you think we're the robbers then, do you?'

'Well, ironically, Sir, the thought had crossed our minds.'

Butch laughed. 'Bank robbers?' he repeated, shaking his head in disbelief.

'Er, look, Sergeant,' Charley said, raising his eyes and smiling. 'I know my mate looks like a bit of an Eyetie, and he may say the wrong thing from time to time, but trust me, he's as British as you and me. He even sings "Land of Hope and Glory". Go on, Butch. Give 'em a burst.'

'I ain't going to sing that.'

'All right. Give 'em a blast of "God Save the Queen", then.'

'Oi, oi!' interrupted the sergeant. 'We ain't conducting auditions, you know. All we want is a look inside that briefcase.'

'Okay then, Sergeant. You win. We give up,' Charley said, handing it over with a smile. 'But as much as I'd like it to be, that bag ain't full of money … stolen or otherwise. Is it, Butch?'

'No, officers,' he agreed. 'It's not. You're going to be bitterly disappointed, mate. Unless you're hungry, that is,' he added in a whisper out of ear shot.

'Well, we'll soon find out, Sir, won't we?' replied the sergeant, eagerly throwing back the flap of the case.

But, when he peered inside, he lost control and burst into hysterics.

'Jam sandwiches!' he cried, tears rolling down his cheeks. 'Bloody jam sandwiches! Go on! Sod off, you pair of buggers!'

He gave Charley back their keys and case while trying to talk over the belly laughter that had spread among his colleagues.

'Get on your way! Oh, and while you're about it, get that blinking motor taxed as well!'

Charley didn't need telling twice, and so without saying another word, he quickly inserted the key into the ignition. But the motor wouldn't start. The battery had gone flat.

'Shit, that's all we need,' cried Butch.

'Leave it to me, Butch,' Charley winked.

'Er, excuse me, officer,' said Charley politely. 'Would it be too much of an inconvenience to ask you and your kind lads for a quick bump-start? Please, Sir, if you wouldn't mind.'

They obliged, and Charley and Butch fled the scene feeling very, very relieved, although Butch still grumbled about the incident. But that was in his nature.

'They got a fuckin' cheek laughin' at us like that. What's a briefcase for if not to put your sandwiches in?' he said, clutching the bag close to his chest, as though it was full of money.

'Oh, come on Butch,' said Charley trying to contain his own laughter, as he wrestled with the steering wheel. 'You must admit, it was bloody funny the way things turned out.'

'I could understand "funny", if when they stopped us, we were both sat there with stockings over our heads and sawn-off shotguns on our laps.'

'Think how much more they'd have laughed if we'd been sat there with a pair of tights still joined at the crotch over our heads,' Charley chuckled.

'Yeah, but we wasn't, was we? We was just two ordinary hard-working businessmen goin' about our lawful business. What possible reason did they have to stop us?'

'I know, Butch. A bummer, weren't it. Do you think it might have been cos we were not displaying a current tax disc? Or could it be that they saw your head suddenly disappear below the dashboard? Or might it be that they mistook you for Mussolini, trying to conceal a briefcase full of stolen money?'

'Er, yeah, when you put it like that, Chas, I s'pose they did have a point. Guilty, Your Honour!' he laughed, throwing his hands in the air in submission. 'Those coppers caught us red-handed with a briefcase full of jam sandwiches. Tee hee hee.'

'Not just ordinary jam sandwiches, Butch. These jam sandwiches are turning up at the edges with all the excitement. Look!' he said, stuffing one into his mouth. Butch, still laughing, did the same.

'You can chuckle now, Butch, but you can think yourself very lucky they didn't have guns with 'em.'

'Why?'

'Why? Cos they would've bloody shot you for the way you spoke back to 'em. And where did you get a word like "tantamount" from?'

'I know. Bloody impressive, weren't it?' Butch giggled. 'Made them coppers sit up and take note, didn't it? I didn't want them thinking we were just a couple of wallies now, did I?'

'What's it mean, then?' asked Charley.

'What, tantamount? I don't know. I got it from that docker bloke. You know, the union man, Jack Dash – the one that's always on the news, spouting and calling for strike action to close the docks down. He uses it all the time.'

'What, that bloke who preaches about twigs and things?'

'Twigs?'

'Yeah, from up on his soapbox in the docks. He tells the workers how the bosses can easily break one twig, but get a bundle of twigs, and they can't break them so easily. "Stick together, lads, and they won't break us!"'

'Yeah, that's what we did, Chas: stick together. Only, we were more like a couple of concrete blocks than a bundle of twigs.'

Butch may have growled a bit whenever he felt threatened, but when it came to vulnerable old ladies, his huge golden heart melted. He was just a big softy underneath all his bluster. He'd often suggest not charging them the full price, like when they carried out a hefty repair for a tiny, frail old lady.

'She can't afford to pay us,' said Butch, with what looked like a tear welling up in his eye. 'She's worse off than we are.'

'Oh, stop it, Butch. Next you'll be telling me that you want to give her one of our jam sandwiches.'

'Hey, steady on, Chas! I wouldn't go that far!'

Charley later pointed out the new Rolls-Royce Phantom in her garage!

Scratching to find the next job, Charley saw Butch dash to answer the phone.

'For us, Butch?'

'Yep, some bloke wants us to stick up some wallpaper for 'im.'

'And?'

'I told 'im yeah, we'll do it.'

'But I've never hung wallpaper before.'

'I have,' said Butch. 'You paste, and I'll stick it up.'

'How much?' asked Charley.

'Seven quid.'

'Seven quid to decorate a room?'

'No, the bloke's done all the stripping and the painting, Chas. All we gotta do is put the paper up cos he can't do it, and for that, we get three and a half quid a piece. Money for old rope.'

And so they started on the job. As fast as Charley pasted, Butch stuck the paper up. Only, when they had finished, big blisters started appearing. As fast as they frantically patted them down, another would erupt elsewhere. By the time the client had returned home, his expensive new wallpaper looked like a moonscape, full of humps and bumps.

'Have no fear,' said Butch convincingly, his fingers crossed behind his back. 'It always happens with this type of paper. Tomorrow, when it's all dried out, it'll be fine. Trust me.'

'Well, in that case, I'll pay you tomorrow,' said the client, thinking that Butch was shooting him a line.

When they returned the following morning, to everybody's surprise, especially Butch's, the paper was nice and flat.

'See? Told you,' crowed Butch. 'Leave it to the professionals. We know what we're doing, don't we, Chas?'

Charley just smiled with relief.

They later found out that heavy paper such as that needed time for the paste to soak in before hanging.

For all Butch's big words and rough edges, Charley was very proud to call him a mate, a true friend. However, they were struggling to find enough work to keep them going, so they decided to call it a day and look for a proper job.

They sold the beast of a truck to an old chicken farmer for half a hundredweight of spuds, £6 10s. in cash, and two dozen eggs, which they divided equally.

Chapter 3

✴

With more hungry mouths to feed than Charley, Butch went out and purchased a cheap, beat-up old BSA 500cc motorbike and sidecar to get around on; whereas Charley, with only one other mouth to feed, was reaching for the stars.

After the almighty backfire that sent wildlife scurrying for safety, Charley climbed on the back of Butch Weston's old combination and they set off for Ted the Tread's, the dodgy second-hand car dealer, leaving a huge cloud of black smoke in their wake. When they got to his car lot, at Basford, Butch parked his old bike amidst the shiny, resprayed used vehicles for sale on the forecourt, which seemed to displease the dealer immensely.

'Hey there! You! Excuse me!' shouted the over-confident car dealer. He swaggered towards them, all teeth and in a wide-awake suit.

'You talkin' to me, or chewin' a brick?' asked Butch, glaring at him.

'Yeah, mate, I am. I hope you're not dumping that old thing there?'

'Cheeky bastard! I'll dump *you* in a minute, "MATE". Talk to me like that…'

'Whoa, whoa!' cried Charley, holding Butch back. 'Please, pay no heed to my friend,' he said, knowing that the car dealer was looking for back-up from a couple of burly lads that were cleaning cars. 'It's just that my mate gets a bit touchy if he thinks someone is being disrespectful to his pride and joy.'

'Oh yeah. I'm sorry, mate,' the car dealer replied, all apologetic. 'I was only joking. Very insensitive of me. I didn't mean to offend.' He extended a hand in peaceful greeting. 'The name's Ted, by the way. "Honest Ted".'

'Honest Ted!' Butch laughed. 'I thought you were called "Ted the Tread".'

'Oh shit,' thought Charley. *'Here we go again.'*

'Yeah, yeah. Very proud of that nickname I am,' said Ted, clearing his throat, behind a forced smile. 'I, uh, I actually got that name cos I tread very carefully when buying in cars to sell.'

'Oh, right. Got it. Silly me,' replied Butch. 'There was me thinking it was cos you painted treads onto bald tyres.'

Wishing to move on, the car dealer hurriedly cleared his throat again.

'Looking for anything in particular, lads?' he asked, inviting them both into his showroom.

'Yeah, a van,' replied Charley. 'I'm lookin' to buy a nice van.'

'A nice van,' echoed Ted the Tread, raising an eyebrow at the prospect of a good sale. 'And how much do you want to pay for this nice van, then?'

'About a tenner.' Charley raised his own eyebrows in anticipation.

When Ted stopped laughing, he took Charley outside into his yard and pointed.

'You see that pile of old crap down the back on the left-hand side?'

'What, that old motor with no wheels on, you mean?'

'Yeah, that's the one, mate. You can have that for a tenner. But, if you was to, say, spend a pony,' [£25] he said, pointing to a scruffy, black, hand-painted 1953 Thames 5QCt van, 'you can have that little baby. The only place you'll get a motor any cheaper than that is the scrapyard down the road at Faringdon.'

'Does it go?' Charley asked, looking down his nose and thinking it was no better than the pile of rubbish it stood next to.

'Go? Go? I'll have you know that little baby runs like a well-oiled sewing machine.'

'Sewin' machine!' laughed Butch. 'My old mum's got one of them, and it's well-oiled, but it don't bloody go, though!'

Ted smirked, wishing Butch would go away. 'As I was about to tell your friend here,' he said, placing an arm on Charley's shoulder, 'put a bucket of water over it, and it'll look good as new. A perfect little runabout. Tell you what,' he said, leading them both into his office like lambs to the slaughter. 'I can see you're interested, so I'll give you a little test ride. What do you say, huh? No pressure.'

Charley grimaced. 'Oh, go on, then.' He had nothing to lose.

'Bones!' Ted cried, leaning out the window. 'Bring that nice little Thames van round the front, would you!'

Although Ted tried to block their view from the window, Charley spotted someone messing about down by the van with a set of jump leads.

'Bad starter, is it?'

'No, no. Not that one, mate,' Ted replied, hiding behind a forced laugh. 'First push of the button, usually. It's just that the battery's gone a little bit flat through lack of use, that's all. Nothing to worry about, though. It'll be goin' in a jiffy…'

'We know all about flat batters, don't we, Butch?' said Charley, thinking back to the other old banger they had.

A few minutes later the old van was out the front, ticking over nicely. And it didn't sound half bad either. While Butch and Charley were busy looking it over, Ted stood there smiling, exposing his brilliant white teeth like a fire and brimstone preacher.

Butch looked back and smiled himself. 'I bet he can even see in the dark with those teeth, Chas.'

'Yeah, I bet he can. Who needs streetlights with 'im around,' Charley whispered, climbing into the passenger seat.

Butch climbed in the back and sat on the floor. 'A bit dark in the back, Ted. Can you smile?' he asked, taking the mick.

Ted was none the wiser, when he turned and smiled at Butch.

'Oh, that's much better,' said Butch, reaching for his sunglasses.

Still none the wiser, Ted proceeded to drive them the short distance around the block.

'Just look how she handles,' he said, throwing the van into a sharp left-hand bend, purposely sending Butch sliding across the floor. 'Safe little motor, this one. Unless, of course, you're sat on the floor in the back, that is,' he remarked, laughing at Butch hanging on for dear life. 'Grips the road like the brown stuff to a blanket. You won't find another bargain like this anywhere. You'll feel like the King of the Road driving this little beauty. In actual fact, talking about kings, the young Prince Charles and his old dad called in here the other day looking for a little runabout, and he took quite a shine to this one. I wouldn't be surprised to see them come back sometime today and buy it.'

'All right. Pull over, then. Let's have a go,' said Charley. 'I wanna know what a king feels like.'

'No. I'm sorry, mate. I can't let you drive it, cos it's not insured for you. But if it was up to me, I'd let you have a go. Course I would. But the law is the law, and you wouldn't want me to break the law now, would you?'

After the short test ride, Charley got out the van and kicked at the wheels. The tyres weren't too bad, the windscreen wipers and horn worked, and the vehicle had two seats – quite a step up from the other old beast.

'I'll give you a tenner, cash, here and now,' said Charley, chancing his arm.

'Oh, do me a favour, mate,' Ted sighed. 'What do you think I'm running, a charity or something?'

'All right then. Fifteen quid.'

'Fifteen quid! I got four hungry kids to feed at home. How far do you think that'll go?'

Charley rubbed his chin. 'That's all I got, mate.'

'I'm going to get bloody rich out of you two buggers, ain't I? Ah, but what the hell. What's money when you like someone,' he said, standing there flashing his teeth like the trustworthy preacher again. 'And seeing as I like you both *so* much...'

'Woah, woah. Now I know you're telling porkies, mate,' Charley replied.

'All right. I'll cut the crap. You can have it for a score, and for that, I'll chuck in a gallon of petrol as well. That's the best I can do for you. Take it or leave it. What do you say?'

Charley shook his head.

'You give Prince Charles a ring, see if he'll give you a better price, cos I can't afford it.'

'Have it on the drip then,' [HP] he replied, trying to tempt Charley. 'Spread the cost over a few months.'

'No. I'm not going into debt for a scabby motor. I'd sooner walk.'

'Look. If I let it go any cheaper, my kids won't eat again this week.'

'Think yourself lucky,' grumbled Butch. 'We ain't had a good feed in months, have we, Chas?'

'And he ain't joking, Ted,' said Charley, walking around to the front of the van. 'How about if I give you all the money in my pocket?' – which, when counted out onto the bonnet of the van, was £17/9s/3d.

Ted looked at the money, scratched his head and frowned. 'You sure you ain't got anymore tucked away anywhere? What about the other pocket?'

'No. That's all I got, mate.' Charley pulled out the linings of both pockets.

'Oh, all right. Go on then. I must be bloody mad. Scrape it all up and bring it into the office. We gotta deal.'

'Oh, good! Do I get a guarantee with it, then?' Charley smiled with delight.

'Guarantee – yeah, of course, you do, mate,' said Ted. 'It sounds like luck, and ends in all.'

'I still get the gallon of petrol, though, don't I?'

'What, at five bob a gallon! You must be bloody joking!'

'Hmm. What do you think, Butch?' Charley asked, feeling that he had just struck the deal of the century.

'Yeah, if I had that sort of dough to spend on a motor, Chas, I'd buy it.'

'Go on then, Ted,' said Charley, emptying his pocket out onto his desk. 'I'll take it.'

'Oh, good. I am so pleased. Perhaps I can now shut up shop and take my family on holiday,' said Ted, trying to make a joke.

He then gave Charley the log book, keys and a bill of sale with the words "Bought as seen. Tried and tested" scribbled across it.

Charley Henry felt dead chuffed driving home in his new van. He sounded the horn a couple of times, and even though it wasn't raining, he turned on the windscreen wipers. To Charley, it was a dream come true having a motor that worked for a change. But then, after only a couple of miles, the engine started to overheat. When he stopped and lifted the bonnet to investigate, steam was spitting and billowing from the radiator like an old traction engine.

'Cor blimey that's a bloody shit ain't it!' said Butch stopped his bike in a cloud of smoke to help, 'I'll go and get some water.'

'No, no. Hang on, Butch. There's a ditch full of it over there. All we need is something to collect it in.'

Butch scrabbled around inside his old sidecar and found an empty bottle. Once the van had cooled down sufficiently, they filled the bottle from the ditch and started to fill the rad. But as fast as they were pouring the water in, it was just guzzling back out again through a number of holes in the face of the radiator.

'Shit!' said Charley, pacing up and down, thinking how they could block the holes.

'We could always fill the rad with concrete,' Butch joked. 'That would stop the water coming out.'

'Ha ha. Very funny.'

'All right then. I'll go and get some chewing gum,' he said, firing up his bike with the usual cloud of smoke. 'I'll be back in a minute.'

Butch returned with a tin of liquid radweld that he got from a nearby garage. When they poured it into the radiator, it reduced the leak to just a small weep, and so Charley was able to drive the van home.

The following day, Charley went out in his new van and found a job with "King Publicities". They supplied, built and erected all the advertising board banners and hoardings onto the motor racing circuits throughout the British Isles, including the Isle of Man. The main works were situated at Greenwich in South East London. Charley was attached to their smaller Dartford branch, which covered all operations to the Brands Hatch circuit, in Kent.

It was an easy job, and Charley wasn't expected to write anything. And, as he lived less than 4 miles from the circuit, he was able to drive straight there from home each morning while the rest of the lads travelled the 12 miles out from Dartford in the firm's new, shiny white van.

Charley's hourly rate was 7 shillings [35 pence], which equated to £14 per week. Like most jobs back in those days, there was no sick pay or the like to rely on, and so if you didn't turn up for work, you didn't get paid. Therefore, short of actually dying, most people made every effort to get into work, as did Charley on that ill-fated Friday morning when the gearbox in his old van packed up during a violent thunderstorm.

Charley had set off for work extra early because he needed to collect something from the other side of Dartford. As he left Dartford for Brands Hatch, bright flashing lightning began to light up the oppressive dark skies for miles around. The intense heavy rumbling that followed shook the very ground beneath Charley's feet. The torrential downpour that ensued totally swamped the roads, making them look more like rivers. It was as though the end of the world had come. Even the windscreen wipers that Charley was so proud of couldn't cope with the deluge. Nose pressed firmly to the screen, he caught sight of a very bedraggled elderly lady standing patiently at a zebra crossing. Charley did the decent thing and brought his van to a stop and waved her across.

'Thank you, young man, and be lucky!' she cried, waving her hand, as she scurried across a torrent of surface water guzzling down the road.

Charley smiled and waved back. *'It's not me who needs the luck'*, he thought, *'sat in a nice dry van.'* But then, when he tried to pull away, he couldn't get any forward gears. He pulled and pushed the lever every which way, but the only gear he could get was reverse. So, rather than lose any pay, he reversed the van through the appalling storm the remaining nine miles out to the Brands Hatch circuit. When he finally got there, he not only had a very stiff neck, but the gearbox had disintegrated altogether, rendering the vehicle totally inoperable.

After his day's work was done, he phoned the kiosk number at the caravan park.

'Hi. You're through to Quick Clean. How may I help you?'

Charley disguised his voice and asked how he could get a big dollop of bird shit off his windows.

'Yeah, very funny, Chas. You want Butch?' he grunted.

'Yes please, Jim.'

Butch dropped what he was doing, fired up his bike, and like something out of *Thunderbirds*, he went to Charley's rescue. He lashed a length of frayed rope to the bars that held the sidecar onto the motorbike and then, almost pulling the sidecar off in the process, he towed Charley home through the lanes. A hair-raising experience to say the least. Not only did the rope break a couple of times, leaving Charley high and dry in a very dodgy position in the road, but there were occasions when he lost sight of Butch completely, through the thick smokescreen his bike was laying.

Early Saturday morning, while Butch was at work, Charley took his few old spanners and walked the six miles to the car breaker's yard at Faringdon.

'What you after, mate?' asked the greasy car breaker, turning off his oxygen and acetylene gas-cutting lance.

'A gearbox for a Thames 5QCt van.' Charley cast his eyes over the old motors stacked up in the yard.

'We ain't got no van, mate, but there's half a dozen old Thames saloon cars down the back. Go and take a butchers. If you want one of the gearboxes, you'll have to take it out yourself.'

'Are they any good?' asked Charley, hoping.

'No. Course they ain't. They've been scrapped, ain't they? But the gearboxes might be all right for another few miles.'

'Yeah, but what one, though?'

'Ah, well, that's the 64-thousand-dollar question, ain't it? The motors were all brought in on the back of a lorry, so you pay your money and take your choice.'

A good couple of hours Charley sweated getting the gearbox out of one of the old cars. Totally covered in grease, he carried the gearbox on his back all the way home, hoping that it would be all right. By late Sunday evening, his old van was up and running again, and ready for work the next day.

And yet, after all that effort, Charley still lost a day's pay, because his daughter decided to make her grand entrance into the world early.

It all started about 5.30am on 25th September 1965. Charley ran round to the payphone in the wooden kiosk and called the midwife. He explained that Barbara had started labour.

'No. She can't have. The baby's not due for another three weeks.'

'I'm telling you she has. The waters have broken and the baby is on its way now. Is there anything I need to do?' asked Charley anxiously, thinking that she wasn't going to come out in time.

'Yes. You can stay calm for a start. First child – nothing will happen for hours yet. Just go back and reassure your wife. Tell her I'm on my way.'

Charley tried to do just that, but at 6.45am, the baby's head was sticking out and they still had no midwife in attendance. Charley didn't know whether to pull, push, stick or twist, but then Barbara gave an involuntary push and the helpless little baby just slid out onto the bed all by itself. By the time the midwife arrived, their new baby daughter was screaming her head off.

The following day, Charley returned to work, full of the joys of fatherhood, and boldly asked his boss for a pay rise. His boss stalled him, saying that he needed to catch Arthur King in a good mood before putting such a request to him. Every payday thereafter Charley asked the same question, only to be given the same answer.

A month or so later, whilst working out on the track at Brands Hatch near to Paddock Hill Bend Charley noticed a white chauffeur-driven Rolls Royce limousine cruising very slowly around the circuit towards him.

'Hello. What have we here then?' he asked, drawing his workmate's attention.

Out of curiosity, John turned to have a look for himself.

'Oh my god,' he replied quickly, tearing his eyes away in a state of anxiety. 'It's Arthur King! Whatever you do, Chas, don't look at him. Just get your head down and keep on workin' until he's gone.'

'Sod off, John! I'm not going to pass up a golden opportunity like this. I'm going to ask him for a pay rise.'

Charley enthusiastically downed his tools.

'No, no! You can't do that!' cried John, as though Charley would be risking his very existence.

'Why ever not?' Charley felt confident of his intentions.

'Cos he's "Arthur King", the big powerful boss man down from Greenwich. That's why not!'

'"King Arthur" – no better person to ask then, is there?' He stepped into the path of the Rolls, flagging it down. 'The buck stops here. The "King" of the company won't be able to pass my request on like Martin, will he?'

'Oh! Bloody, blimey…' mumbled John tensely, trying to hide as the big limousine came to a standstill at Charley's feet. 'You've done it now; you've bloody done it now, you silly bastard! We'll probably both get the sack!'

After a few anxious seconds, with barely a sound from the engine, one of the rear dark-tinted windows slowly opened, and Charley got his first glimpse of the infamous Arthur King. Huge man, white suit, black shirt, white tie, red braces, like a mafia godfather, he was sat there as large as life on the back seat, puffing on a fat hand-rolled Cuban cigar. Charley swallowed hard and began to think that perhaps John was right after all.

'Well? What do you want?' he growled.

Charley's mouth became very dry, and he was momentarily lost for words.

'Come on! Come on! Spit it out, man!' barked the big boss through a cloud of blue smoke, casually knocking the ash from the end of his cigar.

'I, er, I'm sorry to stop you like this, Mr King,' said Charley respectfully, 'but I need a pay rise. You see, I've just become a new father and I need to put some more bread on the table...'

'Oh, I see,' he grunted impatiently. 'Then you should go through the proper channels and ask Martin Bradstock, not me.'

'With respect, Mr King, I've already done that – er, several times, in fact, and...'

'All right, all right. Enough said. I'll give you three halfpennies an hour.' He stuffed the cigar back into the corner of his mouth and instructed his chauffeur to drive on.

'You jammy sod!' yelled John, wishing he'd asked as well.

'He who dares John; he who dares,' Charley laughed, with relief.

Later that day, Charley got a real dressing-down from Martin for going over his head in that way,

'Nobody has ever, ever, stopped Arthur King like that before,' he said angrily. 'He's absolutely fuming! What on earth possessed you? What were you thinking of...?!'

'A pay rise, Martin. I was thinking about a pay rise, cos I've got a family to feed now. I didn't try and kill him or anything. Besides, he can't be that bothered about it cos he's agreed to give me an extra five bob a week.'

Chapter 4

※

Apart from the wages, Charley Henry enjoyed working at Brands Hatch because there was never a dull moment. At lunchtime, Charley and his workmates would often play a competitive game of football against the Brands Hatch boys on the grassy area between Paddock Hill Bend and the Bottom Straight. There were no rules to abide by, just good-humoured foul play on both sides, which they all enjoyed.

During the run-up to the 1966 Formula One British Grand Prix, the place was buzzing with activity, from a big Hollywood film company to a unit of the British Army, complete with a full military marching band that was to start the big day off.

'Look!' said Charley. 'Ain't that James Garner over there?'

'No! That's big John Wayne,' said Chris, convincingly. 'I'd know him anywhere.'

'No, you prat. That's Clint Eastwood!' voiced Brian.

'It is!' said John, squinting to focus better.

'What, Clint Eastwood?' Charley was not fully convinced.

'No! James Garner!'

For all their assumptions, it was indeed James Garner. He was at Brands Hatch, along with a whole host of other film stars, to make the award-winning Cinerama blockbuster film, *Grand Prix*.

The day the film crew shot the big scene with James Garner in the burning racing car, the pits were full of commotion, for it was the track directly fronting the pits where all the exciting action was to conclude.

Standing on the flat roof of the toilet block in the pits, John and Charley had an excellent aerial view of the entire sequence of events as they unfolded. Primarily, they were up on the roof to erect a huge back-to-back Esso sign. Unaware that anything thrilling was about to happen, they were both busily engaged with fixing the sign. But then John became distracted. From the corner of his eye, he saw smoke billowing from one of the racing cars rounding Clearways Bend.

'Quick! Quick! Look, Chas!' he cried excitedly, shielding his eyes from the sun. 'The bloody car's on fire!'

Both John and Charley, unfamiliar with the film plot, watched with bated breath, as the smoking racing car travelled at speed along the Brabham Straight. The film sequence was very cleverly staged. From the end of the pit lane, prior to the start of Paddock Hill Bend, an identical smoking car was pushed out onto the circuit, creating the illusion that the original car had just screeched to a halt, whereby James Garner, in true Hollywood style, scrambled miraculously from the driving seat, seconds before the car became engulfed in flames.

'Cut!' the film director yelled, waving his arms in the air. 'It's all yours now!' he shouted to the firefighters waiting by.

With the fire being extinguished and the film crew patting themselves on the back for a well-shot action scene, James Garner made his way over from all the commotion towards the very toilet block that John and Charley were working on.

'I think he needs the bog after that!' said John, stepping closer to the edge of the flat roof to get a better look at him.

'I'm not surprised – he's just climbed from a burning racing car! Excitement can sometimes affect people like that. Look at you – you've only gotta see Arthur King coming and you want to shit your pants.'

James Garner couldn't help but notice Charley and John leaning over the parapet. Thinking they were perhaps autograph hunters, he gave a warm smile and began to make light-hearted banter.

'That's the most important place on the track!' he hollered, sounding every bit the all-Texan cowboy.

'What – up here on the toilet roof?' Charley frowned, giving the impression that he didn't entirely understand the quip.

'No no. The "john",' James Garner said, with a cheesy grin, thinking that his friendly little joke was a bit too subtle for the English peasants to understand.

'John? I'm John,' John said, also frowning like a halfwit. 'My old mum, God bless her, she always said that I would be important one day.'

'Impotent more like,' Charley grinned. He hoped that James Garner would soon catch on and see that they were only joking with him, but instead he, too, began to frown.

Unsure, he felt the need to explain that a "john" back home was a toilet, which, of course, both Charley and John knew from all the American films they had seen over the years.

'Mr Garner,' John said, keeping up the pretence of not understanding, 'I've been called many things in my lifetime, but nobody has ever called me a toilet before.'

James Garner was totally mystified and returned a very sickly grin, but then a few seconds later he laughed heartily.

'All right. You got me! Where is it?' he asked, swivelling his neck 180 degrees. 'You're bloody good, I'll give you that much. You almost had me going there for a minute.'

'Where is what?' Charley asked.

'Why, the camera of course! This is Candid Camera, isn't it?'

'Er, no, not exactly, Mr Garner. It's just our wicked sense of humour.'

'He's right, Mr Garner,' John confirmed.

'No, no. I'm not falling for that one,' he said, still looking for a concealed camera.

'I'm telling you, Mr Garner, there is no camera. We're up here to fix this Esso sign. That's all.'

For a minute, James Garner looked almost disappointed, but then he returned a loud chuckle.

'Ah, you British, you sure are something else! I'll never fully understand your humour. It's been nice talking with you boys.'

'And with you also, Mr Garner,' replied Charley, smiling. 'Have a nice day!'

John gave a big toothy grin. 'You've got to have a laugh, Mr Garner. Life's too short to be serious all the time, isn't it?'

'You betcha. I'll go along with that,' he replied, sticking his hand up to bid a friendly farewell.

'Have a nice day! Have a nice day!' John repeated, taking the mic out of Charley.

'Yeah, it's what all the Yanks say. I had to make him feel at home, didn't I?'

'You bloody creep.'

'I may well be a creep, but he'll soon forget me; whereas *you* he'll never forget, cos every time he goes to the bog, he'll think of *you*.'

The day before the actual Grand Prix, all work, including filming, was suspended on the race circuit until the qualifying time trials for the grid positions had been completed by the racing drivers. But come 5pm, Charley and his workmates had been given the green light and the circuit was all theirs once more. They had approximately five hours of reasonable daylight left to complete their massive workload before the start of the Grand Prix. Their crew of six split up into three pairs and then sped off round the race track to different locations to erect large wooden advertising hoardings.

Both John and Charley had driven out to Hawthorn Bend to erect a 20' x 4' Dunlop sign. Its siting was crucial in as much as it had to be picked up by the TV cameras, as the racing cars rounded the bend. This meant clearing a small scrubby area of undergrowth. Grabbing the sickle from the back of the van, Charley began to swipe vigorously at the vegetation while John untied the sign. The long, slender 18-inch curved blade of the sickle ripped through the undergrowth like a hot knife through butter. Whilst raking away the cut vegetation, Charley found that one small pliable sapling had defied the sickle. He took hold of the sickle once more and lunged down at it several times, but each time the blade passed, the stubborn sapling just sprang back up again. Determined not to be beaten, Charley physically bent the sapling down and stood on the very tip to hold it taut, and then with his attention focused firmly on the very centre of the blade, he lunged down with full force, driving the point of the sickle deep into his leg, severing the femoral artery.

'Shit!!' cried Charley pulling the vicious blade from his leg and dropping it to the ground. Whilst manhandling the large sign, John caught sight of Charley's leg spurting blood three feet or more from the wound. He immediately released his grip, dropping the sign to the ground, and rushed to Charley's aid. In his eagerness to help, he tried desperately to lift Charley and carry him over to the van.

'Get off me and go and start the motor!' cried Charley, hobbling over to it. Climbing in, Charley jammed his foot up against the dashboard and clasped both hands tightly around the wound. As the blood continued to pump through his fingers, John, like a Formula One Grand Prix driver, raced the van flat out along the Derek Minter Straight before throwing it, with tyres squealing, into Westfield Bend. Down into Dingle Dell, John's vision was becoming impaired by Charley's blood on the windscreen.

Adrenaline rushing through his veins, John was driving on pure instinct. As they entered Stirling's Bend, John's foot was still hard down, scattering their tools and equipment all over the place. By the time they reached Clearways, John was desperately trying to wipe the blood-soaked windscreen with his hand, to see where they were going.

Alerted by the squealing tyres and high-revving engine were workmates Bob and Chris. Seeing the firm's white van, spattered with blood, go screaming past into Clark Curve, with the back doors flapping wide open, they quickly discarded their tools and scrambled into their own motor and gave chase along Brabham Straight.

John finally skidded the van to a standstill on the starting grid in front of the pits. Luckily for Charley, there were still a small number of enthusiasts opposite, in the stands by the Grovewood Suite. One of them, who had a modicum of medical knowledge, cupped his hands around his mouth like a megaphone and shouted across, 'You must get his leg up higher than his heart, or he will be dead in seven minutes!'

A marshal, overhearing this started to panic.

'Don't just fucking stand there like a fucking doughnut!' yelled John. 'Go and phone for a fucking ambulance! NOW! And be quick about it!'

While the marshal ran into the Grovewood Suite to make the vital call, Charley, given the circumstances, was relatively calm, laid flat across the seats of the van with his leg held high through the open door by Chris. Having been driven more than one and a half miles from the other side of the circuit and the fact that the nearest hospital was approximately twelve miles away at Dartford, he got set to thinking, *'Seven minutes – would I even live long enough to get to the hospital? Do I write my last will and testament in my own blood on the side of the van?'* Then he remembered that he couldn't spell, and that he didn't have anything of value to leave anyway, so he didn't bother.

With Charley's blood still pumping, and running freely across the track over the newly painted grid boxes, John ran to the fence and cut a length of straining wire, whilst Bob rushed and fetched two pieces of batten from the back of the van. Together, they made a crude tourniquet that resembled a large cheese wire, which, when tightened around Charley's leg, reduced the blood flow considerably.

Charley was very lucky that day, having his good workmates to hand with their improvisational skills, and, of course, the unknown soul in the stands who took the trouble to relay the vital lifesaving instructions. Charley gave all credit to West Hill Hospital for their kindness and skill in repairing his severed artery.

At 12 o'clock that night, Charley was discharged from hospital and given a ride home in an ambulance. He was given strict instructions by the doctor in A&E to keep his injured leg up, and totally supported, for a few days.

However, by day two, Charley's leg had swollen to almost twice its normal size. He was in such severe pain that Barbara called the doctor out.

'I think the damaged artery is probably leaking internally. You could also have formed blood clots, and there is a strong possibility that infection has set in as well.'

He then strolled over to the wooden kiosk and called for an ambulance, which took Charley to Joyce Green Hospital.

Originally, Joyce Green was an isolation hospital for contagious diseases, built towards the end of the Victorian era out on the marshes at Long Reach, near Dartford. The sprawling, self-contained complex of historic buildings, including that of a four-mile tramway, was erected on the 315-acre site. Laid solely for the horse-drawn ambulances, the ancient tramway linked all of the detached single-storey wards of the hospital to the terminus of the River Thames ambulance service at Long Reach pier.

On his arrival, Charley was put into a large general medical ward containing two dozen or more male patients. They were from all walks of life, and every one of them was suffering a different ailment.

Whilst Charley was very grateful to the NHS for his free treatment, there was no privacy in that archaic ward, not even a curtain to pull around his bed.

They did, however, have a set of mobile folding screens, but whenever the patients heard the squeal from the oil-starved wheels of the screens being dragged along the ward, it usually meant that somebody was having an enema – being prodded and poked about by groups of young student doctors – or the infamous bed bath, or they had died.

Charley had nothing to compare the experience with, because other than when he was born in the British Hospital for mothers and babies alongside the River Thames during an air raid over London during the Second World War, he had never stayed in hospital before. It was entirely new to him.

On his first day at Joyce Green, he felt the sharp edge of the Matron's tongue. Dave, the male nurse of the ward, came to Charley's aid.

'As you've just found out, Charley, it's very unhealthy to call the Matron a nurse. It's a wonder you're still alive.'

He then went on to educate Charley regarding hospital life, the nursing staff and how to address and recognise them by their different uniforms. He was a real pleasant character, one who made the lives of the patients just that bit more tolerable.

Charley's adjacent bed neighbour on the left-hand side was a middle-aged guy called Albert, a colourful cockney character with a good sense of humour, and a very serious heart problem to go with it. On the other side was the original Tommy Atkins, an old soldier of the Second World War who, apart from breaking wind every five minutes, told Albert and Charley of his endless wartime stories. They didn't even get any peace when Tommy was asleep, because his snoring shook the entire ward.

When it came to bodily functions, Charley found that being confined to bed was a total loss of dignity.

'What about when I want to empty the old pipe?' he asked Dave.

'Use the bottle, Charley,' he replied, pointing to the cabinet.

'I can't do that! What about the other end?'

'Just wave your hand and we'll bring you a bedpan over.'

'No way, Dave. I'm not using one of them things. The bottle's bad enough.'

Four days had passed, but Charley had passed nothing regarding the brown stuff. Dave gave him the nod that an enema had been ordered from above and that it was soon to be looming his way.

'Look, Dave. If I can just get to the little boys' room down the end of the ward, everything will be okay and you can save your soapy water for the washing-up.'

'No. I'm sorry, Charley. You can't go down there yet, because your leg must remain flat on the bed at all times. You can't risk putting it on the ground at this stage of the game.'

'Well, I'm sorry, too, Dave, cos I just can't use a bedpan. And there's no way you're giving me an enema either.'

'All right, Charley. If that's how you feel, the best I can do is a commode.'

'A what?'

'A commode.'

'Look, whatever you do in your private life, Dave, has got nothing to do with me,' Charley joked.

'You'll love it, Charley. It's got all the luxuries of a real toilet, except you don't have to pull the chain. I do that for you. It's on its own wheels. I'll bring it over. See what you think.'

'What about the modesty screens?'

'Yeah. I'll bring them over as well.'

'There's no denying it, Dave, I do need to go, and badly at that, but it's bloody embarrassing all the same.'

'Look, don't worry, Charley. Once the screens are around your bed, you'll have complete privacy, and nobody will ever know what you're doing. You can just sit there, like a royal personage on the throne, enjoying yourself.'

'What about Albert? He'll know.'

'He's asleep. Look at him.'

'Okay, Dave. Let's do it then, before he wakes up.'

So Dave pulled the screens around Charley's bed, fetched the commode and ridged the board up to keep Charley's leg supported.

Charley had only been sat on the throne for a couple of minutes when he heard Albert hollering.

'Cor blimey, Dave! Bring that pole over and open this window, will you? I can't breathe here!'

The next time the screens were pulled around Charley's bed was when he was subjected to the legendary blanket bath by two pretty young nurses.

'I must warn you both,' said Charley, feeling somewhat embarrassed, 'there is a very sensitive area on my body, and you shouldn't touch it under any circumstances.'

The girls gave a naughty giggle. What they must have been thinking, God only knows, but it was too late – one of them had touched it. The soap was kicked from her hand, clean over the screens. The young brunette dashed through the screens to try and catch the soap, but it had already landed with a thud onto Albert's bed, which made him cheer, 'You fill your boots, Chas, mate! You'd pay a fortune for that sort of treatment up town.'

'Ticklish feet – so that's the sensitive area to avoid, is it?' said the slender blonde nurse, with one hand over her mouth to prevent her from laughing too loud.

'There is another one, but that's a bit further up. I'll stop you when you get there.'

Again, she let out a naughty giggle.

'Under my arms,' Charley said.

In the bed opposite was an old boy who would sleep all day; but then, after dark, like a vampire, he would come to life and start singing at the top of his voice. Not that that mattered much anyway, because the ward was such a noisy place there was always something to keep the patients awake.

After being stuck in bed for 10 days solid, Charley was going stir-crazy. He begged Dave to let him get up.

'Ask the doctor. He will be making his rounds this morning.'

The year was 1966, and the whole country was gripped with World Cup football fever.

'I've *got* to see the match today, Chas!' said Albert, all excited. 'It's England v Argentina in the quarter-final. A few good punch-ups there, I reckon.'

Albert was a massively keen football supporter, who would go to any lengths to see the game.

'I'm going to ask the doc when he makes his rounds today if he'll let me go and watch the match in the TV room at the end of the ward.'

'What a bloody good idea, Albert. I'll ask as well.'

'But you said you don't like football, Chas?'

'I know I don't, but if it gets me out of this bloody bed for an hour or so, I love it. Especially if, as you say, there will be a punch-up or two, cos I like watching boxing.'

'You crafty old sod, Chas.'

When the doctor came round they both asked him together, Albert pleading their case very well. He said that if England was to win this match, they'd go on to play Portugal in the semi-final.

'Hmm,' the doc sighed, rubbing his chin. 'If you,' he said, pointing to Dave, 'get Charley into a wheelchair with a board attachment so as to keep his leg up, he can go and watch the match.'

'What about me?!' cried Albert.

'Ah, well, I don't know about you,' he said, tormenting Albert, 'because you mustn't get over-excited.'

'I won't! I won't!' replied Albert, almost having a heart attack through fear of not seeing the game.

'Tell you what, Doc,' Charley said, to wind Albert up. 'I could tell 'im all about it when I get back to the ward.'

'What a good idea! Would that be all right with you, Albert?'

'No! No! I gotta see the game myself, Doc!'

'Oh, all right then. But you, Charley, you must make sure he doesn't get too excited, and you, Albert, you make sure he keeps his leg up at all times.'

There was only the two of them in the room watching the small black and white TV. Charley made sure that he was sat by the fire bucket, ready to throw it over Albert should he get too animated. The game was really tense and many times Charley reached for the bucket.

It was another four days before Charley was finally let out of bed under his own steam. He couldn't walk without a zimmer frame because his ankle joint had seized up through lack of movement, but once he was able to hobble about on two sticks, he was discharged and went home.

Upon presenting the sick note from his doctor to the DHSS, Charley received a small percentage of his wages, for which he was very grateful. But then, to his astonishment, he received full pay from his employer, which helped tremendously.

Charley was off work for a total of eight weeks, but come the day that he was to return, Martin Bradstock sacked him.

'It's got nothing to do with me, Chas, I can assure you,' he said holding up his hands in embarrassment. 'It's A.K. He's got the bollock ache cos you didn't write and thank 'im for paying you while you were off sick.'

'Look, Martin. I know this may sound a bit corny, but I was going to do that on my return...'

Martin interrupted. 'Oh, I see. Well, look. All is not lost, Chas, cos A.K. wants to see you before you pick your cards up. He's a funny old bugger, but his heart's in the right place. So just go and see what he's got to say for himself, eh. Oh, and grovel a bit. That should do the trick. He'll most probably give you your job back then.'

Charley Henry was a proud man. He'd never been sacked before, and he wasn't going to grovel to get his job back. He secured another job, but he did go and pay Arthur King the courtesy of a visit. He felt he owed him that much at least.

'How's the leg?' asked the big man, looking over the top of his glasses, as Charley limped into his office with a stick.

'Much better now. Thank you, Mr King,' Charley smiled.

'Had plenty of time to think in hospital, didn't you?' he grunted.

'Yes, as a matter of fact, I did, Mr King. It was pretty boring having all that time on my hands with nothing to do.'

'You could always have dropped me a line and thanked me for paying you. That would have given you something to do, wouldn't it?' he griped.

Charley felt awful being put on the spot like that. He didn't want to humiliate himself by saying that he couldn't spell, let alone write a letter.

'For what it's worth, Mr King,' trying not to sound like a total creep, 'I was going to shake you by the hand on my return to work and thank you personally for your kindness in paying me while I was off sick. I know you were under no obligation to do so cos the accident was entirely my own fault – and I accept full responsibility for it, even though the DHSS referred to it as being an industrial injury.'

Arthur King looked taken aback.

'Er, perhaps I've been a trifle hasty,' he said raising an eyebrow, while extending his hand as a gesture of forgiveness. 'Let's say no more about the matter, eh. Fit enough to start back today, are we?' he added warmly.

'No. I'm sorry. I can't do that, Mr King, cos I've found another job now, and I start tomorrow. You see, I need a safe steady job cos I'm about to apply for a mortgage to buy a house.'

'You've got a safe job here, and I will give you a glowing reference for the building society.'

'Thanks, but no thanks, Mr King. I'm already committed now.'

'Well, there is always a job here if ever you want one.'

Chapter 5

✳

Charley Henry's new employment was with a major timber preservation company. It was a dirty job, but as Charley said, *for a few pennies more*, it was worth it. The job involved the gutting, repair and chemical treatment of old buildings that were severely affected by dry rot and woodworm. The only good thing Charley had to say about it was the money he was taking home: in excess of £19 most weeks. And so, with the extra £5 a week coming in, he was able to get a £3,400 mortgage on a very run-down three-bedroom semi in a good area, close to the park. Charley's logic was that a fully refurbished property in that location would be worth considerably more than he paid for it.

His first ambitious step onto the property ladder proved to be very demanding. Not only were the renovation works gobbling up most of his wages, he still had to find the £25 a month to pay the mortgage. Charley was going into work most mornings totally exhausted from working on the house till midnight, seven days a week.

Totally focused on the house, Charley didn't give a thought to the toxic mixture of chemicals he was being exposed to during his daytime job – and nobody from the company warned their employees of any health hazards either. The only safety equipment given out were a mask, goggles and rubber gloves. Oh, and a fire extinguisher, because the toxic spirit-based chemicals they sprayed each day were highly inflammable, as one of Charley's workmates found out when his spraying lance touched and shorted out some dodgy wiring within a roof void he was working in. The bright flashing sparks instantly ignited the poisonous vapour, setting the whole roof ablaze. It was a miracle the lad ever got out of there alive.

The local papers had a field day with pictures of the burnt-out house plastered all over their front pages, with captions such as *"The Timber Preservation Company has now resulted into cremating the woodworm, as opposed to spraying them with the lethal chemical"*

Up until the day of the fire, it was common practice for Charley and his workmates to crawl about under small floor spaces and in tiny roof voids, spraying the inflammable chemicals. For a measly few pennies more, Charley had risked his life for more than four years working in that harmful environment, spraying what is now a banned substance.

During this time, his son was born; like his sister, he, too, was very eager to get out into the world and make his mark. Weighing in at just 4lb, he climbed into the ring two months prematurely. He was extremely weak and severely jaundiced and had to be placed in an incubator to give him the best chance of survival.

Alarm bells began to ring at the hospital when his body weight dropped under 3lb. The look in the nursing Sister's eyes said it all.

'Have you thought of a name yet?' she asked compassionately. 'We can't keep calling the little chap Baby Henry now, can we?'

Picking up on her concern, Charley was scared shitless. He turned to Barbara, but she was welling up and unable to speak. With a choking lump in his throat, he turned back to the Sister and said, 'Samson. His name is Samson, cos one day, that little fella is going to be very strong.'

The Sister smiled. 'Hello Samson,' she whispered, stroking the back of his tiny little hand with her forefinger. She then drew her pen like a sword and wrote the name Samson Henry in big bold letters onto a new identity card, displayed on the incubator for all to see.

Charley's workmate George insisted on buying him a pint to wet the baby's head.

'Cheers and good health to young Samson!' he said with warm sincerity, raising his glass.

'Sam. We've decided to name him Sam. I think he's had a rough enough start to life without making him a target for all the bullies of this world. Can you imagine what his schooldays would be like with a name like Samson? He'd be challenged every single day.'

'Yeah, you're probably right, Chas. Kids can be bloody cruel without even knowing it, can't they? Anyway, you're a lucky old sod, mate, having a son and heir. I would give anything for my missus to fall pregnant. Goodness knows we've been trying to have a little chivvy of our own ever since we got married, but it don't look as though we're ever goin' to have one…'

'Yes, you will, George,' Charley replied, taking a swig of his beer. 'Just stop trying so hard and it will happen all by itself.'

And sure enough, a week or so before Christmas that same year, George broke the good news to Charley. He was so excited that he couldn't stop talking about it. But sadly, on Christmas Eve, George died suddenly. His grief-stricken widow said that his respiratory system had failed him during the early hours of the morning, and that he'd died in her arms, horribly, gasping for air.

The news was like a hammer blow, which stunned, and deeply saddened, Charley. Shortly after paying his respects at George's funeral, Charley began to think that perhaps the toxic chemicals they both breathed in on a daily basis may have caused, or even contributed to, the demise of his workmate.

The year was 1969. With no wish to join George in the graveyard, Charley left the job and became self-employed once again, scratching out a living by doing small building works. Having completed his apprenticeship, Charley's brother Alan had also become self-employed and so they would often join forces and scratch along together to earn a few pennies more.

'Can you give me a hand to repair and re-point some chimney stacks?' Alan asked, having secured what he thought was a good job.

'Yeah, all right then, Al. How many, how much and where is it?' replied Charley, eagerly.

'There's 6 altogether, 15 quid and it's Ray Morgan's house.'

'You're kidding me? What, Re-Spray Ray's house, you mean – the second-hand car dealer in Long Hexley?'

'Yeah, play our cards right and we'll get a lot more work from 'im,' said Alan, rubbing his hands together.

'Yeah, I'm sure we will at 15 quid. Are you completely mad or something?'

'It's a job!' barked Alan in reply. 'We can't afford to be too bloody choosy.'

'Look, boy. I know we need work and all that, but we can stay at home and lose money. But that's not the point here. That bloke's bloody loaded. He's just bought that house from that multi-millionaire Henry Benston. And rumour has it, he paid £33,000 for it. And he only got that by selling crappy old cars. Look at the heap of old shit he sold me last year!'

'Well, at least have a look at the job,' Alan said, as he climbed into his van.

'Go on then,' Charley replied, jumping into the passenger's seat.

Charley shuddered, as he gazed up at the huge 60% pitched roof of Morgan's house, with its tall chimney stacks rising 12 foot above the ridgeline.

'You're bloody crazy, Al. You want me to climb up there and risk my neck for 15 quid?'

'No – seven and a half quid. And out of that, you've gotta pay your half of the scaffolding costs as well.'

Charley shook his head and grimaced. 'Now I know you're bloody barmy. Must be that bump on the head from that cricket ball you had…'

'He who dares!' replied Alan, bursting with energy. 'You've gotta start somewhere.'

Charley sighed. 'You're gonna get bloody rich taking on jobs like this,' he grumbled.

Later that same evening, whilst having a drink with his mate Benny, Charley overheard Ray Morgan bragging to his mates in the pub.

'I've got a cheap price from the Henry brothers to re-point all my chimneys.'

'How cheap?' probed one of Morgan's mates, thinking that he could get him a better deal.

'15 quid.'

'How much?' he laughed, as though Alan and Charley were a couple of halfwits.

'15 quid. I'd have gladly paid 'em 85 to have that lot done!'

'Would you?' thought Charley.

'D'you know what, Benny? I'm gonna pay that flash bastard a visit at his car lot tomorrow. See whether I can wipe the smile off his face.'

When Charley got to Morgan's car lot, he explained to Re-Spray Ray that Alan had only just finished his apprenticeship and that he was a bit green as to pricing work.

'How green?' Morgan frowned, thinking that Charley was about to mug his wallet.

'65 quid,' said Charley quickly.

'What, you want me to pay you 65 quid just to point three chimneys?'

'No, Mr Morgan – 80. And that's for all three pairs of stacks.'

'But you just said 65?'

'Yeah, plus the original 15 that Alan quoted.'

Morgan took a deep breath and groaned. 'Go on then, 80 quid it is.'

'I don't believe it!' said Alan, laughing. '£80!'

'No – £40,' said Charley. 'Half of that is mine, don't forget. Stick with me, kid, and you'll earn plenty of wonga.'

They hired a 60-foot triple-extending ladder, which barely made the top of the gable end where the first pair of stacks rose up from. Another matching pair were at the far end of the building. The third pair were midway between the two gables.

They couldn't afford proper scaffolding, so they built a timber makeshift platform from some old second-hand boards and 4x2s, which they hauled up and carried along the ridge like a couple of circus clowns. Even while standing on the rickety platform which they'd precariously strung across the ridge, they still couldn't reach the top of the chimneys.

'I've got an idea,' said Alan, rushing down to grab an equally rickety old pair of steps from the back of his van.

'Don't even think about it, Al, cos even with 'em placed on our wobbly platform, we still won't reach the top of the chimneys.'

'Yeah, we will. Trust me. You stand on the top rung first, and then I'll climb up and stand on your shoulders.'

And so the death-defying act began. Only, for them to reach the chimney tops, they both had to stand on tiptoes, which caused the platform to shake even more. To achieve some kind of stability, Charley reached out and wrapped his arms around the chimney and hugged it tightly. Whilst Alan was raining dust and debris down onto Charley's head, Charley called up and reminded him about the rotten old rust bucket of a car full of filler that Re-Spray Ray Morgan had tucked him up with.

'Oh, yeah! What goes around comes around Chas, don't it? I've got a paving slab in the back of my van. I'll cement it on the top of the chimney that serves the lounge. That'll give 'im a nice little surprise at Christmastime, wont it?'

'Yeah. I'd love to be a fly on the wall when he lights a nice yule log fire in the inglenook!'

Nice thought, but they never did it.

Alan and Charley were always out on a limb in those days, taking on impossible jobs and risking their necks for a few pennies more. However, in going their own separate ways, they both started taking on bigger and better jobs. Seizing the opportunity to make a few pennies more for himself, brother Albert gave both Charley and Alan their own trading account to supply building materials at an agreed trade discount.

One day, on a visit to Albert's yard to collect some building supplies, Charley found the shop had been totally wrecked.

'What the bloody hell's happened here?' he asked Albert's manager, Brian, who was attempting to clear up. 'A car crash, was it?'

'No – it was your brother Alan. It all happened after a heated exchange with Bert. Alan grabbed a claw hammer from the display board and then started to smash the place up.'

'Bloody hell!' said Charley. 'Bert didn't try and stop him, then?'

'No way!' replied Brian, trying to keep a straight face. 'The way Alan was swinging that hammer, Bert just stood back out the way and let him do it.'

Alan would have good reason to do that, and Charley couldn't wait to find out what it was. He drove to where he knew Alan was working.

'You'll never guess, Al … I've just passed Happy's yard and it looks as though there's been a big gas explosion there.'

Alan laughed. 'Serves the bastard right! D'you know what he said to me?'

'D'you want to buy a cheap claw hammer?'

'That's a laugh! I know 'e's our brother and all that, but that bastard wouldn't give you anything cheap. The only reason I rearranged his shop like that is cos he welshed on the agreed discount. Can you believe it? He said that he wasn't going to make me rich. I wouldn't mind, but I could have got a better deal at Jonesy's. And now cos of that bastard, the job's plunged into debt. And I can't ask for any more money either, cos I gave a fixed price.'

As Charley said, it was tough out there being the only breadwinner in your family.

Chapter 6

✳

Charley was happy that Barbara, being a good caring mother, wanted to stay home and bring up the children. Being an avid reader, she would often read a complete book in a day. However, things started to go seriously wrong for them when Barbara began to read endless books on the occult. In no time at all, she had become completely spellbound by them.

Their friends Benny and Jenny and Don and Jan came around for a fish and chip supper one evening. For a bit of fun after the meal, it was suggested that they try and make contact with the dear departed. And so, copying the sequence of events described in one of the books that Barbara had become obsessed with, letters of the alphabet were scribbled onto scraps of paper and positioned in a large circle on top of the dining room table. An upturned drinking glass was then placed in the centre of the circle and the lights were dimmed. Starting with Barbara, they all began to place their fingertips very lightly on the upturned glass.

'What happens now?' asked Charley, not having read any of the books.

'Ask if there is anybody there,' Barbara said.

'Is there anybody there?' asked Charley, looking under the table and laughing.

'No, you've gotta be serious and ask properly or the spirit world will think you're just making fun of 'em,' Barbara snapped.

'Oh, okay okay. Is there anybody there?' Charley asked, in a low spooky voice, still laughing, by which time everybody else was also laughing – everyone except Barbara.

It seemed like a harmless bit of fun at first – nobody ever expected anything to happen – but then, the glass began to move very slowly around the table top, keeping inside the circle of letters.

They all laughed, accusing one another of pushing it. But then, when a question was put to whatever was moving the glass, things started to get a tad ghostly. Highly energised, the glass zoomed around the table top, pushing the letters out of the circle faster than anyone could possibly read them. As they all became captivated, trying to formulate the letters into words, and the words into sentences, a loud rap on the front door startled them all – but it was nothing more sinister than Charley's brother Reggie.

Taking his seat around the table, Reggie began to mock the idea of communicating with the dead.

'If you believe all that old crap, you want your heads testing. Next, you'll be telling me you've conjured up an old Indian Chief or something.'

'None other than Big Chief Sitting Bull,' joked Charley, 'and he's already done one or two astonishing things…'

'Like what?' asked Reggie, challenging them to convince him?

'Well, after he told us all about the Battle of the Little Bighorn, he said that you were gonna come round!' joked Charley.

'Yeah, I bet he did. I s'pose he told you what I would be wearing as well, didn't he?'

'Well, funny you should say that, Reggie,' said Benny. 'He started to, but then you disturbed him. Forgive the pun, but he stopped dead when you knocked on the door.'

'Yeah, I bet he did,' said Reggie, laughing. 'Look, just to prove you all wrong…'

He delved into his pocket and produced an old tobacco tin.

'What's all this then? Need a fag to calm your nerves then, Reggie?' Charley asked.

'No, Chas,' he replied, casually tossing the tobacco tin into the centre of the circle, narrowly missing the glass.

'What's the tobacco for then?' asked Don. 'Are you going to invite the Chief to smoke the old peace pipe?'

Again, everybody laughed, including Reggie.

'No, course not. We ain't got no pipe for starters.'

'Well, then, perhaps the old Chief will bring one,' said Charley. 'It's only fair, 'cos you've supplied the tobacco.'

'In order to prove that one of you buggers is pushing the glass, just ask the spook to spell out the name that was once on the tin lid.'

'What d'you want it in, Apache or English?' Don asked, poking more fun.

'Oh, come on, Don. We want it in English,' said Benny. 'If it's in Apache, we won't know whether he speaks with forked tongue or not, will we?'

'Just cut the crap and do it!' Reggie shouted.

'Not much of a test, Reggie,' Charley said. 'We all know you smoke Old Holborn. Why don't you ask him to roll you a fag instead – that would prove it!'

'No, not the name of the tobacco in the tin, you prat! There are the worn-out remains of an old transfer on the tin lid. It's the name that was on the *transfer* that I want your old dead Chief to spell out. Do that and I'll become an instant believer?'

Startling everybody with a loud piercing scream, Jan pulled quickly back from the table.

'The glass!' she cried. 'It just moved all by itself! I saw it! I bloody saw it!'

'Don't be bloody daft!' said Don, hastily removing his hands and feet safely back from the table. 'You imagined it.'

'I didn't! I'm bloody telling you, I didn't!' she said, looking evidently shocked. 'The glass moved all by itself. I swear it did. I bloody swear it.'

Jan's reaction seemed real enough, but Reggie was not convinced.

'Look, just put your fingers back on the glass,' he said, 'and I will prove that it's just a load of old bollocks.'

Reggie stood back to observe, hoping to see who was pushing the glass.

To everybody's astonishment, the glass pushed the letters I-N-N-S-B-R-U-C-K out of the circle.

Reggie was the first to gasp. Totally flabbergasted, his eyes bulging and his heart pounding, he cried, 'That's impossible! Bloody impossible! Nobody but me could have possibly known that. You can scrutinise the lid all you want, but you won't see the name.'

The three girls were visibly disturbed. They hurried away from the table and sat apprehensively on the settee.

'Oh, this is bloody ridiculous,' said Charley, breaking up the circle of letters and righting the upturned drinking glass. 'Time for a nice cup of tea, I think,' he said, trying to regain the composure.

'I ain't goin' out in the kitchen on my own,' said Barbara, showing the whites of her eyes.

An hour or so later, without any letter whatsoever being on the table, Charley carefully turned the glass face down. After the four lads each placed a fingertip very lightly on it, Charley asked if the spirit was still there. To everyone's disbelief, the glass started to move slowly across the table.

With the girls scared shitless, Charley stood up and said, 'I can assure you all, it ain't me pushing it. Cubs' honour, it isn't.'

'Nor me,' said Benny, through an uneasy smile.

'Well, don't all look at me!' cried Don, pulling his hands well clear of the table again. 'I didn't do it!'

'Piss off back to your reservation!' hollered Reggie.

'Don't antagonise it, Reggie,' said Barbara, fearing the worst.

Despite eventually throwing the glass, and all the letters, into the dustbin, Barbara truly believed that their house had become haunted as a result of their dabbling with the unknown. She became deeply troubled by mysterious noises and apparitions. It became so bad that she was afraid to stay in the house on her own, whilst Charley was at work.

Out of complete desperation, Charley and Barbara contacted the local vicar, the Reverend George Baron. To their huge relief, he understood and was very supportive. He went to their house and carried out a number of exorcisms, claiming to have cast out evil spirits. But, instead of their lives returning to normal, the situation got graver: Barbara truly believed that she herself had become possessed by the devil.

They were both under enormous strain and living in absolute turmoil. Charley was going to work each day totally exhausted through lack of sleep because Barbara was in such a state of mental torment. Just when he thought things couldn't get any worse, he received a panicked telephone call at work from Shirley, a neighbouring friend, who Barbara had confided in.

'I don't know how to tell you this, Chas,' began Shirley nervously, 'but Barbara was up here this morning having a coffee, nice and calm one minute and absolutely petrified the next. I had only just put the biscuit barrel down on the table when she stood up and screamed out at the top of her voice. And before I could ask her what was wrong, she had jumped straight through the glass entrance doors of our porch! It scared the bloody shit out of me. There's nothing left of our porch; it's all smashed to pieces. I can't believe she didn't cut her bloody throat.'

'Don't worry about your porch, Shirley. I'll soon fix that. Where is she now?' he asked, almost too afraid of the answer.

'I honestly don't know, Chas, 'cos she was off up the road so quickly, screaming her head off. It was though something terrifying was chasing after her.'

Charley's heart sank.

'What about the children?' he asked, with bated breath.

'Oh, they're all right, Chas. Don't you worry about them. You just go and find Barbara. I'll look after the kids.'

Charley searched for many frantic hours before picking up the children from Shirley and taking them home. He then waited anxiously, with an agonising pain in the pit of his stomach. After what seemed like an eternity, he received a very disturbing telephone call. At first, all he could hear was the sound of uncontrollable sobbing. Deeply distressed, Barbara then began screaming hysterically.

'Help! Help! Please, help me,' she begged.

The hairs on the back of Charley's neck rose up, and the feeling of hopelessness sent a very cold shiver down his spine. To appear calm and in control, Charley drew a deep breath and said, 'Don't worry, Barbara. I'm on my way. Just tell me where you are and I'll be right there to bring you home.'

'I think it's Waterloo station,' she sobbed. 'I don't know how I got here. Please, please, hurry! It's gettin' dark, and I'm very frightened.'

Charley was sick with worry. His heart began to sink – he was at least an hour's journey away from her. He tried desperately to calm her, but then the line went dead.

Before dashing out to the car, pumped with adrenaline, Charley phoned Reverend Baron to fill him in, just in case Barbara was able to make contact with him. He then grabbed the children, bundled them up and left them with his mother-in-law, before driving to the station at high speed.

He was so desperate by the time he got to the station that he just leaped out of the car and abandoned it to the yellow lines.

Charging inside, he systematically searched the entire station and surrounding areas several times, but Barbara was nowhere to be found. He even asked a lady to check the woman's toilets, to no avail.

Before returning to find a parking ticket stuck smack in the middle of his windscreen, he ran over and searched the bus station as well – just in case – but she wasn't there either.

At a loss as to what else to do, Charley went home, numb with worry. No sooner had he closed the front door behind him, the telephone rang. Charging up the hallway, he picked up the receiver and said, 'Hello? Barbara, is that you?'

'No, this is Jessops Windows. We are doing a promotion in your area and would like to extend an invitation to you…'

'I don't wish to be rude mate, but I'm not interest…'

'If we could just take a minute of your time…'

'Look, I told you. I'm not interested, so please get off the line! I'm waiting for an important call.'

'But this will only t……….'

'Goodbye,' said Charley and he put the receiver down.

In the time it took to redial the number, the phone rang again.

'Look, I won't tell you again!' Charley growled.

'It's me, Chas. Shirley. I'm ringing to see if Barbara is all right. Have you found her yet?'

'Sorry about that, Shirley. I thought you were that pesky double-glazing salesman again.'

'Oh, them. I'm fed up with them buggers cold calling all the time.'

'A fact of life, Shirley, but back to your question … I had an alarming call from Barbara. She was begging for help.'

'Where is she? Where is she?'

'The call was made from a station up town, but the line went dead. She could be anywhere now.'

'I'm sorry, Chas. If there's anything I can do, just give me a ring.'

'Thanks, Shirley.'

After a further three frantic hours of pacing up and down, willing the phone to ring, Charley received an anxious call from Barbara's cousin Bet, in Devon. Very tensely, she said that she had found Barbara sat in the darkness in her garden, her eyes glazed over, groaning and nodding her head.

'I'm so worried, Chas. She won't even acknowledge me. It's as though she's in some kind of trance or other.'

'Oh, thank goodness you found her, Bet!' said Charley, with relief.

'It was only by chance I did find her, Chas, 'cos I don't normally go out the back after dark.'

'I'm very glad you did, Bet. But look, she desperately needs your help right now. I've got no time to explain, so please just coax her inside any way you can, and lock the door behind her so she can't get out. And don't, under any circumstances, let her out of your sight for a minute! Sit with her all night if necessary. I'll fill you in when I get down there.'

'Okay, Chas,' replied Bet, nervously. 'I'll try, but she scares the bloody shit out of me in this state.'

'You and me both, Bet.'

Charley's father-in-law insisted on going down to Devon with him. He was just about to go and pick him up when Shirley's husband, Frank, came round and offered to drive them both down in his new car.

'Your old banger will never make it,' he said. 'We'll go in mine. It's a fast bugger, and we'll be down there in no time.'

Charley was so desperate to get to Barbara as quickly as possible that he accepted Frank's kind offer without question.

But the journey to Devon was a complete nightmare. First, they ran out of petrol.

'I don't understand it!' said Frank, tapping the fuel gauge. 'It's reading half a tank. Look!'

Then, there were the massive delays with endless roadworks, road closures and diversions. As a result, they got lost. It was as though there really was an evil force trying to stop them from getting to, and rescuing, Barbara. The final straw came when the clutch gave out on Frank's new car, leaving them all stranded in pitch-darkness somewhere on the Salisbury Plain.

It was an impossible situation: pouring with rain, gone midnight, miles from anywhere, not a soul in sight. Worried sick, Charley wandered off away from the car and whispered, 'Lord, as you know, I'm not a religious man, but right now I desperately need your help, please.'

As if by divine intervention, a battered old Series One Land Rover came looming out of the darkness and stopped right there at Charley's feet.

'You got a problem, mate?' the chirpy driver asked, leaning out of the window.

'Yes,' replied Charley, with a heavy heart. 'The clutch has gone on our motor.'

'Want a lift somewhere, then? I'll take you anywhere you want to go.'

'That's very kind of you,' replied Charley, thinking that all was not lost. 'We're desperately trying to get to Sunbury in Devon, so if it's not too much trouble, I would appreciate a lift to the nearest phone box so we can make the necessary arrangements.'

'I'll do better than that, mate!' replied the Good Samaritan jovially. 'I'll take you all the way! I'm going down to Exeter myself, and I could do with the company.'

True to his word, in the early hours of the morning, the kind man dropped Charley and his father-in-law, John, right outside Bet's house. Frank stayed with his broken car in the rain, somewhere on the Salisbury Plain.

'Thank goodness you've come!' said Bet, opening the front door. 'She's in the other room. The door is open. I'll go and put the kettle on.'

When Charley and John peered into the room, they saw Barbara sat on the floor in the corner, panting like a dog and staring into the abyss. When they entered, Barbara became alert and extremely agitated. She was scared of everything and everybody.

'It's all right, Barbs,' said Charley, reassuringly. 'Relax. We're here now, and you're very safe. I won't let anything harm you. I promise you.'

'She's been like that the whole time,' said Bet, bringing the tea through.

Both Charley and John spent a long, agonising night trying to get through to Barbara, without any success at all.

'We've just got to restrain her and take her home, John,' said Charley.

Not knowing what else to suggest, John agreed. At daybreak, mentally and physically spent, they grasped an arm each and escorted Barbara to the station. Stood on the platform, waiting to board the train back home to Kent, Barbara looked absolutely petrified, almost as though she was being abducted. Onlookers kept their distance, but it didn't stop them from gawping and talking among themselves. Charley was expecting one of them to call the police, but they didn't. He tried to ignore everybody else and spent the whole journey wondering what to do for the best. With deep pain and anguish in his heart, he tried talking the problem over with John.

'She's convinced she's possessed by demons, John. She needs help desperately and yet if I take her to the doctor's in this state, I'm scared they'll commit her to a mental institution.'

John didn't have any answers either. He was just as scared and concerned as Charley.

'I'll support you in whatever decision you make, Chas. You know I will,' he said sincerely.

John was a man of high integrity, and Charley had enormous respect for him and for the extremely hard life he'd led. He knew what it was like to suffer, having been through several traumatic theatres of the Second World War, including that of the Normandy landings, which he rarely spoke of.

'I remember returning home when it was all over. I went to Erith Council to put my name down on the tenders list to repair war-damaged properties. And I was told by some pompous arrogant git down there that they only looked after those who had looked after them during the War.'

'That's bloody disgusting, John,' Charley replied, feeling deeply angry inside. 'What did they think you were doing during the War? Sitting on your arse at home by the bloody fire drinking tea all day?'

'I must admit, I was a bit aggrieved.'

'Aggrieved? I bet you were, John.'

'I got my own back, though, cos that Christmas, 1945, when things were still a bit tight, I took a saw and climbed over the locked gates of Erith park and cut the top six foot off their Christmas tree and took it home.'

'Good for you, John! Although I must admit, I'd have taken the whole bloody tree!'

'The thought had crossed my mind, Chas, but then it was over 20 foot tall!'

They both laughed for a few minutes, but then their thoughts soon returned to Barbara.

'I'll try the vicar first, John, cos he seems to have good knowledge of these things. We'll use the doctor as a last resort.'

So, when they got to John's house, Charley telephoned the reverend and arranged for him and three others from the church, to come to their house that same evening. But Barbara was still afraid that the house was haunted and didn't want to go home to it.

'Look, Barbs. The vicar is going to come and sprinkle a bit of holy water around and carry out an exorcism ceremony and cleanse the house of the evil.'

Convinced that that was the only answer, she agreed to go home and take part in the exorcism. Yet, as soon the vicar arrived, Barbara became very scared and tried to escape. Charley did his best to restrain her, afraid she would jump through a window and run away again, but she gained enormous strength from somewhere and broke free from his grasp, whereby the vicar immediately lifted up his hands and asked the Lord Jesus to bind whatever it was that was controlling her.

Charley was astonished. It was unreal. This can't be happening, he thought, but it was. Other than making an eerie, unearthly groan, Barbara had become totally paralysed.

Charley felt utterly powerless throughout.

The vicar was about to continue when the doorbell rang. Charley's brother Alan, unaware of the proceedings, charged straight into the lounge, dancing and singing in a silly high-pitched voice, *"Polly put the kettle on"*.

'Oops,' he said, stopping dead, his mouth gaping wide open.

'As you can see, Al, not a good time. I'll fill you in and give you a cup of tea another time.'

'Er, okay then, Chas. Sounds good to me.' Alan flicked his eyes around the room, trying to make sense of it all. 'See you later!' He then climbed back into his van and drove away none the wiser.

Charley really didn't want to see Barbara committed to a mental hospital and so he was inclined to believe that she really was possessed by an evil spirit or the like.

Before continuing, the vicar claimed the protection of the Holy Spirit for all concerned. Then, in the name of the Lord, he placed his hands on Barbara's head and began to challenge the evil. Unable to move, she began to make that same spine-chilling growling noise from deep within her throat. It was very disturbing for Charley to watch, but within a few minutes the tortured look began to drain away from her face. It was as though he really had cast out any demons from her. It was truly amazing, miraculous even. She had been freed from her torment. As a result, Barbara became very religious.

However, within a few short months of finding religion, Barbara felt the need to confess to Charley of her indiscretions: with a self-professed devil worshipper that she'd been involved with prior to the haunting. It may have initially freed her from her own punishing conscience, but the devastating news, coupled with the plaguing thought of her with others – and the devil worshipper – was too much for Charley to bear. Before that, he would have willingly laid down his own life to keep her safe, but now he just wanted to walk away. But he couldn't just up sticks and leave: he had two small innocent children to think of, and they needed him more than ever now.

In his deep despair, he began to think that perhaps the heavy burden of guilt that Barbara had been carrying around inside her may have just pushed her over the edge. All of the house haunting, the being possessed by demons and, ultimately, her salvation by God was just a load of old bollocks conjured up by her own mind.

To add to his despair, Charley then received the disturbing news from the school doctor that his daughter had a serious heart murmur.

'Make an appointment to see your own doctor immediately,' he said, handing over a note to pass on, 'and then he can arrange for further tests for your daughter.'

Without hesitation, Charley and Barbara did as he suggested, but as they were so worried, they called in to see the vicar on the way. He laid his hands on their daughter and prayed for healing, after which they went on to keep the appointment with their doctor. To their absolute joy, he could find nothing wrong with their daughter's heart.

'As a precaution,' the doctor said, looking over the top of his glasses, 'we'll send her for tests at the hospital.' But they couldn't find anything wrong either.

With all the turmoil, Charley had forgotten to pay his account with his brother Big Albert. The day after the payment was due, angry Albert came round in his brand-new expensive Stag sports car and sat outside Charley's house yelling and ranting about how he was going to slap a writ on Charley for just £36. Charley was so incensed that he gave Albert a cheque there and then and told him to stick his account up the same orifice that Alan did earlier that month. They didn't speak again for another 14 years.

After a lot of soul-searching, Barbara and Charley both agreed to put their own lives on hold, stay together as a family unit and bring up their children together. The only possible way they could achieve that was to sell up and move far away. It was a very hard decision for Charley to just walk away from all the contacts he had built up over the years in his small-job building business. But, for his children's sake, he did.

So, in 1971, they sold up and sunk every penny they had into the purchase of a large, un-mortgageable, dilapidated detached country house called Oakland's on the edge of a Dorset village, far away from Kent.

Before Charley could actually move away and get on with the rest of his life, there were two things he needed to do. The first was to go and see Vicar Baron and thank him for all he had done for him and Barbara; the second was to go and find, and then sort out, that devil worshipper.

Charley knocked on the door of the vicarage and was greeted by the young curate's wife.

'Hello. Is George there?'

'No, I'm sorry,' she smiled politely. 'He's just popped over to the church. You can find him there.'

Charley was just about to thank her when George's dog, a large powerfully built Labrador, who she was afraid of, pushed by her and tried to get out to the garden. Charley, being the perfect gentleman, tried to block the dog's path and push it back inside the vicarage, but the dog, totally out of character for such a placid breed, began to make the most ferocious snarling noise. Displaying no fear, Charley stared the dog in the eye and tried to command his authority. The dog had other ideas and stared back, bearing his teeth vehemently. The curate's wife began to scream, and for a split second, Charley took his eyes off the dog. Seizing the opportunity, it sprang up for Charley's throat like a wild monster. Instinctively, Charley threw out his arms to protect himself and, somehow, managed to grab it by the neck, by which time its jaws were up dangerously close to Charley's head. It was as though the dog had now become possessed by the devil.

Its heavy body was twisting, bending and turning every which way, working in perfect harmony with every bit of sinew, bone and muscle that it had. Its head, throughout the sustained attack, was relentlessly and viciously lashing from side to side, trying to shred Charley's face and arms. Charley couldn't let it go because it would rip him to pieces for sure; but he knew that he couldn't hold onto it for much longer either. He was beginning to lose strength. When his arms sagged under the sheer weight of it, the dog's back feet would make contact with the ground and then it would leap up for Charley's throat again.

In a desperate attempt to snap the vicar's wife out of her trauma, Charley yelled, 'Push the door wide open!' She responded instantly without thinking. Once she was safely out of the way, Charley took a deep breath and mustered the last of his strength to swing the heavy Labrador back and forth to gain enough momentum to launch it up into the airspace of the hallway. The plan was to quickly grab hold of the door and slam it tight before the dog landed. However, as he let go, its teeth ripped deep into Charley's flesh. Charley ended up with 16 stitches in the back of his hand, and 6 in the base of his thumb.

Despite the stitches, the following day Charley went in search of the devil worshipper, who he once knew as a biker acquaintance. Charley was to learn from the devil biker's wife that whilst he was fighting the mad dog, her husband was conducting a satanic ritual within a darkened room in his house.

'He forced me to watch!' she said, still trembling from her ordeal. 'It was terrifying! I've never been so scared in my life – he was brandishing a large ceremonial dagger at the time.'

'Where is he now?' asked Charley anxious to know.

'Back inside the loony bin, locked up in a padded cell where he belongs, thank goodness. I hope they throw away the bloody key this time!'

'This time? The loony bin? You mean he's been there before?'

'Yeah, about three years ago he had a breakdown and sexually abused my daughter ... I'll never forgive 'im. But this time, 10 minutes into his creepy ritual, he went absolutely berserk and started to smash the house up. At that point, I took my chances and made a run for it and called the police. The next thing I knew, they came dashing to the house with the men in white coats and wrestled him to the ground. Put him in a straightjacket and carted him away, kicking and screaming. He was then sectioned and detained under the Mental Health Act for the foreseeable future.'

Short of actually breaking into the asylum, there was no way that Charley could ever get to him. Because unlike the mad dog which tried to eat Charley alive, the crazy devil worshipper was locked away inside a very secure unit.

Chapter 7

※

Having said their goodbyes to all their friends and family, Charley and Barbara packed up and left behind the comforts of their newly renovated house in Kent and headed off in convoy [one battered overloaded Ford transit van and a fully packed Ford Classic car] for Oakland's, their new dilapidated country house on the outskirts of Buckleywood village in Dorset.

As there was no agent involved in the purchase of Oakland's, they had arranged to meet the vendor at the property at 12pm, to hand over the key. Helping them with the move was Barbara's brother Harry, who was between jobs at the time, had no money and was therefore in no hurry to get back home.

Upon arrival at Oakland's, they ploughed their vehicles up the overgrown winding driveway to see an old boy with a long white bushy beard sat smoking a pipe in the sunshine on a time-worn tree stump. Wearing a battered old brown corduroy jacket, cloth cap and a red neckerchief, he looked up and saw the two vehicles come to a standstill, but he made no attempt to get up and run away.

'Look! There's an old tramp over there,' said Barbara.

'No! That's no tramp – it's a garden gnome,' Charley joked. 'He'll soon scarper when we get out of the motor.'

Getting ready to challenge the tramp, they climbed out of their vehicles, but the old boy just stayed seated, puffing away on his pipe as if he owned the house.

'Perhaps he comes with the place! 'The gardener maybe?'

'Gardener?' said Harry, casting his eye over the garden. 'That's a laugh, innit?'

'Fine morning,' said Charley to the old tramp.

'Yes – it's very pleasant,' replied the old boy, in a rugged Dorset accent. 'Mr and Mrs Henry, I presume?'

'Now I know we bought 'im with the house,' whispered Charley from the corner of his mouth. He then cleared his throat. 'Er, yeah, that's right. How do you know that?'

'Oh, I knows everything what goes on in this village. I got something for you.'

'Oh, yeah? And what's that, then?' asked Charley, thinking of a nice slice of homemade Dorset apple cake.

'The keys,' the old boy replied, jangling them in the air. 'Old Ted couldn't make it this morning. Got called away he did, unexpected like, so he asked me to meet you here and give you the keys on his behalf.'

'Thanks, er…?'

'Zachariah Gabriel', he said. 'But you can call me Zack if you like.'

'Okay then, Zack. Thanks. And thanks for bringing the keys around. Very good of you. You haven't got wings on your back by any chance, have you?'

'Wings?' he frowned, wondering why Charley had asked such a stupid question.

'Well, the Archangel Gabriel, he was a good chap, and he had wings on his back, didn't he?' Charley smiled.

'You're not from round here, are you?' said the old boy, scratching his head, trying to understand the joke.

'Er, no, Zack. We're from Kent.'

'Ah, well that's not from around here, is it?'

'No, Zack. You're right, it isn't. It's Kent…'

'But you've got a London accent?'

'Yeah. That's probably cos north-west Kent abuts London, Zack.'

'Oh, right. So what do you do to earn your corn then, lad?'

'I'm a builder, Zack.'

'Ah, but we've already got one of they in the village. He's a bit pricy, mind. There is another two who call themselves builders, but they don't even know what end of the shovel to hold.'

'It is a big village, Zack. I'm sure it can accommodate another builder. If not, there are plenty of towns nearby.'

'It's a good job you are a builder, buying a big run-down old place like this ... er, not that it's, er, undesirable or anything. I mean, back along, the house and gardens used to be stunning. The old Mr Jacks and his lovely wife used to host many a fine garden party here. Course, they're both dead and gone now. Still, I'm sure you'll make the place all good again.'

'Yeah, well, that's the plan, Zack,' said Charley, 'but before I can do that, I've got to find some work to pay for it all, and that ain't going to be so easy starting up cold in a new area. Plus the fact I don't know a solitary soul down 'ere.'

A warm friendly smile spread across the old boy's weather-beaten face.

'You know *me*, lad,' he said chirpily. 'I'll start spreading the word for you. Well, must dash now. I can't stand around here all day talking. Things to do, people to see and all that. But before I go, I'll just leave you with this little ditty: *"He who whispers down a well, he will do very well, but he who climbs a tree and hollers, he will make many dollars."* Advertise boy! That's what you must do. You need to shout it from the rooftops that you are here and ready to work.'

He was right, of course, but then Charley didn't have any money left for advertising because he had spent it all on buying the shabby old house. He couldn't even raise a loan at the bank either, because he didn't have the security of a job or any other means of paying it back. Other than the house itself, which, incidentally, wasn't far from falling down, Charley's total worth at the time was the old car and van they arrived in, a bag of tools and 15 shillings in cash. Charley had to stretch the cash to somehow feed them all until he found some work, which wasn't going to be easy, because he still had 22 stitches in his right hand.

Instilled into Charley Henry's psyche when he was a small child were the words of his father: *"Money don't grow on trees. Make do and mend. Buy only what you can afford to pay for. And never, ever buy anything on the drip. And, remember this: a bargain is only a bargain if you've got a use for it."*

With those words resonating in his ears, Charley spent a restless night camping out in the old house wondering just how he was going to provide for his family.

Still tired from the night before, Charley took them for a stroll along the lane and down into the village centre. His main aim was to find and put some food on the table.

To try and boost his self-esteem, Charley pulled his shoulders back and began to think of what old Zack had said to him. By the time they had reached the Post Office, Charley had decided to do as Zack had suggested: some serious shouting. Well, whispering, actually!

'Barbara, let's tell the good people of Dorset that we're here and ready to work!' he said, bursting with ego.

'Yeah, but with your accent, will they listen?' she grimaced.

'He who dares…' said Charley, about to risk 1 shilling [5 pence] on their first advertising campaign. 'We must do as me and old Butch did a few years ago…'

'Oh yeah, and what's that – starve?'

'No! We've got to speculate to accumulate.' And he started to dictate the words he wanted Barbara to write down on a card, which he then took inside the shop and asked the lady behind the counter to display in the window, with the other cards.

The lady took Charley's shilling and immediately inserted his card amidst all the others, many of which were advertising old bikes, lampshades, prams, etc. for sale.

'Worth a try, I suppose,' said Harry. 'What have you got to lose?'

'A shilling,' said Barbara.

'We've got to start somewhere, Barbara. Beggars can't be choosers,' Charley said. 'If that shilling investment only brought in one job, it would be worth it. Even if we only made a couple of quid, we could buy some food.'

'Hey! Look, Chas!' Barbara pointed to one of the cards. 'Someone's only trying to sell an old pair of hobnail boots!'

'Oh, yeah! Are they First or Second World War?' asked Charley, reminiscing.

After they all stopped laughing, they continued on and found a greengrocer.

'Those spuds you got there, mate – how much for the whole bag?'

'Are you that hungry then, boy?' the greengrocer joked. 'A hundredweight of spuds take a lot of eating.'

'Bloody starving, mate.'

'Well, in that case, you can have one whole bag for 12 bob,' he said, smiling.

'What about 10 bob?' Charley replied, eagerly awaiting his response.

'Ah, well, that's not quite 12 bob, is it? We can always take a few out,' he grinned broadly, showing his teeth.

Charley smiled back. 'Not worth breaking the bag open for 2 bob surely, is it?'

'Oh, go on, then. 10 shillings it is, but don't you go telling anyone else I let you have 'em that cheap, will you?'

'Have no fear about that, mate, 'cos I don't know anybody to tell.'

The greengrocer laughed. 'Everybody knows somebody, lad,' he said.

Charley smiled and grabbed the spuds. And then struggled all the way back home with them.

After two weeks of eating nothing but potatoes, washed down with only tap water, Charley smiled at Barbara and asked what was on the evening menu.

'For tonight's meal, we have spuds, and for afters, we have more spuds.'

'At least we're free,' said Charley, counting his blessings.

But no sooner had he said that when his past caught up with him. His house was under siege from Detective Sergeant Dave Biggs of the Flying Squad, Scotland Yard.

'Come on! Come on! Open up!' he cried, bashing on Charley's front door. 'I know you're in there. You can't hide from me!'

'Okay, okay! I give up! Put the battering ram down cos I can't afford a new door! I'm coming out.'

Charley couldn't get the door open fast enough.

'Good to see you, Dave,' he said, extending his hand to his very good friend he used to go sea fishing with, back in Kent. Dave, Iris and the kids were down in Dorset enjoying a family holiday.

'A bloody big house you've got here, Chas,' said Dave, looking around. 'Gonna take a lot of wonga to do this old place up, even for you.'

'Tell me about it, Dave,' said Charley, thinking that perhaps he'd bitten off more than he could chew.

'Glad you moved to Dorset, are you, Chas?' asked Iris.

'Er, it's early days yet, Iris. Ask me again in six months' time.'

But Charley was already thinking that he'd made the wrong decision in moving to Dorset. Although Charley was overjoyed to see them all again, he was also extremely embarrassed, because he couldn't even offer them the hospitality of a cup of tea since they didn't have any. He tried to bluff it out, but Dave was no fool: he knew Charley was up against it. And so, as he climbed into his car to leave, Dave insisted that both Charley and Barbara be their dinner guests that evening at their hotel.

'Your brother-in-law can babysit, can't he?'

Harry nodded. 'Yes, of course, I can.'

Both Charley and Barbara felt very guilty tucking into a lavish three-course meal with all the trimmings, washed down with a nice bottle of red wine, while Harry and the children were back home with only potatoes, washed down with the finest tap water.

It was the most perfect summer's evening, and after the exquisite meal, Barbara and Charley, with their stomachs full to bursting, strolled with Dave and Iris along the seashore like millionaires.

As the sun started going down, Dave suggested finishing off the evening in the hotel bar. Reality kicked in for Charley – he felt like a pauper. With only 4 shillings left to his name, he tried to make excuses as to why they should leave and go home.

'Don't be daft, Chas! The night is young! Come and have a drink! Barbara can drive. Can't you, Babs?' he insisted. He was not going to take no for an answer.

'Dave, the meal was really smashing, mate, and I'd love to stay and have a drink with you and talk about the good old times we've had, but the plain and simple truth is I'm a bit skint at the moment.'

'A few drinks won't break the bank, Chas,' he said, grabbing hold of Charley's arm.

'Look, Dave. Thanks all the same. You're a good mate and all that, but I can't go into that bar with you. My conscience won't allow it, cos when I say skint, I mean absolutely bloody dead skint, cleaned out, stony broke, potless. I wouldn't even be able to buy a drink in return.'

'I know that, mate. Why do you think I invited you both over here in the first place? I'm not a detective for nothing. I could see you were a bit brassic, mate. Especially when the kettle didn't even go on.'

'Er, yeah. Sorry about that, Dave. Tea right now is a luxury we can't afford.'

Before Charley knew it, Dave had taken a fistful of notes out of his wallet and stuffed them into Charley's jacket pocket.

'Now you're coming back to the bar for a drink, and that's final, even if I have to drag you there myself. If you really feel you must stand a round, then you buy it out of that, all right? If you need any more, just say the word.'

As the evening wore on, Charley admitted to Dave that he may have made a big mistake in moving to Dorset.

'Don't get me wrong, Dave. I like Dorset, it's a smashing county – but it's not home. I feel as though I don't belong here. I sunk all my dough in that old house. And now I've got to work my bollocks off. That's if I can find any work to pay for the renovation work.'

'Oh, you'll do it, Chas. If anybody can, you can. I know you can.'

After a smashing evening, they left the hotel bar around midnight. Charley tried to give Dave back the remainder of his money, but Dave refused to take it. Charley felt really humble having a good genuine mate like that. Dave was one of life's really nice people. A true friend. One who asked nothing in return.

'Always remember this, Chas,' said Dave. 'No matter where you go in the world, you've still got all your mates, so everywhere is your home to you.'

'You're quite a philosopher, Dave, aren't you?'

'S'pose I am, really.'

'Thanks, Dave. And here's one from the old Chinese philosopher: *Man with no front garden always looks forlorn.*'

Dave laughed. 'Go on, Chas. See you soon, mate. Perhaps we can arrange a fishing trip one day?'

When they got home Charley emptied out his pockets on the table. There was just over £10 in cash. At that precise moment in time, it was a vast fortune to Charley, because it bought some much-needed food and it put some petrol in his van.

Chapter 8

※

Charley was badly missing life back in Kent – the place where he had lots of friends and he could always find plenty of work as well. In Dorset, Charley was nobody. And he knew nobody either. He had no mates, no contacts, no work, no money, and very little food left to feed his family with. Feeling totally isolated, he seriously contemplated moving back home to Kent. He talked the problem over with Barbara, and they both agreed that it would make perfect sense to do so, but only after Charley had renovated the old house.

In his heart, Charley knew it was time to look for a job before they all starved to death. He decided that any surplus money from his salary would be ploughed straight into the restoration work on the house. He also knew that until the house was fully restored that all of his spare time would be taken up working on it.

However, one day, the telephone rang with an enquiry from the ad Charley had placed in the post office window.

'Hello? Is that Mr Henry, the builder?' asked a softly spoken lady.

Charley's heart began to race with anticipation. 'Er, yes, yes, it is. What can we do for you?' he asked, trying to create a good professional impression.

'My name is Miss Hargraves, and we have lots and lots of work needing doing. When are you able to come round to give us an estimate, please?'

It was like music to Charley's ears. 'Lots of work,' he mouthed to Barbara, who was standing close by. 'Weeks, months maybe,' he mouthed again, excitedly.

With his heart beating rapidly, Charley took a deep breath to compose himself and replied, 'As it so happens, Miss Hargraves, I'll be passing the end of your road in the next half an hour. I will call in then, if that would be convenient to you?'

'Oh, splendid! Splendid! Thank you so much. You are so kind, Mr Henry. We'll be waiting for you at the gate.'

Charley didn't even know where the road was. When he eventually found it, he was immediately pounced upon by two very excited elderly twin sisters named Agnes and Gertrude. Wearing brightly coloured matching knitted jumpers and woollen hats, they were both trying to speak at the same time. In their eagerness to show Charley the work they wanted doing, he was hurriedly marched towards the open garage.

'I don't know why it is, Mr Henry,' said Agnes, adjusting her spectacles, 'but we can't seem to get any builder to do our jobs for us.'

'Yes, that's right,' interrupted Gertrude, picking up a clipboard and pencil from a tall box in the garage. 'Once we've recited our long list of repairs, they make their excuses and leave – and they never come back.'

'She's right,' said Agnes, nodding her head in agreement. 'I can't understand why, because we have all the stuff to do the work, right here in this garage. Look,' she said, pointing to a pile of old bits on the floor.

They were like an old-fashioned music hall comedy double act.

'Replace the broken gutter bracket on the garage,' read Gertrude from their list of jobs, in order of priority. Agnes, mouthing along in unison, enthusiastically rushed over and pointed out the damaged bracket to Charley.

'Okay then,' said Charley.

Quick as a flash, she turned and ran into the garage and held up the new bracket for him to see.

'We also have the screws and a screwdriver to fix it with.'

'Okay…' said Charley, hoping that their list would contain some larger jobs.

Agnes then rushed over to the other side of the garage, bent down and picked up a small length of timber from the floor and held it up.

'Nail this new paling to the front picket fence,' she said, galloping ahead of her sister.

Gertrude frowned. 'It's *my* job to read out the jobs!' she complained. 'I've got the list. You just get on and hold the stuff up for him to see and let me do my job.'

'Yes, of course. Sorry about that Gertie, dear,' Agnes replied, slightly red-faced with embarrassment.

Gertrude continued. 'We do have the hammer and nails and some creosote and a brush. Next, fix the new hinge on the garage door. You will note we do have the screws and a screwdriver.'

Their list of small trivial jobs just went on and on. Charley stayed there for the next five hours doing them, during which time the two old sisters must have brought him out at least five huge mugs of tea and four slices of their homemade cake, three pieces of which Charley managed to squirrel away into his van for Barbara and the children back home. Charley earned £2 and 10 shillings on that first job, which he gave to Barbara to get some much-needed food.

The post office window wasn't really the tallest tree in which to holler from, but, as Charley said, you couldn't get much else for a shilling.

The following morning Charley heard someone pounding on his front door with what sounded like a closed fist. When he opened it, he found a tall, well-dressed man of about 75 years old, wearing a deerstalker hat and sporting a well-groomed handlebar moustache.

'Hello. My name is Wing Commander Johnson-Smythe,' he said, in a posh, husky voice. 'I'm one of your neighbours ... ah, well, the third property down the lane, actually. Sorry about bashing on your door like that, only I didn't think the bell was working.'

'That's all right, Wing Commander. It isn't. What can I do for you?'

'Well, correct me if I'm wrong,' he said, stroking his moustache with the forefinger and thumb of his right hand, 'but it's my understanding from old Zack that you're a builder...'

'Yes, that's correct. I am.'

'Oh, jolly good! Glad to see you've bought the old place by the way – it certainly needed a builder to buy it. I'm sure you'll make it very nice one day. Anyway, as I was saying, what I've actually come round for is to see whether or not you would be interested in doing any building repairs. Not for me, you understand. You see, I'm the President of the Orchid Growers Association, and it's for one of our members, a Miss Forbes-Wallows, that I enquire. She's a trifle enigmatic, but she's a jolly good-hearted, honest, straightforward woman to deal with. Not terribly worldly wise though – bit of a target for the more unscrupulous builder, if you get my meaning.'

Enigmatic or not, Charley assured him that he would go and see her and that he would treat her right. After driving past several times, he eventually found her rambling old Victorian house, tucked well away from view behind a very tall, sprawling rhododendron hedge.

Strolling through the substantial rusty entrance gates onto the property, Charley saw, walking towards him, a tall, thin, slightly hunched figure of an elderly lady wearing a shabby overcoat, scarf, mittens and a balaclava. She was either an old ghost or Charley had passed through a time warp when he walked through those gates.

'Good morning. Are you Miss Forbes-Wallows?' Charley made a conscious effort not to stare at her attire.

'Oh, good gracious! Me? No!' she replied, in a clipped, well-honed voice of authority. 'I am her live-in companion. And whom might you be?' she asked, raising an eyebrow awaiting Charley's response.

'My name is Charles Henry,' he replied, thinking that perhaps he should have sprung to attention before answering her.

'Ah, yes. We've been expecting you, Mr Henry. Just wait there,' she ordered, pointing to a worn flagstone on the ground, 'and I'll go and fetch Miss Forbes-Wallows for you.'

Charley found the whole experience a bit unreal, almost dreamlike, being ordered to stand there like a naughty schoolboy. She may have looked like a tatty old scarecrow, but she had an uncanny air of firmness about her and so Charley did as he was told. Just when he thought he was going to awaken from the bizarre dream, the old lady returned with a very petite raggedy scarecrow dressed in the same attire, small enough to fit comfortably under her armpit.

'This is Miss Forbes-Wallows,' she announced. 'And this,' she said, looking Charley up and down, 'is Mr Henry.'

The tiny old lady stretched out her fragile bony hand, as though she were royalty.

'I'm so pleased to meet you, Mr Henry,' she said gently. 'Thank you so much for sparing the time to come round to see us. The Wing Commander has told us all about you.'

'I'm pleased to be here, Miss Forbes-Wallows. Now, what can I do for you?'

Charley fully expected to hear, from the way they were both dressed, that the central heating had broken down.

'It's my bedroom ceiling, Mr Henry.'

'What about it?'

'Why, it's fallen down, Mr Henry! I've had Cobstock, my manservant, remove all the bits from the floor, but he's not confident enough to put up a new ceiling for me. Will you do it for me, please?'

Charley measured up there and then and gave her a price to do the job. When he returned with the sheets of plasterboard for the new ceiling, he heard the unmistakeable sharp tones of the companion.

'Cobstock! Cobstock! Madam said you are to go and give Mr Henry a hand. And be quick about it!' she barked.

Charley heard a loud clatter, followed by a banging door. A wizened old man appeared, wearing a frayed white shirt, black bow tie, waistcoat and crumpled trousers. It was as much as he could do to walk, let alone lift heavy sheets of plasterboard up the staircase. To give the old boy his due, he showed willing, hurrying over breathlessly, limping and dragging his right leg.

'That's all right, old timer,' said Charley. 'Thanks for the offer, mate, but I'll be able to manage 'em on my own. You can carry all of the scaffolding up for me if you like?'

'What!' he gasped. 'Take WHAT up?'

'I'm only joking, Mr Cobstock!'

The old boy then smiled with relief and started to shiver. 'Blinking cold out here, isn't it?' he said, rubbing his hands together.

'It's not much warmer inside the house, is it?'

Mr Cobstock winked at Charley and gave a little chuckle. 'I don't care, because I'm working in the greenhouse this morning. Or, perhaps I should say, the hothouse, because it's so lovely and warm in there.'

Charley could never understand the logic of Mrs Forbes-Wallows and her companion living in a freezing cold house, while their precious orchids enjoyed a nice, warm environment. Charley found the whole experience very amusing. He was fascinated watching them, in their pecking order, going about their daily lives.

The next time Charley was summoned by Miss Forbes-Wallows she sounded more than a bit distressed on the telephone.

'Mr Henry! Can you come round immediately please? It's Cobstock. He's driven into the gate post and knocked it down! It's still got the gate attached to it, and it's blocking the drive. It's causing such an obstruction and nobody can get in or out. The three of us have tried to move it out of the way, but it's much too heavy for us.'

When Charley arrived, the first thing he noticed was poor old Cobstock's head hung low in shame. As he surveyed the damage, the two old ladies came over to pour a bit more scorn on him and, of course, to tell Charley how reckless Cobstock had been.

After the ladies went back inside, Charley winked at the old boy. 'Don't you worry, mate. I'll soon get you off the hook. That post was ready to fall down anyway. Look – it's absolutely rotten.'

'Oh, she won't believe you,' he sighed. 'She thinks I'm wild and irresponsible. They both do. They think I did it on purpose, you know.'

He was right: Miss Forbes-Wallows would not budge no matter how hard Charley tried to tell her that the post was rotten.

'I know that you're only sticking up for Cobstock, Mr Henry, which is most gallant of you, but he must learn to take his medicine like a man.'

While Charley was busy fixing the new gate post, Cobstock had changed into a chauffeur's uniform, complete with black peaked cap and leather driving gloves.

'I've got to take the two old moaners to the shops,' he whispered. 'I suppose they will ignore me all the way there and back as well.'

'Well, at least you'll have a peaceful ride,' Charley joked, trying to cheer him up.

Charley stood and watched the old fella carefully back the big, black pre-war Humber Super Snipe limousine out from the garage. After struggling to close the dilapidated garage doors, he drove the limo around to the front of the house to collect the two women. They, of course, deliberately kept him waiting. So, to look busy – and to get back into their good books – Cobstock began to rub a polishing cloth over the car until they both decided to come out. Yet, when they did, they made no attempt to get into the limousine. The old boy had to limp round and hold the door open for them both, with his head bowed so as not to make eye contact with them.

Charley had to laugh: all three of them were like a ghostly apparition from a bygone age. He had to keep pinching himself to make sure that he wasn't dreaming it all up.

Charley did many more repairs for them. One time he was asked by Miss Forbes-Wallows to go round to Cobstock's bungalow and replace the rotten fence that had blown over in the wind. He was greeted by Mrs Cobstock.

'Hello. Is Mr Cobstock in, please?' he asked, respectfully.

'Who shall I say wants him?'

'My name is Charley Henry and I've come to erect a new fence for you.'

'Ere! Albert!' she shouted back down the hallway. 'Did you hear that… Mr… there's someone out here actually calling you Mr!'

She then turned back, smiled and invited Charley in for a cup of tea and a biscuit before he started work on the fence.

'What a lovely warm and cosy place you have here,' Charley said, trying to make polite conversation.

'Oh, it's not ours, is it, Albert?'

'No,' said Cobstock. 'It belongs to the Duchess.'

'What – Miss Forbes-Wallows?'

'Yes. It goes with the job,' he replied, slurping his tea.

'Oh, I see,' Charley pondered, trying to get his head round it all. 'Why doesn't *she* live here, then, and put you in the big, cold house that's falling down?' he joked.

'What – *her*? She wouldn't do that! The Duchess and the Sergeant Major living in such a small humble abode as this? The Duchess was brought up on a big country estate, you know. I know because I used to work for her father. It's the only job I've ever had. I started straight from leaving school and worked my way up.'

'*Up to what?*' thought *Charley*. 'Why doesn't she live on the estate now?' he asked, sipping his tea.

'Oh, that's because her father died and the estate was sold off in order to pay off the death duties.'

'Was it a nice estate?' Charley asked, devouring the last biscuits on his plate.

'Oh, yes, it was once … but then he wouldn't have anything done to it unless it was falling down, so the place fell into a bit of a ruin.'

'Oh, I see. So, she takes after 'im then…'

'You can say that again – but she doesn't have to. She's got plenty of money, you know.'

'It makes you wonder who the fool is then, doesn't it?' Charley said, returning his cup to the table.

Old Cobstock looked over to his wife and winked, and then they both laughed heartily.

Chapter 9

※

'Word must be getting around now, Chas, 'cos the phone never stops ringing,' Barbara said.

'Yeah, most of 'em don't want to pay, though – not a proper price anyway. The word probably is, give that bloke a ring, 'cos I've heard he works for nothing.'

But then one day Charley's path crossed with Doug Langsdale, a long-established, well-respected chartered structural building surveyor.

'Hello, old boy. I've been hearing some pretty good reports about you and I was rather wondering whether or not you would be interested in tidying up some of the condemned building projects which I have become involved with.'

'Yeah, I would!' Charley replied, eager to know more. 'What does the work entail?'

'Ah. Now … how best to describe without scaring you away … I suppose I could best define the work as dealing with the aftermath of *"Messrs Botchit & Scarper"*. They have left quite a trail, you know.'

'Oh, I see. And you want me to rectify their shoddy work, do you?'

'Er, no, not exactly, old boy. It's too bad for that. It's more the case of pulling it down altogether and starting again.'

Even though Charley agreed to join Doug's list of approved contractors, pricing the work was still fiercely competitive. And what's more, it wasn't particularly enjoyable work either because, more often than not, it meant dealing with very aggrieved people whose anger often spilled over on to the new contractor. As far as most of them were concerned, the word "builder" was a foul, sticky, smelly thing that you wiped from your shoe.

However, it was a step up from all the other jobs that Charley had been surviving on. For Charley to handle the volume of work, he took on a couple of lads on a casual basis. All the time Charley had work, so, too, did they. Charley never turned anything away. In fact, he undertook some impossible jobs from Doug Langsdale, jobs where the people should really have vacated their homes while he and the boys carried out the major structural building works.

One of the more trying people was Mrs Shorefield, with her huge luxury residential "condemned" barn conversion. Like so many gullible people, she was lured and then snared by a very cheap price, impressive talk and lots of empty promises. The whole experience had left her very bitter and twisted towards all builders, good or bad. She gave Charley and the boys such an earbashing that their ears were bleeding throughout the six-month duration of her project.

'He said he could do the job okay!' she cried over and over again, driving everybody insane. 'So, why couldn't he build then, eh? You tell me that! Go on! Tell me! Why did he destroy my property like this then if he was a builder?!'

'Mrs Shorefield,' Charley replied, 'he wasn't a proper builder; that's why. Didn't you think to check him out before you employed him? Anybody can buy a shovel and call himself a builder. Whether he knows how to use it is another matter…'

'Check him out first? Well, he looked like a builder!' she snarled. 'And he sounded as if he knew what he was talking about as well! Besides, he was much cheaper than all the rest.'

'Look, Mrs Shorefield, if someone said they were a top brain surgeon and they offered you a cheap price, would you let 'em operate on your head without first checking 'em out?'

'What's that got to do with a botched building job?!' she retorted.

Charley was tempted to tell her about peanuts and monkeys, but then there was no talking to her because she wasn't listening.

By the time Charley had finished her job, he was mentally and physically exhausted. He had nothing left in the tank whatsoever. At home that evening, Charley fell to his knees, shaking uncontrollably. He felt as though he was going to vomit blood.

'Barbara, I've had enough,' he said. 'I need to sleep for a couple of weeks.'

While Charley slept, Barbara arranged a week's holiday at a caravan site in Beer, in Devon, and a second week in a cottage in Brixham, for him to recharge his batteries.

Chapter 10

In 1976, with the restoration work to Oakland's now completed, it was time to make the decision to stick or twist. Charley was torn between Kent and Dorset, mainly because things were at last starting to happen in Dorset, plus he had made a number of good friends and many contacts there. He talked it over with Barbara again, but she had no preference either way. Charley finally decided they would stay in Dorset.

Charley was tempted to sell up, and purchase one of two properties that had caught his eye. The first was an old shack, together with five acres of land, in the slightly more rural area of Dorset. The asking price was £20,000 for the freehold. The second, and more intriguing of the two, was the once majestic Sterlington Hall. Now in a state of total disrepair, the huge manor house, with 15 acres of land and a small cottage, was being offered to the market by way of informal tender. The guide price quoted by the agent for the entire freehold estate was a mere £15,000.

'Why is Sterlington Hall so cheap?' Charley asked the selling agent. 'Has there been a gruesome murder there that I don't know about?'

'Oh, if only it were that simple,' he sighed. 'It's an executor's sale, but unfortunately, the bank, which is executor to the late Miss Frinstanton's estate, cannot offer full vacant possession, because it seems that they have a legal issue with the former tenant, now-turned squatter, occupying the cottage and land.'

'Squatter?' repeated Charley.

'Yes, and a very unsavoury character at that. He has actually barricaded himself inside the cottage and is refusing to leave. I wouldn't mind, but he signed an agreement with the old lady when he first moved into the cottage, which basically said that, in the event of her death, he would vacate the property within three months. She was cremated almost four months ago now, and he's still there.'

'Well, that's it then. He's got to go,' said Charley.

'Not as simple as that – the cheeky sod has now written to the bank stating that he is going to claim a possessory title by way of 12 years' continuous unchallenged possession.'

'Have you got a copy of the agreement from the solicitor who drew it up?'

'Ah well, that's just it – the old lady drew it up herself.'

'Oh, I see. Well, providing it was properly witnessed, there shouldn't be a problem, surely?'

The agent grimaced. 'I don't know that it was ever witnessed,' he said. 'You see, the late Miss Frinstanton was a bit odd at the best of times. And I think she was suffering from dementia towards the end. Rumour has it that she used to talk with the dead … probably something to do with her dementia.'

'What has the bank said about it all then?'

'Well, that's just it – they don't want to know. They don't want the agro of it all. They just want the easy way out, to discharge themselves of their duties and dispose of the estate as soon as possible, for whatever they can get for it, hence the low guide price.'

'The bastards! They're no better than the squatter!' said Charley. 'Take the old lady's money and then promise her the earth, and then as soon as she's dead and gone, shirk their bloody responsibilities!'

'That seems to be it in a nutshell,' the agent replied. 'All I can say is, that for a bit of aggravation, someone is going to get the bargain of the century.'

Charley was very tempted to have a go.

'You say this bloke is also staking a claim to all the land as well?'

'Correct. He alleges to have used it all to graze his horses uninterrupted for the past 12 years and, as a consequence, he thinks he has the legal right to claim the land as his own, thereby denying the true owner access forever more. Even the old grass tennis courts, would you believe? Ever since we've been marketing the estate, the cheeky sod has strung a barbed wire fence within a few inches of, and right around, the manor house itself, totally isolating it from the land altogether.'

'He sounds a real nasty piece of work.'

'Oh, he's that all right and no mistake. He's been very aggressive towards most people who have been up there for a viewing. What it wants is for somebody with enough guts to buy the place and physically chuck him off. Let the squatter take the court action. If he dares, that is. He'll probably run a mile. His sort normally do…'

'Hmm … well, the price is certainly cheap enough,' said Charley, anxious to go and have a look around, 'and I like a challenge … so when can we go and view the property?'

'Excellent!' said the agent with a beaming smile. 'I was rather hoping you'd say that. I'll give you the key – you can go right now if you like – but be warned, the squatter is extremely abusive towards any other prospective purchasers.'

'Other purchasers? You mean he's put a bid forward as well?'

'Er, yeah, he has. Well, if you can call it a bid, that is. You see, he thinks by scaring everyone else away, he'll stand a good chance of stealing the place for a pittance.'

Forewarned, Charley left the estate agent's office with the huge key to the manor house in his pocket. Despite it being a dark, damp and miserable winter's afternoon, he and Barbara drove over to view the late Miss Frinstanton's estate. Approached via a long and winding tree-lined driveway, the enormous Sterlington Hall looked very cold and unwelcoming, parts of its façade crumbling away.

'It looks a bit spooky to me,' Barbara said, peering from out the car window. 'Like one of those old houses you see in horror films,' she added.

'Well, it's a good job I brought along a string of garlic with me then,' joked Charley, as he climbed out the motor enthusiastically.

Walking towards the substantial pair of solid oak front entrance doors, Charley tried to put Barbara at ease from the cloak of eeriness that seemed to shroud the property.

'Sounds like someone eating a bag of crisps,' he said.

'What does?' asked Barbara, tensely.

'The noise of our boots crunching on the gravel.'

'Come on, Chas. I don't like it here. Let's go.'

'Oh, come on, Barbs. We're here now.'

Charley took the huge key from his pocket and inserted it into the massive lock.

'All right then, but just a quick look, and then we go, all right?'

The old lock was stiff to operate at first, but after a bit of vigorous wobbling, the giant levers inside the lock gave way, making the most ghostly clanking noise that echoed back, deep inside the building.

Barbara swallowed hard and gave an uneasy grin. Before she could change her mind, Charley had pushed one of the heavy doors open to the unnerving whine of the oil-starved hinges. Before them lay the massive entrance hall, with a magnificent stone cantilevered winding staircase rising to the upper floors. Heavy dust-laden cobwebs hung trailing to the floor, where lay the fallen debris of plasterwork from the tall, once ornate ceilings. A patchwork of wooden laths grinned down.

Stepping over the threshold and into the hallway, Charley immediately felt uninvited. Without commenting, he looked back to see Barbara physically shudder as she entered.

Showing the whites of her eyes and breathing rapidly, she said, 'This place is haunted, Chas!'

'No, you're imagining it,' Charley smiled. 'It's only a big old empty house – nothing to be scared of here. It's not like we can hear some of that loud spooky organ music playing,' he joked.

'I couldn't live here, Chas,' she replied, shivering.

'All right. We don't have to buy it, but let's at least have a look around. You never know, you may change your mind.'

'I won't do that,' she quickly replied.

'Look, if there is anything haunting the building, it's probably the ghost of the old lady come back to put the record straight.'

'What – with the nasty squatter for not honouring the agreement he made?'

'No, the bloody nasty bank she entrusted. I can hear the bastards now – *"Oh, don't you worry, Miss Frinstanton. You just sign here and pay us the humongous arrangement fees, and then we'll look after everything when you have gone."* No doubt they will take a huge slice of the proceeds of the sale as well.'

Despite his jokes, Charley could see that Barbara was extremely uneasy about the manor.

'This is no ordinary ghost,' she said, rolling her eyes. 'These walls contain a very evil presence…'

'What, like the tax man, you mean?' he smiled. 'Look, whatever you think, all old buildings feel a bit spooky at first, especially semi-derelict ones. Ask any builder who's restored one. More so if it was major structural work that disturbed the past. He'll soon tell you about scary nightmares.'

'No matter what you say, Chas, I couldn't live here, not even if they gave it to us for nothing,' she said still shivering, as though someone was stood on her grave. 'I really don't like it.'

'All right then, Barbs. You go and sit in the car while I have a look around.'

'I'm not going to sit out there on my own! I'm staying with you, so let's make it quick! But if I get really scared, you'll come out with me to the car, won't you?'

'Done. Let's go.'

And so they started to walk around, their footsteps echoing throughout the building. Barbara was so spooked that she stayed very close to Charley. The deeper they ventured into the building, the more unfriendly the atmosphere became. There were even parts they couldn't get to because the floors had partially collapsed. Charley was not usually sensitive to ghostly happenings, but on that occasion, he found the atmosphere inside that old place overwhelmingly bad. With the memory of his last brush with evil still raw in his mind, he took Barbara out of the manor house and over to see the humble shack and five acres instead.

Accessed via a dead-end gravel track barely a mile long, and with just 30 other properties on similar sized plots backing onto hundreds of acres of open forest, the old shack was a peaceful paradise. In fact, it was the most perfect place in which to live and bring up their children.

A community of chicken farmers sprang up there shortly after the First World War by returning veterans trying to rebuild their shattered lives. Graylings Rest was the name of the shack, after the Grayling brothers, who were both stretcher bearers on the Western Front during the Great War. They, like so many others who came back, were deeply and mentally scarred by their wartime experiences. The only place they felt safe enough to lay their heads to sleep was in the deep hole in the ground which they had dug and covered with corrugated iron. It was only as their confidence slowly returned that they built a small shack above ground level in which to live and yet, they still retained the sanctuary of their dugout under the shack.

Sadly, in 1960, fowl pest, the virulent chicken disease, ripped through the entire community, forcing the farmers that were left, out of business. Many of them were too old to start again, so they just sold up and drifted away.

People from all walks of life were buying up and redeveloping the old shacks, as they came onto the market. Barbara was very relieved when Charley suggested doing the same. While they waited for the laborious planning process to work, they actually moved into the property.

It may have looked a bit run-down, a shambles even, but they found it very cosy inside that old shack, for it had the most amazing air of peace and tranquillity about it. In fact, they found the whole area to be an undisturbed haven teeming with wildlife. The wild deer would come right up to their back door, and as dusk fell, the air would fill with the haunting call of the owl and the cry of the fox. The only downside they suffered was the unmade lane, which was full of deep potholes that they had to drive over every day.

The day after they moved in, while they were still unpacking, they had a visit from an elderly lady.

'My name is Mrs Baker,' she introduced herself, 'and I collect 10 shillings a month from every neighbour to help towards the maintenance of our lane. I trust that we can rely on your donation as well, can we?'

'Yes, of course you can, Mrs Baker, but I think I can do better than that cos I have a JCB at my disposal. I will scarify and blade the road surface free of charge – if that's all right with you, of course.'

Charley Henry got to know the vast majority of people in the neighbourhood while doing the road. They accepted that he was a builder and that he used some of the old buildings on his land as makeshift workshops and a store.

'It's all very nice having our road flat and free of potholes,' commented Charley's next-door neighbour, Burt, as they stood talking in the sunshine across the five-bar gate that fronted his property, 'the only trouble is, it will encourage people to drive faster.'

No sooner had Burt said that, when they heard the loud roar from a vehicle being driven at speed without an exhaust silencer. Looking towards the general direction of the noise, they noticed a huge dust cloud rising. Before they knew it, a car with its roof cut off, containing six or more drunks, shouting, swearing and throwing empty beer cans out the car, came hurtling past, smothering them both with choking dust.

'Where the bloody hell did they come from?!' shouted Charley, dusting himself down.

'Oh, it's that bloody lot from Murdoch's old shanty town!' said Burt, furious. 'They're a bloody pest, they are!'

'Murdoch's? Who the bloody hell's Murdoch?' asked Charley, angry that they had violated the peace.

'Oh, that be old Mrs Murdoch,' Burt grimaced. 'She's a bitter and twisted old bag. They say she used to be a councillor back along. I'm surprised you haven't seen her on the telly – she often makes the local news,' he said. 'They make her out to be a bit of a Robin Hood. A robbing bitch is more the like. The council has been trying to shut her little operation down for years, but she keeps on finding more and more loopholes.'

'Shut her down? Down from what?' Charley was eager to find out.

'Oh, she dragged 30 or more huge tatty old caravans onto a parcel of land, just down the lane a bit. All without planning permission, I might add. She then filled them with the most disgusting undesirable lowlifes you've ever seen. Most of them are druggies. None of 'em work, they live off the DHSS – who, incidentally, pay their rent directly to the old witch, would you believe! You wouldn't want to cross any of them bastards either. While most people go out to work, they think it their God-given right to go out and thieve their way through life to feed their habit. The sooner the council get off their fat arses and clear them off, the better. I've got no time for any of 'em.'

'Who – the council?' Charley joked.

'No! That bunch of assholes down there.'

'So, I take it you wouldn't invite 'em in for a cup of tea then, Burt?'

'A cup of bloody arsenic maybe! They're just a bunch of thugs, especially the one they call 4x2 – he's more than a bit mental.'

'Hasn't anyone ever stood up to them before?'

'Oh yeah, old Mick a few doors down the lane had a go once. It all kicked off after he tethered his goat out the front of his place to eat the weeds down. Mick went back indoors for a cup of tea, and left the goat happily munching down the weeds. 4x2 came ambling by with a big vicious dog on a bit of rope…'

'Oh yeah, and what happened then?'

'4x2 only let the dog start eating the back legs off Mick's goat. Thought it was funny, he did.'

'No!'

'Yep, just stood there laughing.'

'Oh my gosh. What happened next then?' Charley asked, with bated breath.

'Uh, well, hearing the goat cry out, old Mick looked out the window to see what was wrong…'

'Yeah…'

'Yeah, and when he saw what was happening, the air went blue. Course Mick grabbed his 12-bore shotgun…'

'No! You're kidding. What did he do? Shoot the dog then?' asked Charley, hanging on his every word.

'No. He charged out front and pressed the barrel of the 12 bore right up against 4x2's head.'

'No!'

'Yep. Gave him one second to take his dog and fuck off, or he would blow his head off.'

'Bloody hell. And did he?'

'What – blow his head off?'

'No – run away.'

'Oh yeah, he ran all right, shitting his pants, as it happens. In fact, he ran so fast that the dog couldn't keep up with him.'

'So, what happened then?'

'4x2 called the police.'

'Yeah, and did they come out then?'

'Oh yeah, they came all right, blue lights flashing, sirens wailing and everything. Course, 4x2 was jumping up and down in the lane outside Mick's place demanding they arrest him.'

'And did they?'

'No, 'cos they couldn't find no shotgun. Oh, they did a complete search of Mick's house and outbuildings all right, but all they found was an old broken air rifle.'

'So, what happened to the shotgun then?'

'Oh, I took that before the police came, and I gave Mick the old broken air rifle and told him to say that he threatened 4x2 with that. Course, 4x2 was jumping up and down saying to the police how it was a 12 bore pressed against his head…'

'So, how did it all end up then?'

'Oh, the police read Mick the riot act for using threatening behaviour with a broken air rifle.'

'Blimey.'

'We all call Mick "Wild Bill" now.'

'"Wild Bill"?' repeated Charley.

'Yeah, "Wild Bill Hickok", the famous sharpshooter of the Wild West.'

'Sounds like you have all the fun up here, Burt. So, where is this Murdoch's place then?'

'You can't miss it,' he said. 'It's about a quarter of a mile down the lane on the right-hand side. Mind you, it's a bit overgrown now, but you do have to pass it on your way out.'

'Back to the old car … do they often charge up and down the road in that?' Charley asked, fearing for the safety of his children.

'Not normally, no – that's a new game they've got, and that's all down to you!' he joked. 'Nice new flat road surface – they've come out to play on it, ain't they?'

'Come out to kill someone, mores the like,' Charley replied.

'When the road was full of deep potholes they just used to mooch about in small groups. So, be warned, and never leave anything unattended. Or, if you do, be sure to nail it down. Oh, and be sure to sleep with one eye open as well, because they like to creep about after dark.'

'Oh shit, you've really cheered me up now! Do you know anyone who wants to buy a cheap old shack?' said Charley, thinking that the haunted manor house and squatter would have been far less aggravation.

With a huge disheartening sigh, Charley asked Burt if the council kept the residents informed as to possible site closures.

'No, not normally, no. They don't seem to care about us lot up here in this little backwater.'

Just as soon as Charley had finished talking with Burt, he telephoned the council for an update. They told him that they had, in fact, taken out enforcement action against Mrs Murdoch some time ago, and that she had appealed their action, and so they were powerless to do anymore until the appeal had been determined.

A couple of months later, Charley received a letter from the council confirming that their enforcement action was upheld by the planning inspector and that the site would soon be cleared. However, bloody-minded Mrs Murdoch refused to accept the defeat and ignored the decision altogether, which attracted huge interest from the media. Eventually, she was summoned to the county court, and there she was ordered to clear the entire site forthwith. Leaving the courthouse snarling like a wounded animal, she declared emphatically to the television news team that she would defy the court order and that she would sooner go to prison than clear the site.

A few months later, the court issued the notice that would send her down, unless, of course, she signed over the power of attorney to her solicitors for them to instigate the site clearance. Reluctantly she did sign, and Charley and his neighbours rejoiced it was finally all over.

Mrs Murdoch's tenants were given notice to quit the site, but before the neighbourhood had a chance to celebrate, gypsies started to take up the land. It was alleged that the disgruntled Mrs Murdoch, by way of revenge on the council, and the community at large, for their complaints, gave unofficial permission to a group of English gypsies to occupy the site free of charge. As a result, the community was back to lobbying the council once again.

Chapter 11

✳

Charley's neighbourhood took on the feel of a lawless Wild West town. With tension growing daily, Charley met with a group of his neighbours and, together, they decided that a day of action was needed. The plan was to telephone the Chief Executive of the council, one by one throughout the day, and badger him on the issue of the Murdoch site. Of course, after the first few calls, it was his secretary who took the brunt, but the Chief got the message loud and clear.

Charley backed it up the following day with another call, requesting a meeting with the Chief Executive; and to his surprise, he got one.

'Believe me, Mr Henry, I do sympathise with you, and all your neighbours, and I can assure you that we are doing everything in our power to resolve the issue.'

'With respect, Mr Preston, I've heard it all before. Look, just come down to the site yourself and sit outside for a couple hours and you'll see what we have to put up with.'

'I do sympathise with you, and your neighbours,' he repeated, 'who, incidentally, jammed our switchboard solid yesterday, Mr Henry, but the legendary Mrs Murdoch is now claiming that the gypsies are occupying her land without her permission and, as a consequence, she says that she is powerless to do anything about it.'

Charley tried to force his hand. 'What about her solicitors? I thought they had the power of attorney? So, what are they doing about it then?'

'Ah, yes, well I was coming to that, because we have, in fact, been exerting a lot of pressure on them to get on and comply with the court order.'

'Oh, good. So, I can go back and reassure my neighbours that the site clearance is imminent, can I?'

He grimaced. 'Er, no, not yet you can't.'

'When then? People are living in fear down there.'

Frowning, he replied, 'All right. Well, the situation is, we've been given to understand by Murdoch's solicitors that they're experiencing problems in finding anyone who's willing to go in there and risk their men and machinery.'

'I see...' said Charley, totally exasperated.

'Perhaps now, with all the facts to hand, you can understand—'

'Understand!' Charley interrupted. 'You're the local government for goodness sake! Surely you must be able to do it?'

'Not without going back to court we can't.'

Without thinking about the consequences, Charley told him that he would do it himself.

The Chief Executive gasped. 'What – you ... *you'll* do it?'

'Yeah, I will. Not that I really want to, mind, but I will. All I need from you is the proper written authority.'

Preston was so anxious to wash his hands of the problem that he didn't even stop for breath. Lunging for the telephone, he rang Murdoch's solicitor to relay Charley's offer. Before Charley had left Preston's office, he and the solicitor had arranged a site meeting between them.

'I warn you,' said the puny solicitor, all pinstripes, briefcase and bulging eyes, as they ventured up the driveway of the site, 'they're not a particularly friendly bunch in there.'

'I'm not expecting 'em to put the kettle on or anything, if that's what you're thinking.'

'Kettle?' he asked, thinking Charley had flipped.

'Yeah, you know, make us a cup of tea and all that.'

The scrawny solicitor was so tense that he didn't even crack a smile.

However, as was expected, they were both given a very noisy, hostile reception. They were colourfully ordered to leave the site while they could still walk – and not to return unless they wanted to die.

Charley could see the solicitor quaking in his boots, though, to be fair, he did manage to pull himself together and try to reason with the gypsies. He explained that the county court had instructed the total clearance of the site, which meant they were all there unlawfully.

Unfortunately, he failed to get his message across. His sharp suit, bits of paper, posh voice and choice of words were alien to them. They took the view that he was talking down to them, as though they were just a bit of shit on the ground. Taking the piss, they called it, and so they retaliated with their own choice of words: abuse.

Thinking that they were about to be lynched, Charley quickly pulled the solicitor to one side.

'Come on! Let's get out of here!' he whispered. 'I've seen all I want to see. Just give 'em the bit of paper and let's go!'

As Charley and the solicitor made their retreat, the gypsies tore up the papers and discarded them to the ground. Once safely out in the lane, they both breathed a sigh of relief.

'Now you see just what you're up against, Mr Henry, are you still keen to go back in and clear the place?'

'No, I'm blinking not! Only a bloody fool would go back in there if he didn't have to.'

His voice heavy with disappointment, the solicitor replied, 'I can't say I really blame you for changing your mind, Mr Henry. You're only human after all.'

'Who said anything about changing my mind? Look, I live in this lane, and I have two young children to think of.'

'Come again? What was that?' he asked, hanging onto Charley's every word.

'I said I can't wait to go back and get me head bashed in. So, when can I start?'

The tension drained from the solicitor's face.

'Excellent! Everything's in order, so there's nothing stopping you from going in today if you want...'

Charley gave an uneasy grin. 'Only the gypsies.'

Quick as a flash, the solicitor unbuckled his briefcase, got out a notice and stapled it to a fence post.

'That should dissuade any further gypsies from entering the site,' he said, dusting his hands off.

'Oh, good! I feel much better now, knowing that bit of paper's going to stop 'em...'

'I've done my best. I can't do any more than that,' the solicitor said, shaking Charley's hand before sprinting over to his car and climbing in.

'Oh, before you go, there's just one other—.'

But the solicitor was already racing away.

Like a lemon, Charley stood alone in the lane with the problem. He didn't sleep much that night through worrying. He kept tossing and turning, trying to formulate a strategy plan. His first thoughts were to go blazing in with a big gang of blokes for protection; but then he didn't want to push the gypsies into a corner, because they might feel compelled to fight their way out. Charley only wanted to clear the site, nice and peacefully, without any fuss, police or bad publicity. The last thing he wanted was a war on his hands.

It was almost the morning before he had finally devised his approach: to only take Big Jake along with him. Jake was one of Charley's most trusted building labourers and, as his name suggested, he was a big menacing-looking man. In reality, however, he was a very gentle giant.

Charley also decided on his 12-gauge shotgun as a precaution against the rats that they would undoubtedly meet on site. And, lastly, he decided to use the element of surprise and go in there the following morning at first light, to catch them as they slept. Charley was to roar onto the site, with his JCB, closely followed by his back-up, Big Jake, in the van.

Well, that was the plan anyway, so Charley informed the police of it, just in case he needed their help in a hurry.

Chapter 12

※

With the excitement about to start, Doug Hodges, the chairman of the residents' association, was hiding under his bed wearing a crash helmet and safety goggles.

It all kicked off at approximately 5.30 am. Dawn was just beginning to break when Charley and Big Jake got to the site. There, foiling their well-laid plans, were two old cars parked nose to nose, blockading the entrance.

'Shit. They're ready for us, Jake,' mouthed Charley, looking back from the JCB.

'Oh bollocks, that's all we need,' mouthed Jake in reply.

Before they knew it, all these blokes were running full pelt towards the barricade, raging. Five or six of them were gypsies; the rest were 4x2 and his cronies. Charley swallowed hard, thinking the worst – but the men stopped and stayed on their side of the barricade.

'Good morning, lads! I hope we didn't disturb you, but we're here to clear this site, in accordance with the court order. I'd very much appreciate it if you would please back up your cars and grant us access.'

'Fuck off! You ain't fucking coming in here, mate, and that's fucking final!'

Charley tried to calm the situation with a few polite, well-chosen words – only to make matters far worse. Politeness equated to weakness in their eyes. So Charley decided to wave the paperwork out the door, as his white flag, in the hope of a pow wow.

'This gives us all the necessary authorisation to enter and clear the site forthwith,' he said.

'Forthwith? What's that fucking supposed to mean then?'

'It means right now. TODAY,' replied Charley, from the safety of his cab.

Their spokesman, a huge, mean-looking fella, in a dirty old string vest, tatty jeans and wellington boots, stepped forward. He raised one of his thick-set tattooed arms, pointed a massive forefinger and bellowed, 'Take your fucking bits of paper and shove 'em up your fucking arse!'

Charley tried to think.

'Are you fucking deaf or something, mate?'

'Okay then,' Charley said, screwing up a single sheet of paper and tossing it out the cab. 'We'll forget the paperwork for now then, shall we? But we've still got a job to do, and as unpleasant as that may be, we're going to do it. So, we'll start by crushing the empty vans first. That'll give you all time to move out, nice and peaceful like.'

Charley had lit the blue touch paper on a keg of dynamite.

'If you don't get that fucking JCB out of here now, I'll fucking smash it up! Do you get my fucking drift?!'

Charley didn't flinch.

'I'll ask you again: are you fucking deaf or just plain bloody stupid?!' he roared.

'I heard you,' Charley replied, making ready to pick up the shotgun from the floor of the JCB, 'and I won't let you do that.'

Incited by his mates' war cries, the massive man ran over to the fence and ripped a post clean out of the ground with his bare hands. Wielding the post, he strode towards Charley, bawling, 'D'you want some of this then, eh?! EH?'

'*Oh shit,*' thought Charley. '*Here we go…*'

Charley picked up his shotgun and looked him straight in the eye. Seeing the gun, the big fella hesitated.

Confident he now had control, Charley made his way down from the machine – seemingly fearlessly – clasping the gun in his right hand.

'You were saying, mate?'

Charley held the bloke in a cold, steely stare till, still clutching the fence post, he dropped eye contact and stepped back into the safety of the crowd.

Keeping his poker face, Charley breathed a long sigh of relief. He was fairly certain that his subliminal message regarding the shotgun had taken deep root.

Suddenly, a loud cry rang out from the back of the bunch.

'What you fucking going to do? Start shooting us all, then?'

The remainder of the mob jeered in support.

'I'll do whatever is necessary,' Charley declared.

The reception committee then huddled together and began talking in whispers. Having said nothing up to this point, Big Jake climbed out of the van and joined Charley.

'Well done, Chas. They won't do anything now. Not now they've seen the gun, they won't.'

Charley wasn't entirely convinced, and his heart was pounding.

'It ain't even loaded, Jake. The only two cartridges we got are under the seat of the van.'

'Yeah, but they don't know that, Chas, do they? A shotgun speaks volumes, mate, and there ain't any man in his right mind who'd ever dare challenge someone holding one.'

'That's what scares me, Jake, cos half this lot aren't in their right mind. Look at 4x2 and his mates! They're all spaced out on the old wacky baccy … or worse.'

'Yeah, I bet most of 'em have still got needles stuck in their arms,' Jake replied.

'Yeah, just a load of pricks, ain't they? The way that one's walking it looks as though he's got one stuck up his arse.'

'What – that one with a smile on his face, you mean? Seriously though, Chas, what are we going to do if the mad bastards rush us?'

'Fucked if I know, Jake. I s'pose I'll have to point the gun at 'em and say "bang!"'

'And if that don't work?'

'I could always bash 'em with it, I s'pose, but I don't think 4x2 would even feel it, Jake.'

'Look out, Chas, they're making a move…'

The mob, led by the big bloke with the fence post, walked back and stopped about 20 foot in front of the JCB. In complete silence, they fixed their eyes on Charley and Jake. Charley knew their plan was to try and unnerve them, and to a certain extent it worked: there was a total stand-off. Whilst Charley couldn't stop looking at the fence post, the mob couldn't take their eyes off of Charley's shotgun.

Eventually, it was Charley who broke the silence.

'We can't just stand around here all day!' he shouted. 'We've got work to do. So, if you're not prepared to move the cars for us, then I'll just nudge 'em gently aside with our JCB, all right?'

They made no reply, so Charley took the initiative and said to Jake, 'We're going in, mate! Get in the van and stay close to me.'

He then climbed back up into the JCB and fired it up. The mob stood fast. Placing the shotgun across his lap, Charley then revved the engine, as if to say 'I mean it, I'm coming through', but there was still no response. As a further gesture of his intentions, Charley slowly lifted the front bucket and opened up the jaws to expose the bulldozer blade. Still nothing. And so, with a very dry mouth, Charley slowly inched the machine towards the barricade, pushing the old cars aside like discarded matchboxes. The mob was dispersing!

'They've fucking given up!' Jake yelled, jumping from the van and leaping onto the foot plate of the JCB. 'Look! Most of them are scampering down the lane!'

Charley broke wind in relief.

'Ha! Steady on!' Jake laughed. 'You might shit yourself!'

'Too late, Jake! I've already done that, mate. I can't take the excitement anymore.'

Whilst they were busy clearing a suitable area to light a fire, they noticed that a good proportion of 4x2's cronies were packing up their belongings into black plastic bags and leaving the site. It was also apparent that the gypsies had brought along their own caravans and set up camp slightly away from the main rubbish-strewn, rat-infested camp of 4x2 and Co. Many of the old caravans were empty and some had been stripped of their aluminium panels.

'Come on, Jake. Let's get on with it.'

As they started to crush one of the empty caravans, they were set upon by an ugly, uncompromising pack of "women" Their threats and bad language were far worse than the reception committee they first encountered.

'Just ignore them, Jake,' Charley said – though harder said than done.

'Oi, oi! I'm fucking talking to you!'

A revolting, sour-faced lady proceeded to tell Charley and Jake that their menfolk had gone to round up a hundred or more troops.

'And when they've beaten the living shit out of you two arseholes,' she screamed, 'they're going to dig a fucking great big hole with your JCB and fucking plant the fucking pair of you in it!'

She also informed them the men were going to occupy the remainder of the empty caravans. With no desire to enter dialogue, Charley clambered into the JCB and drove it into all said static caravans, damaging them beyond habitability.

When he looked back, he saw Jake walking towards him, donning pair of ear defenders that he'd got from the van.

'What a good idea, Jake!' Charley said, when he handed him a pair also.

Knowing that Jake and Charley could no longer hear them, the wailing witches gave up and left them alone.

Charley's young son Sam turned up on site about 10 am, with a flask of hot tea and sandwiches.

'So far so good, Jake,' Charley said, as he munched down a sandwich.

'I thought we were done for when that ugly old cow started yelling the odds. Can you imagine waking up next to that every morning?'

'I'd rather not, Jake.'

Pouring another drop of tea from the flask, Charley looked to Jake and said, 'Well done, mate. I'm sure we're over the worst now.'

'I wouldn't be so sure, Chas!' he replied, looking back towards the entrance.

'Bloody hell!' Charley cried, on seeing an even larger mob approaching, armed with iron bars and pieces of wood. Charley told young Sam to quickly cut across the fields and go home. With Sam safely out of the way, Charley grabbed hold of the shotgun and charged over to the van to get the only two cartridges they had. Hurriedly breaking the gun, he inserted the cartridges into the chamber and got up onto the roof of the JCB. Jake grabbed a pick handle and scampered onto the bonnet.

By the time the jeering hecklers had reached them, they were holding a strong, high position of defence.

It was much like a scene from the epic *The Battle of the Alamo*, where John Wayne and his men were overpowered and beaten to death. Thinking that's what they had coming to them, Charley was of a mind to fire a warning shot over their heads.

Meanwhile, unbeknown to Charley and Jake, Wendy Martin, whose property overlooked the site, had witnessed their desperate plight from an upstairs window and had made a frantic telephone call to the police.

As Charley's finger hovered nervously on the trigger, a wizened old man raised both arms aloft, instantly silencing the siege. You could hear a pin drop as he shuffled his way towards the front. The wrinkled and weather-beaten old boy wore a battered grey trilby hat, a red ragged cravat around his scrawny neck, a brown-checked threadbare jacket and a pair of dark brown corduroy trousers tied with a length of frayed rope. He may not have looked the toughest, but he certainly commanded respect.

On reaching the foot of the JCB, he just stood there, chewing on tobacco, with dark brown spittle oozing from the corners of his mouth. His broken, blackened teeth resembled a row of bombed-out houses. He stared up at Charley. No one dared breathe during the silent war of nerves. The old boy appeared to be summing up, ready to pass sentence on Charley and Jake.

Suddenly, he spat out a dark brown residue. When he finally spoke, it was with a gravelled croak.

'What's this – you're going to shoot one of ours?' He spat to the ground again.

Charley gulped. He told him that he hadn't threatened to shoot anyone.

'What's the gun for, then?' he roared.

'What – this one?' Charley replied, raising the shotgun, unwittingly scattering the mob. 'I brought it along to shoot the rats.'

Once they'd regrouped, the old boy moved on to Big Jake. Detecting a bit of gypsy blood, he asked that he be allowed to speak with him alone.

'You have my word that no harm will come to him – or you – while we talk together.'

Jake turned to Charley and nodded before jumping down with the pick handle. Jake then went to one side with the old boy and Charley was left stood on top of the JCB, guarded by the mob.

After many anxious minutes, they both shook hands and returned. The old fella then singled out the tattooed bloke in the string vest who'd confronted Charley and Jack earlier.

'Was it 'im that threatened to smash up your machine?'

Taken aback, Charley needed time to think.

'I won't ask you again,' he growled.

'Uh … yeah … yeah it was.'

'Did you threaten to shoot 'im?' he forced?

It was like Charley was on death row, fighting for his life.

'No, I didn't,' he answered. How he wished that he was anywhere else but there!

'Did you point the gun at 'im – or anyone else – when you came in here?'

Charley shook his head. 'No, I didn't. I was just holding it.'

The old boy then looked over to Big Jake and nodded, before giving the tattooed bloke the biggest bollocking that Charley had seen since he worked for his eldest brother, Albert.

'You'll have no further trouble from us, gov,' he winked. 'Everyone will be gone from here by tomorrow.' He then turned and hollered, 'None of you is to touch their scrap! Is that understood?!'

It was better than having police protection!

The panic over, Charley came down from the machine and shook hands with the old boy.

'Thanks for your help, mate,' he said. 'No hard feelings, eh?'

'None taken, boy,' he winked again. 'Stay lucky.'

He then left the site, closely followed by the rest of them.

The feeling of relief was so tremendous that both Big Jake and Charley collapsed in a heap by the fire. They were drained. They were both still lying there, gazing up at the sky, when the police swarmed in.

Seeing them on the ground, the sergeant naturally assumed the worst and ran over.

'Are you all right?'

'Yeah, we're just having a little rest, mate,' Charley joked.

'Your neighbour Mrs Martin told us that there were hundreds of gypsies here, and that they were about to kill you?!'

'Er, yeah, it was a bit hairy, there's no denying that. But on this occasion, it worked out for the best that you arrived late.'

'You were bloody lucky to get away with it!' he grunted.

Moments after the police left the site, Charley had a visit from the Chief Executive of the council, along with two of his planning officers. Grinning from ear to ear, the Chief remarked how pleased he was now that the site was finally being cleared.

'Er, pleased enough to grant planning approval for my new replacement dwelling?' Charley asked with a hopeful smile.

'Oh, I feel sure that there won't be any problems in that quarter,' he replied, looking over the top of his glasses towards his planning officers.

'You crafty old sod!' Jake remarked, as they left the site.

'It's no use getting older, Jake, if you don't get wiser, is it? Push every button and pull every lever that's available to you: that's my motto. Anyway, enough about that, what else did my mate, the old gypsy king, ask you?'

'Your mate?' Jake questioned, shaking his head.

'Yeah, didn't you see the way he kept winking at me?'

'Winking? He was only doing that cos he fancied you.'

'Yeah, ha ha. Joking aside, what did he say then?'

'Oh, he wanted to know if you were mad enough to use the gun.'

'What did you say then?'

'I told him you were barking. Totally insane.'

'Did he ask why I was wearing "brown" trousers then?'

'No, he'd worked that one out for himself.'

They then both laughed at their near-death experience.

'In all, Jake, a good day, don't you think?'

'Yeah, but we're going to need a bloody lot of skips to clear this site, Chas.'

'No, I don't think so, Jake. Just go over and ask that old bird to open her mouth again and we'll shovel it all in there.'

'On your bike, Chas! I ain't going anywhere near that crater – I might lose my footing and fall in.'

That evening, Charley had a call from Doug Hodges, the chairman of the residents' association.

'Everything go all right, Charley?' he asked, wanting to know all the ins and outs.

'Yeah. You can take your crash helmet off now, Doug. They'll all be gone tomorrow.'

A few days later, Doug circulated a letter to all the residents saying how he, as chairman, had managed to get the site cleared.

Chapter 13

※

Later that same year, Charley was summoned by the county court regarding the clearance of Mrs Murdoch's illegal shanty town.

Approximately eight months earlier, the Murdoch family had issued legal proceedings against the firm of solicitors who had instructed Charley to clear their site. The solicitors were being prosecuted for exceeding their power of autonomy, and Charley was called to give evidence on behalf of the defence.

Charley was extremely busy at work at the time and so the solicitor arranged for the time slot immediately after lunch to allow him to give his evidence and then go back to work. Charley arrived at the court to find the puny solicitor pacing up and down outside.

'Don't look so worried, mate,' Charley said, smiling. 'I'm only a few seconds late.'

'It's not the time that worries me,' the solicitor replied, as he hurried Charley towards the courtroom.

'What is it then?'

'It's that a bit of a problem has arisen: some of the witnesses for the prosecution have made a serious allegation, on oath that you went blazing onto the site with a loaded shotgun and threatened to shoot anyone who got in your way. Is there any truth to that?'

Charley laughed.

'It's no laughing matter – the courts take a very dim view of that sort of thing.'

'All right, keep your hair on! I'm a builder, not a cowboy. And no jokes please – I've heard them all.'

'You haven't answered my question. Did you take a loaded shotgun on site and threaten anyone with it?'

'Welllll … yes and no.'

'What do you mean yes and no? Either you did or you didn't.'

'Yes, I did take a gun on site and no, I didn't threaten anyone.'

'I see. I take it you do possess a current licence for it?'

'Yeah, of course I do. Look, you're making it all sound as though I'm the one on trial here. You saw how hostile they were. Without the sight of the gun, we'd have been beaten to death – and you would still be looking to find someone to clear the site.'

'Point taken. But their barrister will challenge you on the issue, so be very careful how you answer him.'

'The witnesses who made that defamatory statement, were they the gypsies?'

'No, they were some of the original tenants,' the solicitor replied.

'No use calling the old gypsy king then,' whispered Charley under his breath.

'Pardon? Call who?'

'It's all right, I was just thinking aloud.'

When Charley entered the courtroom he was immediately shown into the witness box by the usher, and then sworn in. The barrage of cross-examination promptly began.

The barrister for the prosecution was first.

'Think back to the time when you entered and cleared Mrs Murdoch's site, Mr Henry – were you carrying anything?'

'Er, yes, I was,' replied Charley, his mouth dry. He was unsure where his line of questioning was going.

'Will you tell the court in your own words what it was then?'

'Yes … apart from a tea flask, I was carrying a 12-bore shotgun.'

'"A 12-bore shotgun",' the barrister repeated loudly, as he turned towards the judge to emphasise the gravity.

'What possible reason could you have for taking a loaded 12-bore shotgun onto a residential site where people were still living?'

'I can see that, in the cold light of day, it sounds a terrible thing to do, but I am a responsible licence holder.'

'That still doesn't give you the right to wave a loaded gun around.'

'Look, the gun wasn't loaded when we entered the site, and I didn't wave the *empty* gun anywhere. It's just from my initial visit with the solicitor, I could see the site to be vermin-infested and so I merely took the gun along so we wouldn't be pestered by the rats.'

The judge stopped writing for a moment and looked at Charley from over the top of his glasses.

'When you say rats, I take it you mean the four-legged kind?'

'Yes, of course. What else?'

'Oh, I think you would have been better off taking a Jack Russell along with you,' he suggested.

'Er, with respect, you don't have to feed a shotgun,' Charley confidently replied, now that humour seemed to be playing a part in the proceedings.

The prosecution barrister continued.

'Apart from the rats, Mr Henry, when you actually cleared the site, did you crush, and dispose of, the site owner's car, or for that matter, any cars belonging to the tenants?'

'I did as instructed, and that was to clear the entire site, including the old cars which were lying about the place. I didn't see any vehicle that looked remotely roadworthy.'

'Do you recall seeing a new 20-inch colour TV and a new Hi Fi system plus numerous personal possessions that were being stored in one of the caravans that you disposed of?'

'No, I didn't see anything like that.'

'Did you even take the trouble to look inside any of the caravans before you crushed them?'

'Yes, of course, I did. I had to be sure that there wasn't anyone still inside 'em.'

'No more questions,' he said.

After a few trivial questions from the defending barrister, Charley left the court and went back to work.

Chapter 14

At 9 am, on the first day of April 1979, Charley received an odd telephone call offering him the biggest and potentially the most lucrative job to date. The caller spoke in a heavy whisper and sounded very much like a dirty old pervert in a white mackintosh.

Charley very nearly dismissed the call, thinking it was a friend playing an April Fools' prank; however, he decided to go along with it and try to turn the tables with his own joke.

'Hello? Is that Henry Developments?' came the muffled voice of the mystery caller.

'Look, pal,' Charley replied, 'if you're selling stick sweets, I don't want any, thank you.'

'What? Stick what? This *is* Henry Developments, isn't it?'

Charley was about to tell him to peddle his stick sweet elsewhere, when the caller offered him a huge building project that made him stop and think. The proposed contract was to build 30 new bedrooms and bathrooms, plus all the demolition and refurbishment works to the main buildings.

'Say again,' said Charley, straining to listen. He hoped he might just recognise the voice so as not to make a fool of himself. 'Only, it's such a bad line that I can hardly hear you.'

'Look, I can't talk any louder. My name is Arthur George Bainbridge, and I'm the new owner of the Waterside Motel. If you want the contract that I'm offering, then you'll come to the Motel at precisely 11 am today. You do know where it is, I trust?'

'Yes, I do.'

Yet, Charley was not convinced that it was a genuine enquiry. Perhaps if it hadn't been for April Fools' Day, he might have thought differently. With no way of tracing the call, Charley asked if he could ring him straight back.

'I haven't got time for all that,' continued the whisper. 'Do you want the job or don't you?'

'Yes. It sounds good to me. I'll see you at 11 am, today.'

'Right. Not a moment before, or after!' He then promptly hung up.

'That was bloody weird,' thought Charley. *'It's got to be a wind up. Nobody talks in whispers like that. Unless, of course, he was ill. Lost his voice maybe. No, it's a joke call all right. Or was he trying to hide something? Perhaps he didn't want to be overheard. If that was the case, then why?'*

Charley's imagination was running wild. His mind even turned to Fawlty Towers and the psycho hotel owner Basil Fawlty. What an April fool that would make! Thinking it sounded too good to be true, Charley tried calling a couple of mates who he thought would pull a stunt like that.

'Hi Phil, you seen the local TV news this morning?'

'No, why's that, Chas?'

'Oh, it's that the new owner of the Waterside Motel has been charged with running a brothel.'

'No! Has he really? I don't believe it!'

'Fancy going down there one night, Phil?'

'Now I know you're bloody joking, Chas. Oh yeah, got it. It's April Fools' Day, ain't it? Yeah, nice try, Chas, but you'll have to get up earlier than that to catch me out! Motel? Couldn't you do better than that?'

'I know. Stupid, weren't it? I mean, who would fall for an April Fools' joke about a crazy motel owner?'

Phil laughed, and so did Charley, but still the telephone call bugged him, so he rang a further two mates. But nobody was letting on. Despite his misgivings, Charley believed that a huge job like that would be well worth pursuing – and a welcome change from clearing up all the condemned projects for Doug Langsdale.

After exploiting all the avenues of enquiry, Charley went to the Motel, as requested, but he was 10 minutes early. Remembering what the caller had said about punctuality, he parked up with one eye on the time, the other on the reception area. At four minutes to eleven, he noticed a smartly dressed lady leaving the reception area. She hesitated for a moment, but then quickly climbed into a car and drove away.

Charley thought no more of it. A few moments before 11 am, he walked into the reception, where, lingering in the air, was the smell of strong, cheap perfume.

'*Oh shit,*' he thought, as he reached out to tap the bell on the counter. '*I hope that smell ain't the weird caller. My old mum warned me about blokes who smell like that.*'

Alerted by the bell, Charley was greeted by a pretty young lady who came through from the office door directly behind the counter.

'Hello. My name is Charles Henry, and I have an appointment to see Mr. Bainbridge at 11 am.'

'Are you sure, Mr. Henry,' she said, flicking through the pages, 'because I can't see any appointment in the book?'

'*So, it WAS a bloody wind up!*' He knew it!

'April! April!' cried an anxious male voice through the open door of the office. 'You run along now, and I'll deal with him.'

'*"April",*' thought Charley, thinking he'd been had. '*Why couldn't she have been called May, June, anything other than April?*'

As she left the counter, a creased face emerged, closely followed by a gangly, potbellied body.

'Ah! Mr. Henry, I presume. You made it all right then. My name is Arthur Bainbridge,' he said, with a silly, forced grin. He extended his right hand.

Clutching a roll of building plans in his left hand, he proceeded to roll them out across the counter top. He perched a pair of thick black horn-rimmed spectacles on his nose and began to explain the plans to Charley.

As Charley lent forwards for a closer look, Mr. Bainbridge looked over Charley's shoulder. Somewhat distressed, he exhaled a silent but deep groan. Charley caught another whiff of the strong perfume and turned to see the lady who'd left earlier standing in the doorway. When he turned back to look at the plans, they had disappeared from the counter top.

Under a very nervous smile, Arthur Bainbridge cleared his throat.

'Hello, dear. You're back early … and, might I say, your hair looks lovely!'

'I haven't been yet, Arthur!' she snapped, suspecting he was up to no good.

As she walked towards the desk, Mr. Bainbridge tried to kick the plans that he'd tossed to the floor, under the counter.

'What are you doing, Arthur?' she growled, like a prison warden.

'Oh, nothing dear, just seeing to this chap,' he replied before muttering through clenched teeth something about an eagle-eyed sparrow. Then, turning towards Charley, he confirmed, 'Er, yes that does include a full English breakfast.'

Charley was stunned. None of his mates could ever have arranged such an elaborate April Fools' joke as this.

'It looks like rain,' she said, 'and so I came back for my umbrella because I don't want my hair to get ruined.'

Charley stood there trying to make sense of it all, while Arthur just carried on with the pretense of taking his booking. The lady picked up her umbrella and walked out into the courtyard. Arthur then stopped talking, rushed over to the doorway and watched her drive away.

Charley was flabbergasted by the goings-on.

Confident she had gone, Arthur ran back without explanation and ducked down beneath the counter. After one or two grunts, he retrieved the plans and stood bolt upright with a strange look in his eye. Presuming he was going to roll them out on the counter again, Charley waited, but then, without warning, Bainbridge flipped a cloth cap up onto his head, jammed a pipe into the corner of his mouth and set fire to it.

'*This bloke should be locked up, trying to act as though this is all nothing out of the ordinary,*' Charley thought.

'Right, follow me, Mr. Henry, and I will familiarise you with the premises before showing you the fantastic plans we have.'

Once outside, Bainbridge took off like a steam train, leaving a trail of smoke in his wake. He was desperate to show Charley as quickly as possible everything that needed to be demolished to make way for the new block of 30 ensuite rooms, and the block that was to be retained and renovated.

With one last look over towards the car park, Bainbridge hurried Charley into the dance hall.

'Even all this is to be demolished,' he said, as he raced around, locking all the doors. 'Just a precaution, you understand. We don't want to be disturbed while we thrash out a deal, do we?'

'As you like, Mr. Bainbridge. It's your motel…'

'Right. Now that we're completely on our own, let's get straight down to the business in hand. For starts, what's your first name?'

'Charles, but everybody calls me Chas or Charley, I answer to either.'

Pressing his forefinger to his lips, Bainbridge instructed Charley to shush. After checking every conceivable hiding place, he swaggered back, like he had just taken a massive shot of valium.

'Er, sorry about that, Chas. I thought I heard something.'

He puffed a huge cloud of blue smoke into the air.

'As I was about to tell you, my name is Arthur and so you can call me … Arthur.'

'Okay then, Arthur. It's nice to get things on a friendly basis,' Charley replied, shaking his bony hand.

Like a big business tycoon, Arthur then rolled the plans out across a tabletop and placed a heavy glass ashtray at either end to keep them open.

'While my wife's not around to interfere, Chas, we can get right down to the nitty-gritty. Talk freely, so to speak. No beating about the bush. Lay the cards on the table and do some plain ordinary speaking, er, man to man like. Know what I mean? Cut through all the crap and get straight to the point. Women don't understand how these things are done. Do they?'

'Gosh, if that load of old waffle was getting to the point,' thought Charley, *'best I book a room for the night.'*

'Well, do they, Chas?'

'Er, yeah, sorry Arthur. You're right. I'm all ears. Let's hear what you've got to say.'

Before Arthur began his spiel, he glanced at his watch, took off his jacket and tossed it onto the adjoining table, fancying himself as something of a high-powered executive.

'As you're probably aware, Chas,' he said, stretching his red braces with his thumbs, 'we've only just purchased this dump, and, as you can see from our plans, we intend to take it upmarket considerably, get rid of the old image altogether. Know what I mean? And then once all the building works are completed, we're going to rename the place, call it "The Bainbridge Park Motel". What do you think?'

He let go of his braces with a snap.

'Sounds good to me, Arthur,' Charley replied with an uneasy smile. 'I take it then that you have all the necessary planning and building regulation approvals?'

'Yes, yes, yes, of course we do. Just give me a good cheap price and the job's yours.'

'"A cheap price"? When it comes to major building works such as this, there's no such thing as a cheap price, Arthur. Remember: you get exactly what you pay for.'

'Yeah, I know that, but you must be more competitive than the others if you want this job.'

'Okay, Arthur, just as long as I'm not competing against the James Gang.'

'"The James Gang"? Who are they? Better still, are they cheap?'

'Yeah, they're very cheap, Arthur, but you won't like 'em, cos they can't build – since they're a bunch of COWBOYS. All right at rounding up cows, I believe.'

Arthur returned a cheesy grin.

'Well, seeing as I've got no cows, best you give me your best price then.'

'Okay, Arthur, no problem. If I could just take a copy of the plans away with me, I'll get you an estimate in the post in the next few days.'

'No, no, no, Chas, that's no good to me! You see, I want to know the price NOW!'

He slammed his hand down on the plans like an American General in a low-budget war film.

All the signs were staring Charley in the face: first, the cunningness; then, the sheer panic, closely followed by the desperation; the calm entrepreneur; and, finally, the power-crazed madman. Who was Charley dealing with if not a complete maniac? What was he to do? He couldn't afford to be too choosy – he needed the work.

'Look, you're a professional, Chas. You know what you're doing ... how much things cost ... you should be able to give me a ballpark figure. That's all I want at this stage of the game; a rough idea to work with. Surely you can do that for me, can't you?'

'No, I'm afraid not, Arthur. This is not a run-of-the mill project.'

Arthur's eyes turned cold.

'Well, if you don't want the job,' he growled, 'I'll find some other bugger who does! I may even ask that *James Gang* you were on about just now, see if they want the job!'

Charley thought about the huge contract on offer and so, against his better judgement, he took a deep breath, did a few quick calculations on a notepad and gave Arthur a very rough guesstimate.

'How much!' he cried. 'Cor blimey, you could build Buckingham Palace for that! This is only a humble motel, you know. You better start sharpening your pencil if you want this job!'

'Arthur,' Charley appealed, 'if I sharpened it any more, I would be cutting my fingers. And you wouldn't want that, would you?'

'Better than me cutting my *throat!*' he scowled, folding up the plans. 'I'll find someone else to do the job instead. There must be someone out there hungry enough who will do it cheaper.'

Time to call his bluff.

'Fair enough then, Arthur,' Charley said, walking towards the locked door.

'Speaking man to man, as you suggested, they'd have to be bloody starving to beat the price I just gave you. And I'll tell you this for nothing, Arthur: if you want a proper job doing, you must pay *a few pennies more* than the James Gang. Unless, of course, you ask the proverbial monkeys to do it for you...'

'Are they cheap?' Arthur joked.

'Yeah. Apart from the James Gang, they're the only ones who work for peanuts. Now, the door please, Arthur, because I've got work to do.'

'Er ... hold on a moment, Chas ... perhaps I've been a tad hasty in the matter. What if we cut down on the specification a bit?'

'Yeah, we could always leave the roof off, Arthur! Course it'll let the rain in, but, then, the summer is coming.'

Arthur returned a wry smile.

'I suppose I asked for that, didn't I? But I was thinking more along the lines of knocking off the internal decorating,' he said. 'Me and my son Jonathan could always do a bit of painting. You know what they say – if you can piss, you can paint.'

'Yeah, I've heard that too, Arthur, but there's lots of people out there who can't piss. They leave drips all over the floor.'

'Yeah, I've noticed that in *our* bathrooms. Dirty bastards.'

'When I referred to *drips*, Arthur, I meant *paint* drips...'

'Yeah, yeah, that as well,' he said.

After a great deal of bartering, they eventually came close to an agreed price.

'I can see we are going to get along just famously!' Arthur beamed in victory.

He gave Charley his hand to shake on the deal.

'Now, when my lovely wife comes back from the hairdresser's, all we've got to do is tell her the good news. Er, together, that is. We'll tell her together; it'll sound much better that way. Only, she likes to feel as though she's involved in some small way. You can understand that, can't you?'

'Yeah, I can appreciate that, Arthur. You've got to keep her in the loop, so to speak. It's only natural.'

'Good. So, all you've got to do is tell her that you will be sending us your written estimate confirming the agreed price. Oh, and perhaps you'll just tell her that you don't have a problem with the Motel staying open for business as usual while you carry out the work. Oh, and just one other small detail – tell her about the late penalty charge should you not complete the project within six months.'

'What! Now, you hang on a minute, Arthur. I didn't agree to all that. Surely you're joking. You can't remain open throughout a major rebuilding programme such as this? It's not possible. Not only is it not possible, it's damn right insane to even think of. What about your guests?'

'Oh, sod the bloody guests! They don't even come into the equation.'

'No, I'm sorry, Arthur. It just can't be done; you'll have to close down for the duration. And as far as a late penalty charge goes, if you want me to include that within the contract, the overall price would have to increase considerably.'

'Oh, but I thought that's what we'd agreed,' he said, with a crafty frown.

'No, Arthur, we didn't. We only agreed the price based on normal working conditions.'

'*"Normal"? What am I saying? There's nothing normal about this bloody madman!*' Charley thought.

'Oh, I'm sorry, Chas. I must be getting confused with what the other builders have told us,' he said, cunningly starting off another round of negotiations.

Charley sighed. 'Arthur, it won't be easy you staying open for the duration; however, I s'pose if it meant getting the job, we could give it our best shot. But it would take much longer to complete the project doing it that way—'

'You've got six months only!' he interrupted.

'Okay then, Arthur. We may just be able to meet your deadline if I swamp the job with labour, and we work seven days a week. But I couldn't possibly—'

'Then flood it with labour! Do whatever it takes! Work 24/7 if need be. But whatever you do, this Motel stays open while you do it!'

He banged his hand down on the tabletop gain.

'Arthur….. I'm probably going to regret saying this, but if you can guarantee me very, very prompt stage payments, I'll do it. We'll build around you, and your guests – however, as I was trying to tell you before, I couldn't possibly agree to a late penalty charge.'

'Done.' Arthur shook Charley's hand vigorously in delight. 'We'll clinch the deal with a swift one in the bar. Toast to a successful job and all that. We can fill in my good lady at the same time. I'm sure she'll be very pleased with the outcome.'

Arthur had no sooner put a pint on the bar, when Charley detected that cheap perfume again. He turned to see the lady stood in the doorway.

'Ah, you're home, my little Jaffa cake! We have some very, very good news for you, haven't we, Charley?'

'What have you done, Arthur?!' she cried.

'Oh, your hair looks very lovely,' he said, sweet-talking her.

'Sod my bloody hair! What have you done?'

'Done, dear? Why I haven't done anything, my little wallflower.'

'What haven't you done then?'

'Go on, you tell her, Chas.'

Charley almost choked on his beer.

'Er, no, I think that's your place to do that Arthur, don't you?'

'Arthur!' she roared. 'A word in private!'

'Oh, sorry, dear. Didn't I tell you Mr Henry here is an excellent builder? John and Betty recommended him to us. They said that he is the best builder in the county. And you'll never guess what – he's only given an unbelievable price to do all the building works!'

Anticipating her reaction, Arthur ducked down behind the bar. Charley could see the look of fury in her eyes and so he moved slowly further along the bar.

'Arthur! Arthur!' she screamed.

'Have you seen the peanuts, dear?' he asked, keeping his head down, well out of her reach.

Without answering, she picked up a small dish of peanuts from the end of the bar, walked around and tipped them over his head.

'Oh, good! You've found them, my precious!' he said, standing up, peanuts falling to the floor.

'Now, explain yourself!' she bellowed, slamming the empty dish down onto the bartop.

'Yes, of course. Sorry, dear, I haven't introduced you. This is Mr Charles Henry, a fine builder. Charley, my wife.'

Charley nodded apprehensively, while she continued to grill Arthur through clenched teeth.

'What did I tell you? You know what happened last time.'

'Yes, all right, my little piranha fish. You don't have to keep harping on about that.'

She turned to Charley and smiled. In a softly spoken voice, she offered her apologies.

'I am sorry Arthur has wasted your time this morning, Mr Henry, because we have already decided to instruct Laneways as our builder.'

'That's all right, Mrs Bainbridge. Thank you for letting me know. Laneways are a very good, reliable building company, and you shouldn't have any problems with them at all.'

Charley swallowed the last of his beer, returned his empty glass to the bartop and bid them both good day.

'No, no, please … just wait one minute, Chas.'

Arthur put another pint on the bar before a last-ditch attempt to convince his wife. Pulling her out of earshot, Arthur started to plead his case.

'Look, I know you want Laneways to do the job, but please hear what Charley has to say for himself.'

'I'm done talking, Arthur,' she said, walking away.

'But look, Bev, Charley can do the job much cheaper than Laneways and, unlike them, Charley said that there's no need for us to close down. It's a no-brainer. We get to stay open for business as usual, and we don't lose any money from cancelled bookings. At least hear what he's got to say for himself.'

She turned to face Charley.

'Is that right what Arthur has just told me, Mr Henry? You can do all that work while we stay open?'

'Er, well— '

'Yes, of course he can!' Arthur blurted, before Charley had a chance to voice his own doubts on the matter. 'He's a proper professional builder, isn't he, unlike some of those other wimps you've been talking to.'

He tutted and rolled his eyes up to the tobacco-stained ceiling.

'Oh, shush, Arthur! I was asking Mr Henry. Kindly let him speak for himself.'

'Oh, all right then, my little sunflower. Might I just remind you, dear, who it was that recommended Charley to us in the first place. Hmmm? They spoke very highly of him – very honest, straightforward and trustworthy; easy to deal with. And if Charley said he can do it, then that's good enough for me. Especially at the price I got,' he mouthed so Charley wouldn't hear.

'Oh, shut up Arthur and let him speak!'

'Well, Mrs Bainbridge, as I was saying to Arthur—'

'Forget about him! What makes you so sure that you can do what all of the other builders can't? You see, we've asked a number of them, and they all say the same – it's not possible to stay open.'

Arthur's lanky frame buckled with fear, thinking that Charley would say the wrong thing. He maneuvered his way behind her and began making hand gestures and mouthing instructions over to Charley.

'Well, Mrs Bainbridge,' Charley said, trying to ignore Arthur's gesticulating, 'the choice is entirely yours whether you stay open or not. As I was telling Arthur, it won't be easy working here, or to even finish the job on time if you choose to stay open.'

She quickly turned, to catch him waving his arms in the air.

'What on earth are you doing, Arthur?! she cried. 'Stand still!'

'Damn fly!' he said, swiping at the air. 'Spread disease, they do.'

'Just ignore him, Mr Henry,' she sighed. 'Now, what were you saying about finishing the project?'

'Yes, as I was about to say, if I flood the whole job with labour, and we work seven days a week, I'm fairly confident we can do it on time.'

'See, my little doubter. It *can* be done,' Arthur crowed. His relief that Charley hadn't dropped him in it showed. 'You just leave it up to me and Charley – we speak the same language. We are going to get along very well, aren't we, Chas?'

Charley just forged a smile and nodded.

Embarrassingly awkward though their first meeting was, Charley got the job. Prior to starting, he asked the Bainbridges to sign a binding contract whereby the job would be split into six equal stages and, if the work went according to schedule, Charley would expect a progress payment every month.

Well, that's what Charley thought…

Chapter 15

※

Whilst Charley was pleased to have won such a huge building contract, he was also very mindful of Arthur's mental state. Arthur was on a high, after orchestrating the deal with Charley. He was convinced he was smarter than anyone, especially his tiny wife. In his delusion, he thought he could run the Motel better than her, project manage the new building programme and control Charley and the boys all at the same time. If ever he saw an opportunity of making or saving money, he would go to any lengths to do so.

Tiny or not, however, his wife could control him with just a single glance. Had it not been for her straight talking, Charley wouldn't have taken the job on – at any price.

Charley's first day on site proved interesting. He'd hardly parked his van when Arthur, knowing his wife was watching from the reception window, came strutting over.

'Come on, come on! What time d'you call this?' he barked.

Charley frowned and looked at his watch.

'Why, it's 7.30 am Arthur,' he said. 'Have you got a problem with that? Is it too early for you? Have I disturbed your guests or something?'

'The guests?! No! Sod the bloody peasants!' he cried. 'Don't go wasting any time worrying about them buggers. Their sort won't be coming back here once this place goes up market.'

Charley glared at him. He found Arthur's attitude and his staged act rude and offensive. Charley's body language didn't go unnoticed – it left Arthur unsure how to continue with his little game plan. Through the uneasy silence that followed, he cautiously glanced back towards the reception window. Convinced that his wife was no longer spying on him, he dropped the act and an evil grin crept across his lived-in face.

'It's only my little joke, Charley!' he laughed, removing his pipe. 'The look on your face! It works every time!'

'What does?'

'The old gee up routine. Nothing personal, mate, but we must start how we mean to go on. That's my motto. Keep on top of things, you know. Set the pace. Remind you that the countdown has now begun, and that you've only got six months to go.'

'Cor blimey, Arthur, give us a blinking chance! We haven't even started the job yet! It's only our first morning.'

'Precisely,' Arthur grumbled, poking his smelly old pipe towards Charley. 'So, where's all your men then? I thought you were going to flood the job with labour, so what happened? Got drowned in the flood, did they? Ha ha ha!'

Charley bit his lip and counted to 10.

'I can assure you, Arthur, you'll have no worries regarding our workforce, because, for one, they can all *swim*. And two, they will be here on site, and working, by 8 am sharp.'

'8 am? Cor blimey. Half the day will be gone by then. You'll never get the place finished if you only work part-time. From the way you spoke the other day, I thought we were going to see an explosion of action right from the word go.'

'Woah, woah. Now you just hold up a minute, Arthur. For starters, your brief was for no disruption. That's why we're not starting work until 8 am. However, if it's an explosion you want, I can arrange that for you. We'll start at 6 am in the future. How does that grab you?'

'Good! That suits me just fine,' Arthur grunted. He was confident that Charley was now dancing along to his tune.

'The earlier the better as far as I'm concerned. The more hours you work, the sooner you'll be gone from here.'

Charley concealed his exasperation behind a smile.

'Excellent. I'm glad we've now established the ground rules. There'll be no creeping around worrying about you, or your guests, from now on.'

Arthur swaggered back to the reception area. Charley walked over to his van and poured half a cup of tea from his flask. As he sipped, he started to think of ways of neutralizing Arthur. Once the boys had arrived, Charley gathered them for a quick briefing before starting the job.

'Be on your guard,' he warned. 'There's something not quite right about this Bainbridge bloke.'

'What d'you mean – he's one of *them*, Chas?' said Big Jake, blowing a kiss and waving a limp wrist.

'Well, he's certainly a bloody pain in the arse, Jake, that's for sure. But not in the way you mean. But if you're that concerned, be careful where you stop and tie your shoelaces.'

'He's not the full 10 bob then?' asked Ray, the electrician.

'I'm not really sure, Ray. He's a bloody devious bastard, I know that much. So, be very careful what you say to him. Right, now that's all said, you now know what we're up against. So, we'll spend our time today quietly cutting off all services and stripping out the buildings that are due for demolition, and then at 6 am tomorrow morning, we'll give the mad bastard his explosion.'

It was very peaceful the following morning when Charley and the boys crept on site, not a single light showing from any of the guest rooms.

Jake gave a silent laugh, as did Ray.

'I think they're all still tucked up in bed, fast asleep,' said Charley, looking at his watch. 'Time for an alarm call, don't you think?'

'Yeah! Let's do it!' everybody cheered, punching the air.

Throwing the switch to the arc lights was the signal to simultaneously fire up the plant. The violent sound of the roof being ripped off, followed by toppling walls and crashing masonry, had Arthur Bainbridge running out of the building into the courtyard, absolutely seething.

'Morning, Arthur!' Charley yelled over the noise.

'What d'you mean "morning"? It's the middle of the bloody night, for goodness sake! What the bloody hell do you think you're doing? The switchboard is jammed with all the guests complaining. And her indoors has gone bloody berserk – and I mean bloody, fucking berserk! She's ready to kill someone!'

While Jake joked along with the boys, demonstrating the shoelace diversion, Charley exaggerated lifting his arm to look at his wristwatch.

'"Doing", Arthur?' Charley calmly replied. 'Why, we're carrying out your orders, of course, mate. Don't you remember yesterday you were bending my ear to start this early?'

Arthur scowled, bearing his teeth like a wild, injured animal ready to bite.

'Yeah, but I meant do it quietly! Do it bloody quietly!'

He was on the brink of having a seizure.

'Arthur, your words to me were "Sod the bloody peasants, I want explosive action" – and that's just what you got. We can't carry out demolition work quietly. It's impossible.'

'Yeah, yeah, I know that but—'

Arthur was abruptly stopped by the piercing tones of the tiny Mrs Bainbridge. Red with anger, in her hairnet, pink slippers and dressing gown, the wailing banshee appeared in the doorway of the reception area. Charley looked at Arthur and raised an eyebrow.

'Your call, mate,' he whispered. 'Are you going to tell her or shall I?'

Arthur was so panic-stricken that he began to whimper.

'You've got to help me out here, Chas,' he begged, in a low pathetic groan.

'What was that, Arthur? Didn't quite catch it, mate.'

Charley was enjoying every minute of the show.

Arthur was desperate. He'd have clutched at any straw to save himself from his wife's ranting. As her barrage of obscenities intensified, he pleaded to Charley like a helpless child.

'Sorry, Arthur. I don't see how I can, seeing as we were only following your instructions, mate.'

His spineless frame buckled.

'It's all right, my little petal!' he cried nervously. 'You leave 'em to me, I'll soon deal with them.'

Charley took pity on him and thought he'd offer him a way out, when Arthur suddenly straightened up and began waving his arms around and wagging his finger.

'And don't you ever, ever do that again!'

Charley decided to break his little charade.

'Arthur. Arthur. You can stop yelling now. She's gone back inside.'

But Arthur hardly dare look.

'Look, if it would help to restore the peace with your good lady,' Charley said, chuckling away inside, 'we don't mind rescheduling our starting time. What about 8 am? How does that suit you, mate?'

His eyes lit up and a sickly grin spread across his distorted face.

'Yes! Yes! Yes!' he cried, excitedly. 'I'll go and tell her this instant. That should shut her up.'

With Arthur charging across the courtyard like a halfwit to pacify his disgruntled wife, Ray wandered over. He had a smile on his face and an evil glint in his eye.

'Why don't you bring Mad Ginger over here? I think he'd feel right at home, here in this asylum.'

'Wash your mouth out, Ray,' Charley replied. 'One madman on the job is quite enough, thank you!'

Despite Arthur's extraordinary behaviour, things did settle down on the building front, though he was often heard yelling at his staff and scrutinising his guests.

The longer the boys worked at the Motel, the more easily they were able to spot the genuine traveller. The ones without luggage stuck out like a sore thumb. Seamus, one of the brickie's labourers, always took a keen interest in the guests with no luggage.

'Gee, would you take a butcher's at that!' he exclaimed one day, spotting a very shapely young platinum blonde, with hair down to her waist, in a short black leather miniskirt.

'She's got legs right up to her armpits!'

All those working within earshot stopped and watched her walking on the arm of a fat, balding, middle-aged guy.

'That's got to be her father, surely?' said bricklayer Barry.

'I don't think so, Baz,' said Mike, one of the other brickies. 'Look where his hands are. He can't get the smile off his face!'

'The dirty bastard!' shouted Seamus, his eyes out on stalks. 'How does such an ugly bastard like him pull such a sexy bird as her?'

'Oh, grow up, Seamus!' Charley shouted. 'That loud clap of thunder you heard this morning wasn't a storm brewing: it was that bloke dropping his wallet.'

'Yeah, but how did he pull her then?'

'Oh, have a day off, Seamus!' yelled Jake. 'Look at what he drives! He must be bloody loaded to have a motor like that. I bet you any money you like that in five minutes' time, when they get to their room, she'll be telling him what a rampant stag he is.'

Seamus was practically foaming at the mouth.

'Yeah, is that so? What room do you reckon they'll be in?'

'Probably that one up there with the red light outside,' said Charley pointing.

'Oh, good! Will someone lift me up in the front bucket of the JCB so I can look through the window?'

Barry flicked a trowel full of muck at him.

'Come on, you dirty old pervert! Get some more bricks over here, before I chuck a bucket of water over you!'

Charley's first agreed progress payment was due. He handed the invoice to Mrs Bainbridge, expecting to be paid immediately.

'Thank you, Mr Henry,' she smiled. 'I'll make sure my husband gets it.'

But then Arthur vanished.

Charley asked the boys if they'd seen Bainbridge, but none of them had, so Charley waited and watched for a further seven days before speaking to his wife.

'I thought he paid you?' she said, sounding surprised.

'Er, no, Mrs Bainbridge. He hasn't as yet, and we need our money now. '

'Oh, in that case, I'll send him over straight away,' she said.

But he never came.

One more day passed, and Charley was beginning to get a bit anxious.

'Look, Chas! There he is!' cried Jake over the sound of the concrete mixer.

'You'll have to be quick, he's just getting into his car!'

'Well done, Jake!'

Charley ran over to pounce on Bainbridge before he drove off.

'You stop right there, Arthur! I want a word with you!' Charley grabbed the door handle and pulled it open.

'Not now, Charley, I'm in a hurry. I'll see you later,' he said, pulling the door closed.

'Oh no you don't, Arthur! You'll see me NOW!' replied Charley, pulling the door back open. 'You see, I need our payment cos the job cannot continue without it.'

'Oh, very sorry about that, Charley. I've just used the last cheque in the book. I'll pay you next week when the new cheque book arrives. Is that all right, mate?'

Charley stood his ground.

'No, I'm sorry, Arthur, it isn't. Not only do I have a massive wage bill to pay each week, but my suppliers also want paying.'

'Look, I can't give you what I haven't got, all right!' he snapped. 'You'll just have to wait, won't you?'

'All right then, Arthur. I'll wait until next week ... but all work stops NOW and it won't restart again until your cheque is cleared. Is that all right with you?'

He wound the window down and threatened to get someone else in to finish the job.

'Oh, I think you're forgetting our legally binding contract, Arthur, which, as of now, you're in breach of.'

Arthur got out of the car.

'Right!' he snarled, walking over to the reception. 'I'll see what I can do!'

Needless to say, he found another cheque, which he threw at Charley.

'Thank you, Arthur,' said Charley, pleased as punch.

Arthur just glared at him.

The following day, Arthur was all smiles to Charley and the boys, as if nothing had happened, but when the second payment was due, Arthur was just as reluctant to part with his cash.

'I think it's got something to do with his religion,' Charley told the boys at teatime.

'I didn't know he was religious,' said Ray, scratching his head.

'Yeah, it seems he's an orthodox, tight-arse bastard. I think it would be easier to get a kidney from him than actual money.'

After going through the same routine of leaving countless messages for him, Charley cornered his son, Jonathan.

'What exactly is your job here, Jonathan?'

'Oh, I'm the manager,' he proudly replied.

Charley played up to his self-importance.

'Manager, eh? Pretty powerful man then.'

'Yeperoony! You could say that, Charley.'

'Oh right, soooo, if I was to need something urgently, you're the man to ask while Arthur's away, are you?'

'Yep, I suppose I am, really. What can I do for you?' he asked confidently.

'Money, Jonathan. I need our money NOW. You see, it's long overdue, so if you'd be so kind as to go and get it for me, please, I would be very grateful.'

'Oh, I may be the manager, Charley,' he stuttered, 'but I can't pay you. That's the old man's job. You best ask him.'

'I've been trying to do that, Jonathan, but he insists on playing hide-and-seek with me. As I'm getting a bit tired of that game now, you best go and find 'im – rapido – and tell him that the job is going to grind to a stop in three hours' time. At high noon, in fact – unless, of course, he pays up in the meantime.'

Jonathan looked very embarrassed and began to panic.

'I can't promise anything, Charley, but I will certainly do my best to find him.'

Arthur decided to call Charley's bluff and stay in hiding. And so, as the clock struck noon, Charley picked up an orange traffic cone and walked out into the middle of the courtyard. He raised the hollow cone to his mouth.

'Now hear this! Now hear this!' he cried, loud and clear. 'It's time to stop work, boys, cos we're not getting paid!'

The boys, of course, knew the score and downed tools immediately. Like a lynch mob, they joined Charley in the centre of the courtyard. As if by magic, Arthur appeared, with a ridiculous forced smile on his face.

'Chas! Chas! I've been looking *all over the place* for you. You see, I've been a bit tied up with my solicitors just lately and I've lost all track of time. I think we need a pow wow.'

Charley told the boys to go and have an unofficial tea break, to give Arthur one last chance to come clean.

'Er, I've got a bit of a problem meeting the outstanding payment this time, Chas,' he said.

'You had a problem last time, Arthur, as I recall.'

'Oh, that was just an oversight, Chas. This time, there's been a delay on a property sale, which means that I'm £5,000 short. But if you accept what I've got, I promise you sincerely that I will catch up before the next payment is due. Is that okay, mate?'

'I don't believe you, Arthur. I really don't. I've kept my side of the deal – I've flooded the job with labour, who incidentally want paying; we've worked with you on our case seven days a week, trying to achieve the impossible. All I ask in return is to be paid on time. Is that too much to ask? Well, is it? Only, I can't run this job on fresh air. So, please tell me this is not another one of your delay ploys.'

'No, no, Chas, it isn't. I promise you it isn't. I'm not messing you about, honestly, mate. I will catch up. Trust me, I will.'

Charley gave him the benefit of the doubt and accepted the reduced payment.

There was a general election that year, and history was made: Margaret Thatcher was elected the first female prime minister of the United Kingdom. The day after the election, just for the crack, Charley and the boys painted "WELL DONE MAGGIE" in large blue letters on an 8x4 sheet of plasterboard and affixed it to the top lift of the scaffolding that faced the main road. The reaction from the passing drivers was phenomenal. From people shouting words of support to foul disapproval, hooters blowing, thumbs up and V signs, they had it all.

The time had come for the third payment. Arthur came looking for Charley, who was looking forward to being paid without any agro.

'I really don't know how to tell you this, mate,' Arthur said, 'but my bank has refused further payments until they receive a comprehensive report from the building consultant that they're sending down from Portsmouth. They say that he will be here today, about 11 am, to assess the situation.'

'Look, Arthur, you assured me before we even started this bloody job that your finances were sound and secure, and that your funds were in place, ready to pay me as and when. You're already £5,000 in arrears from your last payment as it is.'

Arthur raised his hands in the air.

'I know, Chas, mate, I know, and I feel very bad about it, believe me. I don't know what that blinking bank is playing at, I really don't. Let's just see what the consultant says before we say any more on the matter. We'll sort it all out after he's gone. All right, mate?'

Chapter 16

※

As the time approached 11 am, Charley kept a conscious eye on the car park. He spotted Mrs Bainbridge climb into her car and drive away. When he turned his attention back to the job in hand, he noticed a tall, casually dressed middle-aged man with his collar turned up and a pair of designer sunglasses perched on top of his head stood gazing at the building works. He had a camera strung around his neck and a clipboard in his left hand. Eager to make his presence felt, he started strutting around the courtyard with an uncompromising look on his face. Confident that he had captured everybody's attention, he began to flaunt his position, taking photos of the job from every conceivable angle. Passing a critical eye, he made exaggerated movements of his head and commenced writing on the clipboard.

'Er, Chas, you seen that prat down there?' asked Barry.

'What, that prick with the sunglasses on his head like a big tart, you mean?'

'Yeah.'

'You can't miss him, Baz.'

'Oh, I won't miss him, Chas,' he replied, poised with a full trowel of muck. 'Just say the word, and I'll let him have it.'

'As much as I'd like to, Baz, just ignore 'im. The way he's acting, he'll disappear up his own arsehole in a minute.'

'I say! You up there on the scaffold!'

Charley ignored him. He called again, only this time much louder. Charley looked down, paying him little attention. Oh, how he'd love to burst his self-important bubble!

'Yes, you!'

'You talking to me, mate?'

'Yes, I am, as a matter of fact. I'm looking for Mr Henry,' he said, knowing full well he'd already found him. 'I've been told that I would find him here on site. Do you know where he is?'

'Well, it depends what you want him for, mate. If it's a job you're looking for, you're unlucky, because the last one was taken about an hour ago.'

'Oh, no, no, no. I can assure you I'm not after a job. You see, my name is Carmody. I believe you're expecting me – I'm the consultant from Portsmouth.' He stared Charley straight in the eye.

'Portsmouth?' Charley repeated, dismissively. 'I don't even know where that is, mate. Besides, I'm not expecting any consultant. What do you consult anyway?'

'Buildings. I'm a building consultant, sent down by the bank, in Portsmouth. I've been instructed by them to come and see you.'

'Me? No, mate, not me. You must be getting me confused with someone else. Look, mate, whatever you're selling, I'm not interested, all right, so go away, cos I've got work to do.'

'But you don't understand, Mr Henry—'

'Look, for the last time, I bank at Winterbourne Wellford. I think it's probably Mr Bainbridge you're looking for.' Charley pointed towards the reception area.

'No, I've already spoken to him, but he can't answer any of my questions and so I rather thought you maybe could fill in the gaps. Oh, and perhaps you would be kind enough to show me around the job at the same time, if that's all right?'

Despite feeling very uncomfortable with the unfolding situation, Charley agreed and jumped down from the scaffold to join him.

'I don't know whether you're fully aware of it or not, Mr Henry,' he said, deliberately slowing his words, 'but I'm afraid I must inform you that all of the power has now been removed from the hands of Mr Bainbridge regarding this project. And so, unfortunately, that means you're now up against the big guns of the bank.'

'Oh yeah, and what's that supposed to mean then?' Charley asked, uneasily.

Picking up on Charley's concern, he increased the intensity in his voice.

'I've been asked by the bank to compile a report on this building project because they are concerned where all the money is going.'

After some considerable time of scrutinising everything he saw, he dropped his clipboard to his side and placed his arm on Charley's shoulder, like a trusted friend.

'Look, Mr Henry,' he whispered out of earshot, 'we don't want any unpleasantness now, do we? Off the record, if you were to offer Mr Bainbridge, say, £10,000 compensation for his loss of trade, I could then go back to the bank with a glowing report and smooth things over. The payments could then be made, and everybody would be happy. What do you say, eh?'

'*I* wouldn't be happy,' Charley replied. 'Far from it.'

'Oh, I don't think you quite grasp the gravity of the situation, Mr Henry. You've got no choice in the matter.'

Charley was stunned. £10,000: that was the price of a modest house. He hadn't done anything wrong. The job was going along on time. The building inspector was happy with the standard of work. Charley needed time to think, but the cocky consultant wasn't about to let up. Sensing victory, he began to pile the pressure on even harder.

'Now you listen to me!' Charley replied, trying to keep his cool. 'I don't know what your game is, but I've a binding signed contract regarding this building project, and as of right now, Mr Bainbridge is in breach of it. Not me – HIM! Now if you really want to help the situation along, you can go and get my cheque that is still outstanding, cos if I don't receive it by midday tomorrow, the job will be shut down and legal proceedings will commence.'

'Okay then. I gave you a chance, but if that's the way you want to play it, we'll do it the hard way. I want you, by 8 am tomorrow morning, to provide me with copies of all your paperwork relating to this job. All your costing, wage books, estimated profits, and a full list of all building materials delivered to site, backed up, of course, up by the invoices. I also want a full list of all contractors on site. If you fail to provide any of the information that I have requested, there will be serious consequences. Do you understand?'

Charley swallowed hard. From the corner of his eye, he could see Big Jake trying to get his attention, and when Charley didn't respond, Jake walked over and interrupted.

'I wouldn't normally disturb you, Chas, unless it was very important—'

'I can't talk now, Jake. I'll see you in a minute after this bloke has gone.'

'But I need a word urgently now,' he said. 'It's very, very important.'

'This better be good, Jake,' Charley said, as they stepped aside.

'There's something not quite right about that bloke, Chas,' he said, rubbing his chin. 'I've seen him here before.'

'What, before today you mean?'

'Yeah. I can't be sure, but I think he was here yesterday.'

Charley was puzzled and needed to gather his thoughts. Without explanation, he turned back to the consultant and told him that the meeting was now closed. But Carmody wouldn't leave it alone. He was confident that he had Charley on the run and about to crack, and so he raised the pressure.

Then, to Charley's surprise, the cavalry came charging in.

'You heard him! Meeting closed!' growled Beano, Charley's old dad. Unlike Barry, who'd asked Charley for permission to chuck a trowel full of muck at the consultant, Beano was shaping up to throw a few punches. He may have been a pensioner, but he was still a very tough man for anybody to take on. He often came in for a few hours each day to help out and in so doing, had witnessed the whole episode. After quizzing Big Jake, Beano was getting ready to insert the consultant's clipboard, and his camera, up his arse.

Outnumbered, Carmody made a tactical withdrawal.

'Don't forget!' he shouted from a distance. '8 am! I will be waiting! You know the consequences if you don't!'

Beano couldn't hide his anger; he was like a rottweiler straining at the leash.

'You'd better hurry up and go, mate,' Charley yelled, 'before I take his lead off!'

Beano knew something didn't quite add up, and he couldn't rest until he found what. Like a super sleuth, he snooped around until, eventually, he identified the man's car. After recording its details on a block of wood, he gave it to Charley.

'Ere, your mate's the local copper. Ask 'im to check that out.'

On the way home that evening, Charley caught sight of his mate Phil's car parked outside the village pub. Taking the block of wood, he went inside to find him.

'Blimey! You look harassed, Chas. Had a hard day, mate?' he asked, concerned.

'I wish it were that simple, Phil.'

After Charley explained what had happened that day, Phil thrust a pint in his hand.

'You get that down your neck, mate,' he said, taking the block of wood, 'and I'll go and make a phone call.'

Within a few minutes, Phil returned, with a big grin.

'Did you say that bloke came from Portsmouth, Chas?'

'Yeah, that's right, Phil. I did. Why's that?'

'Well, he goes a bloody long way to hire a car then, because that registration number you gave me belongs to a car that's on hire from a company in Exeter, Devon. You are sure that's the right car, aren't you?'

'Well, as sure as I can be, Phil. I didn't actually see him go to it myself, but my old man did.'

'Okay, well, let's assume it's the right car. I can't do anything tonight because the hire company is now closed, but don't worry, there will be someone banging on their door first thing in the morning – I've put a request into the Exeter police to find out who it's on hire to, and when I get the info, which should be about half eight, I'll bring it straight over. We can then hit the bastard with it together.'

'Oh, thanks, Phil. You're a good mate. I really appreciate it. But don't come to the site in your police car, will you?'

'Give me *some* credit, Chas!'

By the time Charley left the pub he felt a lot happier, and not because of the drink either. It was the thought of confronting that loathsome man in the morning.

As Charley drove into the Motel car park the following morning, the so-called consultant was stood in front of the reception area as bold as brass. On seeing Charley, he made a dramatic gesture of looking at his watch before striding over.

'I hope for your sake, Mr Henry that you've got all the paperwork that I asked for?'

Charley couldn't believe the nerve of the man. Either he'd given Phil the wrong number to check, or this bloke was the real deal. Charley gritted his teeth and calmly said that it would all be here about 9 am.

'Oh, well, if that's the best you can do,' he smirked, sauntering over to his car, 'I'll just have to wait for it then, won't I?'

Charley's eyes lit up when he saw the car he went to. He'd given Phil the right number to trace!

'That's a nice motor you got there, mate. Is it yours?'

'Yeah, that's right,' he replied, unsuspectingly. 'It is.'

Charley should have walked away there and then and waited for Phil, but he couldn't contain himself.

'By the way,' Charley glared, 'I don't think you're going to like the paperwork that's coming here this morning, old son.'

'Pardon?'

'You heard me!' Charley snarled. 'It'll reveal just who you really are. Car hire company in Exeter, eh? It would appear from the information already in my possession, that you've been telling me one or two porky pies, mister. So, until the rest of the info arrives, I suggest that you go and buy yourself a nice tight-fitting gum shield. Oh, and while you're about it, get one for your mate Bainbridge as well, cos I'll be seeing you both in the reception area very shortly.'

The colour drained from Carmody's face, like water gurgling down a plughole.

'Do you still want me to hand over 10 grand?' Charley spat.

Unable to speak, the man turned and walked quickly over to the reception. Charley became impatient waiting for Phil to arrive. When he finally did, he not only had a big beaming smile on his face, but he was waving a piece of paper in the air. The bloke, fearing the consequences, came out, ran across the car park, threw his case into his car, and raced away, leaving the smell of burning rubber behind. Beano was yelling and shaking his fist. It's a wonder he didn't leap on the bonnet, as the car sped past him.

Phil grimaced. 'Tell me that wasn't the bloke, Chas?'

'Yeah, Phil, it was. I'm sorry, mate.'

'Oh Chas!' he groaned, shaking his head. 'You said you were going to wait for me before confronting him.'

'Phil, I had every intention to, mate, but when I see 'im swagger so cockily over to his car, I just lost it, that's all.'

'Never mind, mate. You're going to love this info – he's only a blinking rep for a tarmac company, that's all!'

'The bastard! The bloody bastard! You wait till I get hold of Bainbridge. He'll have such a bloody lump on his chin that he won't be able to take his pullover off for a week!'

'Chas, Chas. Now calm down, Chas,' said Phil, shaking him by the lapels of his jacket. 'Don't do anything rash … just sit down and think about the situation carefully first. Don't do anything that you may later regret.'

'Calm! Would you be calm, Phil, if that little shit tried it on with you?'

'Don't do it, Chas.'

Charley sat down on a stack of bricks and lowered his head, deep in thought. Thirty seconds later, he jumped up and said, 'I've thought about it, Phil. I'm going over there to punch his lights out!'

Phil laughed. 'Now don't be a prat, Chas!'

He was right, of course. Punching Bainbridge's lights out wouldn't have solved the problem – it would have made Charley feel better, though. The police were powerless to do anything about it because no money had actually changed hands by the conman. And there was no point in taking legal action either – that would only have stopped the job dead, and that wouldn't have suited anybody.

Once Phil had gone, Charley marched over to the reception area to have it out with Bainbridge, man to man.

'I'm afraid he's indisposed at the moment, Mr Henry. Can I be of any help?' replied Mrs Bainbridge, seemingly clueless.

'Er, no, Mrs Bainbridge. There's something I need to give 'im.'

'Oh, you can give it to me, Mr Henry, if you like. I'll pass it on.'

'I don't think so, Mrs Bainbridge. I'll wait to give it to Arthur in person. Thank you.'

'As you please,' she said and carried on with her paperwork.

Shortly afterwards, Jonathan came over on site.

'I've been asked to give you this envelope, Chas.'

'Oh yeah? By whom,' he asked, opening it up to find a cheque covering all the monies outstanding.

'By my father, actually.'

'Oh, I see. Right then, Jonathan. I want you to go back and tell your dear old dad that I want to see him as a matter of extreme urgency, cos we have some very serious unfinished business to attend to.'

Arthur's mind was so severely twisted he thought that by paying his cheque and then going into hiding for a couple of days that Charley would soon calm down and forgive his actions. He was wrong. Charley was angrier than ever. Finally, Charley caught sight of Arthur darting across the courtyard and into the storeroom. Knowing there was only one way out, Charley waited patiently outside for him to emerge. Eventually, the door opened and, very slowly, out popped Arthur's head to see if the coast was clear for him to leave.

'Going somewhere, Arthur?' whispered Charley from the blind side of the door, dropping a length of 2x4 timber into the opening.

Arthur gulped and tried to slam the door, but the 2x4 stopped it from closing. Charley then barged the door fully open, sending Arthur flying backwards.

'What the hell are you going to do, Chas?' he cried in fear.

'You may well ask, you fucking bastard! Try and con 10 grand out of me with that bloody fucking rep, would you!'

Arthur buried his face in his hands, and with a pathetic whimper, he slumped to the floor, like a bag of shit.

'Let it all out, Chas! I wouldn't blame you if you hit me. You've every right to – I deserve it. I'm very sorry. It was a stupid thing to do. Get it all off your chest! Let's clear the air and start afresh. How can I make amends?'

'You can't, Arthur ... you bloody can't. But if you want this job to continue without me pressing charges with the police, or my solicitors issuing court proceedings against you—'

'Anything Chas, anything!' he whined. 'I'll do anything to put things right between us. Just say what you want and I'll do it.'

While Arthur lay on the floor, a broken man, Charley walked around the room. 'For starters, you can tell me where I can find that bloody conman rep!'

'I don't know, Chas. I honestly don't know.'

'Wrong answer, Arthur!' Charley shouted, kicking his feet. 'Don't insult my intelligence! You took the man's booking, so you must have his address and phone number!'

'Oh, I've got that all right, Chas,' he stammered. 'I thought you meant where is he now.'

'Okay, now we've got that one sorted, I want your solemn promise that there will be no more sodding about. Do I make myself clear?'

'Crystal, Chas, absolutely crystal. Goes without saying, mate,' he trembled. 'I'll go straight over and get you the address and phone number. Er, you won't tell my wife what I did, will you? Please, only—'

'Well, that depends on how well you behave in the future, Arthur, don't it?'

Charley couldn't be sure which Arthur feared most: a beating, a visit from the police, legal action or facing the wrath of his wife. Later that same evening, Charley had the extreme pleasure of phoning the conman and venting the last of his anger.

Chapter 17

※

Disgraced and deeply humiliated, Arthur was finally off Charley's case and back in his box – though not before trying to shift the blame for his misdoings onto his wife.

'You have no idea what it's like for me, Charley,' he whined, with his head and shoulders slumped like a down and out. 'I have to live with her 24/7. It was all *her* doing, you know – my wife. She was the one that made me do that terrible thing to you.'

'Oh, come on, Arthur, don't insult my intelligence! If she made you do it, then why was you so anxious to keep it a secret from her, eh? Tell me that.'

'Ah, well, she don't actually know what I did, but she drove me to it all the same. You see, she keeps on winding me up and bossing me about all the time. You have no idea what that kind of pressure can do to a man, day after day, year in, year out—'

'Oh, stop it, Arthur! You'll have me in tears in a minute.'

'I know why she does it, though…'

'Go on, then. Why's that, Arthur?'

'She does it to make me gee you up. You know – to make the job go faster. It's her way of coping, because she's so worried that you won't get the place finished on time.'

'Oh, come off it, Arthur. Do me a favour!'

'Honestly, Charley. I keep telling her to stop worrying because I've got every confidence in you. I know you can do it all right, mate.'

'You sure about that, Arthur?'

'Ah, well, now you come to ask ... perhaps I am just a *little* bit worried. You know, I wouldn't be normal otherwise, would I?'

'"Normal"? That's a laugh, Arthur! You're far from that! Look, if you're that worried, I s'pose I could—'

'Yeah, yeah, I am,' he interrupted. 'I really am. What could you—?'

'Well, seeing as it's you, Arthur, then I s'pose I could risk it. No – perhaps on second thoughts best not to.'

'Risk what? Risk what?' Arthur begged. 'I'm prepared to put up with anything that will hurry the job along!'

'Okay then, Arthur, you've twisted my arm. I will risk it and bring Mad Ginger over onto site. He'll speed things up 'cos he does the work of two, if not three, men. He's like a human dynamo once he gets going.'

'Oh, thanks, mate. I really appreciate it,' he smiled, as though Charley had just become his newfound friend and ally. 'Mad Ginger – hmm, I like that description. I suppose he got that name because he works so fast?'

'Er, no, not exactly, Arthur,' Charley grimaced, with his fingers crossed behind his back. 'Let's just say he's a bit eccentric, shall we – but don't worry, he's a perfect gentleman, and a bloody good carpenter to boot. But be warned: we usually only put him on sites far away from the public.'

Arthur frowned. What on earth was Charley talking about? But then he chuckled. 'You nearly had me going there for a minute, Chas!'

'I'm not joking, Arthur. I mean it. Keep your distance 'cos he don't like to be disturbed. That's why we don't let anybody else work with 'im. Let's just say he enjoys his own company and leave it at that, shall we?'

'Okay, Chas. I'm a man of the world – I can understand that.'

'I don't think you do, Arthur,' Charley said, shaking his head.

Arthur let out a loud laugh. Charley was having him on! 'Well, I'm very pleased, Chas, and I can't wait to see the impact that he'll make on this job.'

'Oh, he'll make an impact all right, Arthur, and no mistake,' Charley said quietly under his breath.

'What was that, Chas?'

'I said he'll be here tomorrow, Arthur.'

Arthur was transfixed watching Ginger at work. 'Nothing distracts him, does it?' he said. 'He's like a well-oiled machine. Just look at him go! Where on earth does one man get so much energy from?'

'It's 'cos he eats a big breakfast, Arthur,' Charley replied, trying to hurry him along. But it was too late because Ginger, unaware that anybody was watching, stood bolt upright, with a strange look in his eye.

'Ah, excuse me, old boy,' he said in a deep, posh voice.

'Who's he talking to?' Arthur whispered, unable to tear his eyes away.

'Who? Me?' Ginger returned, in an entirely different voice.

Thinking that Ginger had overheard him, Arthur was about to answer, but then Charley grabbed his arm and stopped him.

'Yes, old boy. Would you be so kind as to pass me that paring chisel?'

Arthur held his breath as Ginger continued switching voices.

'What – this one here?' Ginger replied, picking up the chisel with his left hand and passing it over to his right.

'That's marvellous!' he said. 'Absolutely marvellous. Thank you so much, old chap. You're so kind.'

'Did you see that, Chas?' Arthur whispered.

'See what, Arthur?' Charley pretended.

'All what he just did. Surely you must have seen it?'

'Oh, *that*,' Charley replied, dismissively. 'Pay no heed, Arthur. We don't want him to think he's something special now, do we? We just put it down to one of his little idiosyncrasies, that's all. Lots of people talk to themselves. Ginger says that it's the only intelligent conversation he ever gets.'

'Yeah, I must admit, I talk to myself sometimes,' Arthur said. 'It helps me to think.'

'Well, there you go then, Arthur. You could be his brother!'

'Yeah, but I don't do it in two different voices. That man's bloody mad! He really believes that he is two different people!'

'Yeah, I know that, Arthur, but for goodness sake, don't tell him that!' Charley said quietly.

'Why not?'

'Why? 'Cos I only pay him for one, that's why! I don't want the other one asking for a wage as well, or else I'll have to charge you for the both of 'em.'

Arthur began to laugh. 'Is he ever a problem to anyone?'

'Only if he thinks they're laughing at him,' Charley replied.

'Oh my God!' said Arthur, instantly wiping the grin from his face.

'I'm only joking, Arthur! Ginger's no problem really, except, of course, if he ever refuses to pass himself the chisel, or he picks an argument with himself…'

'Oh shit, what happens then?'

'Ah, well, then we've got a real problem on our hands, 'cos someone has got to rush in there and bash him on the head with a lump of wood – preferably, a lump of wood with a large rusty nail sticking out the end. That usually does the trick.'

'And what if that don't work?'

'Ah, well, then you've gotta go and bash him again.'

Unable to look away, Arthur quickly stepped behind Charley for protection.

Charley chuckled. 'It's a good job it's not April 1st, Arthur!'

'What's that got to do with it?' he frowned.

'April Fools!'

Totally confused, Arthur gave Ginger a very wide berth and quickly retreated to the safety of the reception area.

'You wicked bugger!' laughed Ray, having overheard the whole conversation. 'Why didn't you tell him the full story?'

'What story would that be then, Ray?'

'You know, the fact that Ginger has a tendency to burst out laughing for no apparent reason, and that he has a compulsion to mimic the odd sound or two.'

Charley smiled. 'No need, Ray, 'cos once Arthur sees the benefits of having the madman around, he'll accept all of his little amusing ways.'

'Amusing ways! That's a laugh. What are you gonna say when there's a full moon then, eh?'

'Don't even go there, Ray…'

'You must warn Arthur, Chas. It's only fair.'

'No, I don't wanna alarm 'im, Ray. But if Ginger does have a funny turn, you'll have to shoot him with that silver bullet we keep for such events.'

'Why me?'

'Cos you're a good shot – and he knows you - he won't suspect anything .'

'What about Arthur, then?'

'No, you ain't gotta shoot 'im as well, Ray. Ever since our little ruck the other day, he's been treating me more like his best friend than his builder. We're like *that*, me and Arthur,' Charley joked, squeezing his thumb and forefinger. 'Having said that, he's still a bloody pain in the arse, the way he keeps changing the specification every five minutes.'

Before the day was out, Arthur was back bending Charley's ear once again.

'Ere, Chas, have you ordered the sanitary ware yet, mate? Only, she who must be obeyed would like vanity units instead of the pedestal basins.'

'Oh, that's a bit awkward now, Arthur,' replied Charley, trying to dissuade him. 'Everything's been on order for weeks now.'

'I've already tried to tell her that, mate, but she won't be put off. Once she has made her mind up, nobody can change it.'

'Would you like me to send Mad Ginger over to have a word with her? He can be very persuasive...'

'No! Don't do that! For goodness sake, Chas!'

'Well, I suggest you go and try again, Arthur, 'cos the en suite rooms are too small to accommodate big vanity units.'

Arthur returned a sickening smile. 'I hear what you're saying, Chas, but there's no talking to her on the matter. She wants to come over after lunch and try to visualise what the vanity units would look like in place. Perhaps you can have a go at her then – see if you can make her change her mind?'

Charley and the boys had hardly finished their tea break when all three of the Bainbridges descended the job.

'Now what seems to be the problem, Mr Henry?' asked Mrs Bainbridge, with a condescending smirk, whilst Arthur, trying to gain her favour, began busily scribbling on the wall where he thought a vanity unit should go.

'I haven't got a problem, Mrs Bainbridge, but *you* will if you insist on the big vanity units.'

Her eyes turned red with anger, but then she quickly composed herself and asked why.

'Because they'd be too big. They would totally overpower the room.'

She grimaced and looked towards Jonathan for support. 'What do you think, Son?' she asked, with a forced smile.

'Oh, I think they would look just the ticket, Mother. And, if it would help to keep the costs down, I could even make the legs up for you 'cos I still have all my pipe and threading equipment,' he added.

She rubbed her chin for a moment before muttering instructions over to Arthur. Totally ignoring Charley, she then turned and left the room.

'Right! We've made our minds up, Chas!' said Arthur, slapping his hands together to conceal his embarrassment. 'Get the vanity units on order, but not the legs – we'll supply them ourselves.'

'Okay then, Arthur. I'm not gonna argue with you. It's your funeral. Don't say I didn't warn you.'

Charley then confirmed their instructions in writing and asked Arthur to sign it.

The next catastrophe to hit the job was Dublin Bob's 50th birthday. Bob was one of the plastering gang, and he wanted to celebrate his birthday in style with a nice pint of Guinness over the pub at lunchtime.

'Will you be joining us for a drop of the old black stuff, Chas?' Bob asked, in his broad Irish accent.

'Er, no thanks, Bob. I think I'll pass on that one. But you have a good birthday, mate. Just one thing to remember, though, Bob: if you can't put one foot in front of the other when you leave the pub, then you sleep it off over there in the beer garden, all right?'

'Oh, that'll take about 15 pints to get to that state, Chas!'

Before they went over the pub, Charley grabbed hold of the other three spreads: Burt, Taffy and Seamus. 'If he comes back pissed, sling him in the back of his van and lock the door, all right?'

'No worries, Chas, mate. We'll look after him,' said Taffy.

'It's not him I'm worried about, Taff – it's what he'll do to the Motel that bothers me.'

Two hours later, the plasterers returned; all four of them were well tanked up and staggering around the site.

'Look at the bloody state of that lot, Ginge!' said Charley, looking on from an upstairs window.

'Bloody disgusting, Chas, if you ask me,' replied Mad Ginger. 'It usually takes me at least three hours to get to that state. Would you like "Him" to go down and have a word with 'em, Chas?'

'Er, thanks but no thanks, Ginge. I think we'll pass on that one, mate. I'll just nip down and chuck 'em all in the back of their van to sober up before Bainbridge sees 'em.'

'By the look of 'em,' said Ray, joining in, 'that should take about three days.'

By the time Charley got down there, Dublin Bob had started singing. 'Come on, Bob. In the back of your van, mate,' he said, opening the back doors. 'Time to sleep it off.'

'That won't be necessary, Chas,' he slurred. 'We'll be no bother, Sir, I promise you. You have my word as a plasterer and Boy Scout – dib dib dib – we'll just sit down here on the grass by the lily pond, and we'll have a nice little cup of tea from the old flask.'

'Yes, we'll do just that, Chas,' said Seamus in agreement. 'We can just sit nice and quietly and watch the fishes.'

'Taffy, if they get out of line, I'm holding you responsible,' Charley said, pointing his finger to drive his message home.

Everybody else on site was working whilst the plasterers lay in the sun by the lily pond totally inebriated.

'It sure is hot,' said Bob, fanning his face with his newspaper.

'Hot is it, you are?' said Seamus, plunging his cup into the pond. 'That'll cool you down,' he laughed, throwing the water over Bob.

Everybody staying at the Motel must have heard the screams coming from Seamus when the plasterers grabbed him and swung him back and forth over Arthur's prized lily pond.

'Chuck 'im in!' yelled Barry, from the top scaffold.

Charley looked down from the balcony to see the huge splash, as Seamus sunk to the bottom of the pond.

Arthur came charging across the courtyard, furious.

'Oh shit!' said Charley. 'That's all we need.'

Ginger found it all highly amusing. 'This should be good, Chas,' he said, rubbing his hands together.

'It ain't no laughing matter, Ginge. If Arthur says anything to that lot while they're in that state, he'll be joining Seamus at the bottom of the pond!'

Ginger cupped his hands and cried, 'Go on, Arthur! You tell 'em, mate!'

Charley's eyes flashed around the job to see all the boys egging the plasterers on to give Arthur a bloody good dunking. Thankfully, Arthur thought better of it before it was too late and opted for the shelter of the Motel. Once the plasterers had sobered up a bit, Charley sent them over to apologise to Arthur and his good lady.

Chapter 18

✺

A young apprentice plumber had start working on the job, and while he was very keen, he had a serious image problem to maintain, which soon got under everybody's skin. He strutted his way around the site like a big tough man, grunting at anyone who got in his way. Because he bragged so openly about his street cred, nobody forewarned him about Mad Ginger. In fact, most of the lads on site couldn't wait to see Ginger's reaction to him – or, in fact, his to Ginger.

The boys on site usually took no notice of the weird and wonderful noises that the Mad Man made while working. But one fairly quiet day, everybody stopped work to look when they heard the sound of what can only be described as a charging bull elephant.

'Sounds like the Madman kickin' off again, Chas,' said Jake.

'Yeah, I heard 'im. It's not a full moon tonight, though, is it?' Charley answered.

Chuckling, they both looked down from the covered catwalk that provided access to all the first rooms, to see what was happening. Almost everybody else on site was doing the same, when all of a sudden, an electric extension cable and reel was seen flying through the air about eight foot above the courtyard; closely followed by some strong words of protest and high-pitched screaming from the young apprentice, who was also seen on the same flight path.

Cheers and applause rang out across the whole site as the not-so-tough guy landed in an unglamorous heap on the tarmac. The only person not out there cheering was Mad Ginger. When the laughter died down, Charley went down and asked Ginger what all the commotion was about.

'Commotion? What commotion would that be then, Chas? I never heard anything – I was too busy workin'.'

'Oh, come on, Ginge. It sounded like a full-blown African safari out there. What went on?'

'Nothing to do with me, Chas, honestly. Unless…'

'Unless what, Ginge?'

'Well, unless it was you know who lurkin' about again,' he said, raising his eyebrows and looking over his shoulder.

'Look, Ginge, you promised me you'd leave *Him* behind. I don't want Bainbridge on my case again sayin' you're scarin' his guests away.'

'Yes, you're right, Chas. If I see *Him*, I'll send him home immediately.'

The only thing the young plumber suffered was injured pride. After he recovered from the shock of meeting Mad Ginger for the first time, he walked over, minus his swagger, and had a good gripe to Charley.

'That chippie, he's a bloody madman!' he cried. 'He needs locking up!'

'Yeah, I know he does, son. He usually is when there's a full moon, but mad though he may be, you must have done something to set 'im going…'

'I didn't do anything!' he whined. 'He just went bloody fucking berserk!'

'I know he may seem a little odd to you, son, but you must have done *something* to wind 'im up. He doesn't normally waste energy unnecessarily.'

'All I did was plug my extension cable into a socket in the room where he was working. That's all.'

'Don't tell me – and you trailed the cable through the door frame while he was trying to fit the door?'

'Yeah, I did, as it happens. I told him to hang around and take a chill pill while I drill a couple of holes, and then he just went bloody crazy.'

'A "chill pill"?' repeated Charley, laughing. 'You're lucky to still have your arms and legs, boy. Look, take my advice, son. If you want to stay alive around Mad Ginger, never, ever stop 'im from workin', 'cos it will seriously damage your health.'

The next major drama to unfold on site was the arrival of the vanity units. Charley walked over to the reception area looking for Arthur. A member of staff directed him to the dining room, where Arthur was enjoying a late breakfast with his wife and son. All three of them smiled and passed the time of day, as Charley gatecrashed their breakfast. After they'd exchanged pleasantries, Charley informed Arthur that the vanity units had arrived, and asked him for the legs that he was supplying.

'Oh shit! I forgot we haven't got them.'

Mrs Bainbridge carried on eating, as though there wasn't a problem.

'When will you have them?' asked Charley, wanting to get on and fix the units.

Still chewing on a piece of crispy bacon, Arthur simply looked up and said, 'Oh, just fix 'em back to the wall, Chas. The legs can go on later.'

Instead of saying what he was thinking – that he was a stupid prat – he responded very politely with, 'I'm sorry, Arthur. That can't be done without the proper support of the legs. The units are much too heavy; besides, the leverage is far too great.'

Charley could sense that Mrs Bainbridge was agitated by his refusal to fix the units, as Arthur had suggested. For a minute, he thought that she was going to erupt. By the look on Arthur's face, so did he. She surprised them, by managing to remain calm. She picked up her cup and saucer and started sipping her tea with her little finger out, like she were a cut above everybody else.

Arthur rolled his eyes up to the ceiling, in fear of what was about to happen next. After a few slurps of tea, she returned her cup to the table and took a deep breath. She then smiled sarcastically and said, 'Seeing as they don't know how to fix them, Arthur, why don't you and Jonathan go over on site and make them all gather round, while you both show them how to do it? And then, perhaps, they will be able to fix the rest of them okay.'

Charley was deeply offended by her condescension. Charley glanced over at Arthur, expecting him to do or say something, but he just sunk down into his chair, choking on his bacon. Charley was about to try and educate the silly Mrs Bainbridge on the practicability of her stupid suggestion, when his attention was drawn to Paul, the plumber, beckoning frantically from the doorway.

'Er, excuse me,' said Charley to the Bainbridge family. 'I'll just go see what the plumber wants.'

'Forget the legs, Chas,' Paul whispered, hardly keeping a straight face. 'The bloody units are too big for the room. We've held one in place, and the door just catches on it. What a dilemma!' he said, with one hand over his mouth trying to curtail his laughter.

'Oh shit! A dilemma, indeed, Paul. But not for us though, eh?!' said Charley, looking back towards the Bainbridges' table, smiling.

Arthur returned a smile and waved back.

Paul chuckled. 'He 'asn't got a bloody clue, Chas, 'as he?'

'He soon will 'av, Paul – when you go over and tell 'im.'

'I ain't going anywhere near 'em, Chas. That's *your* job. Good luck, mate.'

'I don't need luck, Paul, 'cos I shall be very diplomatic when I break it to 'em.'

'This, I've got to see,' he said.

'If you've got any ear defenders, Paul, I'd put 'em on now if I were you,' said Charley before strolling back to relay the explosive news to the Bainbridges.

Arthur looked to see Paul still standing in the doorway. 'What's he want, Chas?' he asked, curious to know.

'Er, good question, Arthur. Well, it's like this. You can forget about the legs.'

'Oh, good show. So, they can fix them without the legs after all?'

'Er, no, Arthur, that's not what I meant. I think you best come over on site with me, 'cos I can explain it better over there.'

'What, right now? Can't it wait? I ain't finished me breakfast.'

'No, Arthur, I don't think it can.'

'Oh, for goodness sake, Mr Henry, just tell us!' cried Mrs Bainbridge.

'Well, it would appear that the vanity units are just a tad too big for the room.'

Mrs Bainbridge totally lost it. Seething, she leaped to her feet, sending the chair flying backwards behind her. Then, spitting fire and venom, she dragged Arthur, whinging, over onto the site. Trying hard not to laugh, Paul and the young apprentice held the unit in position, whilst Arthur tried the door.

'Who the fucking hell measured these fucking units?!' screamed Mrs Bainbridge.

Paul and his apprentice rested the unit to the floor and stepped back. Arthur stood there red-faced and speechless like a naughty little boy about to be caned by the headmaster, whilst Charley made a speedy retreat towards the exit door.

'And just where do you think you're going?' growled Mrs Bainbridge, turning her aggression on him. 'You've got some serious explaining to do!'

'You're dead right, Mrs Bainbridge, I have. I'll be back in a minute. I'm just goin' over to our site office to collect the paperwork,' Charley said, before vanishing through the door.

Pacing up and down outside the site office, as though he were in urgent need of a toilet, was another desperate man with a huge problem on his hands.

'Are you Mr Henry?' he asked, as Charley darted into the site hut and rifled through his paperwork.

'Correct. I am. But I can't talk right now cos I have a bit of a crisis to deal with.'

'Oh, please hear me out, Mr Henry,' he begged. 'This won't take a moment.'

'I'm sorry, but I haven't got a moment.' Charley grabbed a signed copy of Arthur's instructions regarding the vanity units and dashed out the door.

'I've got a good proposition for you!' he shouted, running after Charley as he hurried to sort the Bainbridges out. 'You won't be disappointed!'

'Then scribble your name and phone number down, and give it to that big fella over there!' yelled Charley, pointing to Jake before colliding with Paul on the catwalk, as he made his exit from the room.

'Best of luck, mate,' Paul whispered. 'We couldn't stay in there a moment longer. She's liable to kill someone the way she's ranting.'

'Thanks, Paul, but I don't need luck, mate. This bit of paper should shut her up.'

'What you gonna do? Shove it in her mouth?'

'Nah, don't be silly, Paul. I ain't puttin' my hand anywhere near her big gob – she might bite it off. Besides, you'd need a full load of ready mix concrete to fill that cavern up.'

'What you gonna do then?'

'Just watch and learn, Paul, because the pen, as they say, is mightier than the sword.'

After pausing for a second or two to catch his breath, Charley casually entered the room. 'I think this will explain all, Mrs Bainbridge,' he said, presenting her with the paperwork containing Arthur's signature. She took one look at the paper, and then over to Arthur, before screaming and ripping it into small pieces, chucking them to the floor and stamping on them with both feet. During her frenzied attack on the paperwork, Charley looked over to Arthur for his support, but he was paralysed with fear. So, Charley just watched and waited for her to burn herself out.

After a while, the room fell silent. Nobody uttered a word. After a quiet moment of reflection, she pointed towards Arthur and said, 'You'll have to forgive him, Mr Henry, for he knows not what he's doing. He's not quite the full 10 bob, owing to the fact that when he was born, they shoved his brains up his fucking arse, instead of his head.'

She then turned and stormed out of the room, with Arthur trailing nervously in her wake.

While Charley was picking up the paper from the floor, Paul poked his head around the door and gave an ovation. 'Bravo, Chas! That was bloody marvellous! We'll have to start calling you King Alfred from now on!'

'Why King Alfred?'

'Oh, come on, Chas. Don't you know your history?'

'Yeah, I do, as it happens, Paul. So, tell me – what's King Alfred gotta do with it all?'

'He killed the dragon, didn't he, that's what.'

'That was King George, you prat!'

'Oh, was it?' he replied, scratching his head. 'What did King Alfred do then?'

'He burnt the cakes, didn't he, you stupid git!'

'Oh no, he didn't!' said Big Jake, pushing his way past Paul into the room.

'Oh yes, he did!' cried Mad Ginger, like a pantomime clown, from outside on the catwalk.

Making up the audience from the doorway, Ray yelled, 'He's behind you!'

'That just about sums this job up, don't it?' said Charley. 'What a bloody pantomime.'

'Talking about pantomimes, Chas – that bloke is still down there pacing up and down. I think you might be interested in what he has to say for himself.'

'Oh shit. I forgot about him!' replied Charley, racing from the room.

'I couldn't leave without speaking to you, Mr Henry,' the bloke said nervously, 'because I'm fast running out of time.'

'Okay then. I'm all ears, mate, so let's have it.'

'I have a very large detached Victorian property that was converted into 11 flatlets many years ago, and now it's in need of some improvement. It's in a good position close to the sea and all that.'

'And what, you want me to give you a price to renovate it?'

'Er, no, not exactly, no.'

'Then what *do* you want?' asked Charley.

'Well, you see, the council has served a demolition order on the property because they say that the building is unsafe and liable to collapse at any time. So, unless I comply with the order, they will pull the property down and give me the bill for so doing.'

'So, what do you want of me then?' asked Charley.

'I need someone like you to do the work to get the order lifted, but then I have no money to pay you. So, here is the proposition: you supply all of the labour and materials to do the job, and then once it's done, I will sell the property, and we'll split the proceeds between us. What do you say?'

'How much time did they give you to comply with the order?'

'Six months.'

'How long ago did they serve the notice then?'

'About five and a half months,' he replied, with a huge grimace.

'You've got no chance, Mr!'

'Will you at least come down and see the property?' he pleaded.

'There's no point, mate. The council's probably already warming up their diggers in readiness, as we speak.'

'Oh, don't say that. There must be *something* you can do?'

'No, I can't do anything for you … unless, of course, you want to sell the property as it stands, demolition order and all?'

'No,' he sighed. 'That will take much too long. Besides, I've already been down that road with another builder, only to have him back out at the last minute.'

'Look – as I see the situation, you've got two weeks at best before the diggers turn up, so what if I could sign and exchange a contract within 24 hours of receiving it, and then complete the purchase 24 hours after that?'

'Now you're talking,' he said with a smile. 'Let's get it on!'

'Not without seeing the place first, we don't.'

'Yes, but of course,' he replied full of anticipation. 'Follow me.'

The property didn't look too bad from the front – quite substantial, in fact – but the back of the building was suffering significant subsidence and was in imminent danger of collapse. Nevertheless, they thrashed out a deal there and then, subject to Charley speaking with the council regarding an extension on the demolition. Seeing as Charley was a builder, and that he gave an undertaking to do the necessary work with a given time frame, they approved it. So, Charley agreed to purchase the property from the desperate man, subject to contract.

On his return to the Motel, Charley was pounced on by Arthur, who looked a bit worse for wear. 'All sorted now, Arthur, are you?' asked Charley, out of concern for the smooth running of the job.

'Yeah, yeah, everything's all right now, mate. Her bark is far worse than her bite,' he replied, trying to make light of the matter. 'Er, can you reorder the pedestal basins, please?'

'Already done, Arthur.'

'Oh, good. Er, can you send all the vanity units back all right and get a full refund?'

'I only wish I could, Arthur, but I can't 'cos they were a special order, made to your own requirements to suit this job. Or not, as it now turns out.'

'Oh shit,' he replied with a fearful look in his eye. 'Look, Chas, my ball and chain's going to the hairdresser's at 11 am tomorrow morning, so can you stack all the units in the back of me garage while she's out. I can then chuck a sheet over 'em and tell her later.'

'You'll be lucky, Arthur. The units will completely fill your garage, and more besides. And you won't be able to hide 'em either.'

'I suppose I can always lock the door and say that I've lost the key. That'll keep her at bay for a while.'

'We can always light a bonfire, Arthur. You can then chuck 'em on that if you like. She'll never find 'em then.'

'No, no, don't do that, for God's sake, Chas. She really will start biting lumps out of everybody then, especially when she finds out we still have to pay for 'em. That'll really freak her out.'

'In the garage it is then, Arthur,' said Charley, happy to get shot of them. 'Consider it done, mate.'

About a week or so later, while Charley and the boys were sat down having their lunch break in one of the end units, Mrs Bainbridge kicked the door open, almost breaking it off the hinges, like some sort of stormtrooper.

'I'm not fucking standing for this!' she roared.

'Tell her to sit down then,' whispered Big Jake from the corner of his mouth.

'Why ever not, Mrs Bainbridge?' replied Charley, trying to defuse her. 'We're only having a cup of tea, for goodness sake.'

'I'm not on about your fucking tea break!' she snarled.

Charley sprang to his feet. 'Mrs Bainbridge, will you please moderate your language. You're beginning to embarrass the men.'

'Fuck the bloody men!' she barked. 'I'll talk any way I want! It's my fucking Motel!'

'Then, can we please at least do it quietly, in private outside,' said Charley, walking towards the door.

'I don't know what it is you've got on Arthur,' she growled. 'Why he won't stand up to you anymore, I do not know. Well, I'm telling you this for nothing: I'm taking over from him now, and you won't be able to wrap me around your little finger quite so easily!'

'Woah, woah! Slow down, Mrs Bainbridge. What's the problem?'

'Those fucking vanity units in my garage! That's the fucking problem!'

'Oh, so you'd like us to shift 'em for you, so you can put your car away?'

'No, I want you to fucking get rid of 'em! Send 'em back to where they came from, because we're not paying for 'em!'

'I'm sorry, Mrs Bainbridge, I can't do that. As I was telling Arthur—'

'Fuck Arthur! It's *me* you're dealing with now!'

'Okay. Then I'll tell you. Those units were a special order made specifically for this job, and may I remind you that Arthur did, in fact, sign for 'em and that – you will no doubt recall – I did express my concerns to you both at the time. Now, if you will excuse me, I've got work to do.'

Realising that Charley wasn't going to cave under her hail of abuse, she returned to the reception area, spitting blood. Charley went back inside with the boys to finish his tea break.

'She's a bloody handful when she gets going, ain't she?' said Ray.

'Tell me about it, Ray,' Charley said, with a huge sigh. 'If only I could find a way of silencing her, like we did Arthur.'

'Some hope that is, the size of her gob,' said Graham. 'I bet she could even shatter glass with that voice.'

'Split concrete more like,' replied Charley. 'Why, I bet she could even split the atom if she put her mind to it.'

'When she's not splitting concrete or the atom, do you think she abuses poor old Arthur?' Paul asked.

'There's nothing poor about him, Paul. Ain't you forgettin' what he did?'

'I think what Paul's gettin' at, Chas', said Ray, 'is does she abuse him sexually. You know, ties him up with leather straps and whips him, that sort of thing, only you read about it all the time in the Sunday papers.'

'What sort of papers do you read then, Ray?' asked Graham.

'I think they're both mentally disturbed,' said Mad Ginger. 'I know the signs to look out for. I could always send *Him* over to blow in her ear, Chas. Point out the error of her ways?'

'Thanks, Ginge, but I think we'll pass on that one mate, okay.'

'Do you want me to take a few bricks over, Chas, and brick up the doorway to the reception?' asked Jake. 'Keep 'em both inside until we finish the job?'

'No, that won't work, Jake,' Charley said. 'If the walls of Jericho fell over when Joshua blew his trumpet, that little doorway wouldn't stand a chance against her big mouth.'

It was only the constant banter with the boys that kept Charley sane on the job.

With the new block nearing completion, Charley thought it was high time that they all took a relaxing weekend off to recharge their batteries. They finished up on the Friday night by cutting through a new doorway at first floor level, linking the catwalk of the new building block to the existing building block, whereto they had erected a new secondary indoor access staircase that was to eventually give further access to the upper floors of both the new and old buildings. There was still a lot of alteration work to do before the new access could be officially used, and so Charley placed a safety barrier, together with plenty of danger signs, at the foot of the staircase, to prevent anybody from inadvertently using it before it was safe to do so. He even made a point of speaking to Mrs Bainbridge personally, before leaving the site that weekend.

'Please warn your staff not to use the new staircase as a shortcut, 'cos we've removed a large area of floor boarding from the very top of the staircase right back over to the flank wall. In fact, everything over the old boiler room has no floor, and we don't want anybody balancing across the joist and risking an accident.'

'Thank you, Mr Henry. I'll make sure that all my staff knows that,' she said.

On their return to work Monday morning they found that a large area of ceiling had been broken down over the boiler room.

'Some bastard's been climbing about up there, Jake, and dropped something heavy down through the floor joist,' said Charley.

Charley tried asking the members of staff, but they said they were under strict instructions not to reveal to any of the workers on site what had happened. He even asked Arthur, but he wouldn't talk either. So, eventually, Charley cornered Jonathan.

'It's more than my life's worth to tell you, Chas,' he mumbled.

'It'll be more than your life's worth if you don't tell me,' said Charley, grabbing hold of his jacket lapels, 'so start talking!'

'All right, all right! Put me down, Chas!' he yelped. 'You didn't hear this from me, all right,' he said tensely, adjusting his jacket.

'Understood, John. So, what happened then?'

'It was Mother,' he said, quickly checking over his shoulder to see if there was anyone within earshot. 'She fell through the floor on Friday night after you lot had gone home. It was lucky we heard her cries otherwise we'd never have found her.'

'Cries? Was she badly injured then?' Charley asked, with concern.

'Well, when we found her jammed between the two big boilers, she looked in a pretty bad way, and so we rushed her straight to hospital for X-rays and that sort of thing.'

Charley gulped. 'And what's the extent of her injuries?'

'She has a number of severely bruised ribs, two black eyes and a badly sprained arm.'

'Oh shit. Did they keep her in then?'

'No, they sent her home and told her to put her feet up, but Mother, being Mother, wasn't having any of that. She's over there, bravely manning the reception, as we speak.'

'Okay, Jonathan. Thanks for the info. I'll go and see her after our tea break.'

'Whoopee! It looks as though your prayers have been answered, Chas,' said Ray, grinning away, as he slurped his tea. 'I can't see her comin' over here shoutin' the odds for a while.'

Ginger started to grin, too. 'D'you think me and *Him* should start a whip-round?'

'So, it's all comin' out now then, Ginge. You read the same Sunday papers as Paul!' Ray jeered.

'No! I don't mean a whip-round in that sense, you dirty sod. I mean buy her a nice bunch of flowers.'

'Piss off!' said Jake. 'What, after the way she talks down to us? She got what she deserved. Perhaps it'll teach her some fuckin' manners!'

'You're all heart, Jake,' said Charley. 'Have you no compassion?'

'Not with her, I ain't,' he replied.

With much deliberation, Charley ventured over to the reception and found Mrs Bainbridge sitting hunched over at the counter. She was wearing the most enormous pair of dark sunglasses, and a head scarf, with one arm in a sling and the other clasping her ribs. She was in agony.

'Hello, Mrs Bainbridge. I've heard on the grapevine that you've had an accident, and I'm here to express our very best wishes for a speedy recovery.'

'Thank you, Mr Henry,' she croaked softly. 'And thank all your men as well. It's my own fault: I shouldn't have climbed over the barrier and up the stairs. Oh, and just so you don't think I'm completely stupid, I didn't balance across the joist and slip off – I walked between them, and the ceiling just gave way.'

Who said dreams don't come true: the atom-splitting, fire-spitting dragon's flames had been extinguished. She never bothered the boys again. Arthur was so pleased that he was back in charge that he started bringing Charley out a nice pint at the end of each working day, as the job neared completion.

'Would you book a room here, Chas?' asked Big Jake.

'What, just for a couple of hours, or the whole night?'

'Either.'

'No. I'd sooner stay in a telephone box in the middle of Spaghetti Junction!'

Chapter 19

✷

After the long and dreadful nightmare of the Motel, Charley was totally worn out and ready for a few days off. Unfortunately, time was ticking on the demolition order for the big old Victorian building that he'd purchased. Any further delays, and the council would intervene and flatten it without notice. Charley was juggling that with trying to build his own new replacement home, which had just been approved.

Having underpinned and removed the walls at the back of the condemned Victorian building, Charley was up to his neck in a deep foundation trench, with three floors and a roof suspended over his head, when a Mr Wolfe appeared on site. He crouched down alongside the trench and introduced himself.

'Are you from the council, reference the demolition order, Mr Wolfe?' Charley asked, climbing up the ladder out of the trench.

'Oh goodness gracious, no! Not me!' he chuckled. 'I have been mistaken for many things in my life, but never a building inspector! No, I actually need some building work doing and, as I was telling your man around the front, I've been given your name, with the highest possible recommendation that you know exactly what you're doing when it comes to building works. And, I must say, looking around the site, I'm very impressed with what I see. What on earth is holding everything up now you've taken the walls away?' he asked, scratching his head.

'Magic!' Charley joked. 'It's all suspended in mid-air by pure unadulterated magic.'

'Gosh, that's fantastic. I like the sound of that.'

'What can I do for you, Mr Wolfe?' Charley asked, wishing to move on.

'Some of your magic, please,' he said, opening a small attaché case from which he produced a set of drawings. 'The enchanted Walnut Cottage!' he announced with gusto, trying to convince Charley, and himself, of its potential. 'I'd like your keenest price, please, to refurbish and extend the building, as per these approved plans.'

Charley took the drawings and rolled them out across some scaffold boards, and cast a quick eye over them.

'Sorry, Mr Wolfe. There's a lot of work here, and I haven't got time to do it. You're best off finding another builder.'

'I appreciate you can't drop everything else you're doing and start my job straight away, Mr Henry, but can you at least please give me an indication of the costs involved. And then, if it's within our budget, we will wait for you – providing it's not too long, of course.'

'No, sorry. I can't give you a price off the plan, I would need to see the property first.'

'Fair enough. So, can you come over on your way home this evening?'

'Again, Mr Wolfe, I'm sorry. I just haven't got the time.'

Mr Wolfe was so desperate that he poured his troubled heart out to Charley, telling him that 15 months earlier, he and his wife had gone to a public auction to buy their fairytale dream home. What they bought, however, was a property of extreme nightmares. He'd gotten a bit carried away and bid more than they could afford. Coupled with the spiralling architect's fees and the lengthy, arduous battles he had with the council's planning department, this had all taken its toll on him, his family and his finances. He was left with no other alternative but to sell their safe, comfortable home and put their furniture into storage.

'So, Mr Henry, there you have it. We're now living day to day from black plastic bags in rented accommodation.'

'I see,' said Charley, taking a deep breath in sympathy. 'It must be very difficult for you to keep it together.'

'It is, Mr Henry. Very difficult.'

Being a sucker for a sob story, Charley agreed to meet Mr Wolfe at the cottage at 6.30 pm that same evening. The chocolate-box thatched cottage, complete with sweet-smelling roses around the door, had stood peacefully on the edge of Clovers Wood for the best part of 300 years or more.

'Very peaceful spot you got here, Mr Wolfe,' said Charley, casting his eye around the place. 'I can see why you were so drawn to it. Once through those gates you could be in the last century, or even the one before that.'

Wolfe let out a heavy sigh. 'We thought so at first, Mr Henry, but our elation has now gone. The place has become a huge millstone around our necks. We may even have to sell the property if your building costs are too high for us. I don't suppose there is any chance you want to buy it, is there?' he asked, in hope.

'As much as I'd like to, Mr Wolfe, I've got enough problems with a demolition order to contend with.'

As Charley was about to climb into his van, Mr Wolfe pleaded with him to prepare the estimate that evening. Charley was weary from his day's work and said, 'I can't promise anything, but I'll see what I can do.'

'Oh, thank you very much, Mr Henry! I'll collect it from you in the morning.'

'Like I said, I can't promise, Mr Wolfe. Besides, we start work very early,' Charley replied, trying to put him off.

'That's okay. Take it with you, and I'll come to the site you're working on and pick it up there.'

'I'll see what I can do.'

Charley knew he wasn't going to get any peace from this man and so he prepared the estimate and took it to work the following day.

'Look! I don't believe it!' said Jake, as they approached the site. 'That Wolfe bloke, he's only here already! And from the state of him, he looks as though he's been here all night!'

'Have you got it, have you got it, Mr Henry?!' cried Wolfe, striding into the centre of the road before Charley had even parked his van.

'Yes, I've got it,' Charley replied, passing the envelope through the open window.

Whilst Charley parked up, Wolfe tore open the envelope and skipped quickly over the pages until he found the bottom line. A few seconds later, he let out a loud sigh, as if the end of the world had come. 'It's much the same as the others,' he muttered, scrunching the estimate up in his hand.

Charley turned to see Big Jake about to fire up the mixer. 'Don't start that yet, mate,' he whispered. 'I don't want him diving headlong into the drum to end it all. Go and put the kettle on instead, eh.'

Turning back to console Wolfe, who was now sat slumped on a stack of bricks, Charley said, 'I'm sorry we can't do the job any cheaper for you, Mr Wolfe, but we can offer you a nice cup of tea to soften the blow.'

'Do you take sugar, Mr Wolfe?' asked Jake, returning with three steaming hot mugs of tea.

'No,' he replied, taking the tea from Jake and staring hopelessly into the mug to try and find the answers that he so desperately wanted. 'Can you break the project down into two parts, Mr

Henry? One to cover the restoration works, and the other to extend and complete the cottage. What do you say?'

Charley took a deep breath and, exhaling noisily, said, 'I don't really like doing that, Mr Wolfe, cos to do the job piecemeal would make things a bit messy – and more expensive in the long run…'

'I can't afford to do it any other way, Mr Henry. I just can't.'

Charley took pity on him, and so, against his better judgement, he cut the price to the bone and agreed to do whatever was necessary to make the cottage habitable so they could at least move in. The plan was to completely gut the building right back to the bare skeletal structure and start again. However, by the time they had stripped all the walls of the asbestos-clad panelling that had been added over the years to hide the decay, they found that most of the brickwork that formed the skeletal structure had perished and was crumbling to dust.

Mr Wolfe arrived on site to find Charley looking worried, staring into his tea, much like he did the day he came to collect Charley's estimate.

'Problem, Mr Henry?' he asked.

'No, I always look like this, Mr Wolfe, when a job is about to plunge into debt.'

'What are you saying, Mr Henry?'

'I'll show you. Look here, at the walls,' said Charley, poking the internal brickwork with his finger and watching it crumble away to nothing.

Wolfe gasped. 'I thought you were going to work some of your magic for me, Mr Henry?'

'Magic, we can do no problem, Mr Wolfe, but miracles – they're a bit out of my league, I'm afraid.'

'Oh shit. You're beginning to scare me now, talking like that. It all sounds very expensive.'

'I'm beginning to scare myself as well, cos it'll be expensive to sort out.'

Mr Wolfe started to hyperventilate. 'I can't afford to pay you any more money, Mr Henry,' he whined. 'I just haven't got any more and I can't raise any either.'

'I appreciate your honesty, Mr Wolfe, but just give me 10 minutes to think about how best we can deal with this problem.'

'Okay,' he replied, sounding practically suicidal. 'I'll get out your way and walk around the garden for 10 minutes.'

'Ere, I've just seen Wolfe out there, Chas,' said Jake, walking through the door. 'What have you said to him, 'cos he looks as if he's gonna top himself?'

'Well, it's either him or me, Jake,' Charley replied, still thinking.

'I'll go and get the rope from the van and give it to 'im then. Show 'im the big tree down the bottom, shall I?'

'No, not yet, Jake, 'cos I've made me mind up. We'll jack it up and bosh the walls over.'

No sooner had he said that when Wolfe returned, looking like death warmed up.

'Okay then, Mr Wolfe. I've thought about it, and this is what we're going to do. I gave you a price to make this cottage habitable, and habitable it will be. And so, rather than wasting valuable time trying to patch up the unpatchable, we'll bite the bullet, jack the building up, whip all the walls away and rebuild them. It'll be cheaper for us in the long run.'

'Oh, thank you! Thank you so much, Mr Henry! I'll never forget your kindness in our hour of need, even if I live to be a hundred years old, I won't.'

Charley's run of bad luck didn't end there: he broke his shoulder one evening, diving for a ball while playing cricket. Yet, the more serious injury was to a torn ligament in his arm. Being a small village practice, Charley knew his doctor very well, and the doc, knowing what Charley did for a living, informed him that the ligament would take many months to heal properly.

'You must not, I repeat not, under any circumstances, even think about using your arm to work with,' he said. 'You must keep it supported at all times, in a sling.'

'I can't just stop work, Tim. Wolfe would top himself for sure if I did.'

'Wolfe? Who the blinking hell's Wolfe?' the doc asked, frowning.

'You may well ask, Tim, cos we've just demolished most of his house. And the rest of it, we've got it stood up on acrow props, so stopping work isn't an option open to me right now.'

'Oh, I see. Well, you'll just have to supervise, Charley, because that torn ligament is the only thing that's holding your arm onto your torso. Damage it any further and your arm will drop off.'

There was no margin left on Wolfe's job to introduce any more labour without plunging it even deeper into debt. But luckily for Charley, the cavalry was at hand, because his old mate and one-time business partner Butch Weston knew that he was injured and struggling. He came to Charley's rescue and lent a much-needed hand for a few weeks. Butch's young son, Dan, who had just left school, came along for the work experience.

Charley was unsure who was suffering the most: himself, unable to lift his arm unaided above his waist, or Wolfe, seeing his dream cottage jacked up with no walls around it. Every day without fail, Wolfe would come to the site. The mere sight of the cottage, in that state, seemed to send him into a downward spiral. Slouched, he'd shuffle around the job, his hands in his pockets, like a man in serious mental turmoil.

'It's a good job there ain't no buses running past this job,' said Butch, chuckling. 'The state Wolfe's in, he'd probably chuck himself under one.'

'That's what bothers me, Butch,' said Charley, knowing that Wolfe was a man on the edge, running fast out of time, and money.

But, then, for some unexplained reason, Wolfe just stopped coming to the site altogether.

'Where's that rope gone?' asked Big Jake. 'Anyone seen it?'

'Ere, that's a point,' said Charley. 'Dan, go and take a butcher's in the orchard. See if there's anything other than apples hanging on the trees…'

'Perhaps he's just gone on holiday for a couple of weeks?' suggested Ray.

'No, he can't have. He ain't got no money for that, Ray. There's only one place he's liable to go, and that's the lunatic asylum.'

Dan returned looking distressed. 'Quick! Quick!' he cried, breathlessly. 'Out there! Hanging on the trees!' he said, running back out to show them. Everybody stopped work and dashed down to the orchard, expecting to see Wolfe dangling from one of the trees.

'Where? I can't see anything hanging on the trees,' said Charley.

'Nor me,' said Butch, scanning the orchard.

'Are you all blind?' Dan laughed. 'Look harder! The leaves – they're hanging all over the trees!'

'I'll bloody kill 'im!' Butch shouted.

'Not before I do!' yelled Charley.

'Well, you asked me to see if there was anything apart from apples hanging on the trees, and I told you.'

About a week later, Wolfe turned up on site, alive and well. The strange thing was, he was driving a brand-new expensive estate car. Climbing out, he stood tall, positively glowing all over.

'That's gotta be his twin brother, surely?' Charley watched him strut around like a millionaire smoking a big cigar, in a pair of designer sunglasses.

'If it ain't his twin brother,' whispered Jake, 'he must be drugged up then. There's no other explanation for it.'

'Mr Henry!' called the new, confident Wolfe.

'I think you may well be right there, Jake,' said Charley, from the corner of his mouth. 'He's definitely pumped up on something. As if we ain't got enough problems on our hands without dealing with a junkie as well.'

'There's only one way to find out for sure, Chas…'

'How?'

'Ask him to roll his sleeves up, and while you keep him talking, I'll take a butcher's at his arms.'

'His arms?'

'Yeah, it's what they do in films. They look for puncture wounds.'

'I'll have a go, Jake.'

Before Charley could say any more, Wolfe had reached them. In a deep self-assured voice, he asked Charley for a private word.

'Yes, of course, Mr Wolfe. What is it?'

'It seems I've been left an unexpected legacy, and so we're now in a position to pay for everything. Will you please carry on and complete all works for us.'

'Thank fuck for that,' thought Charley, utterly relieved.

'Oh, well done, Mr Wolfe. I would be very pleased to. I'm glad that fortune has smiled on you at last.'

'Oh! Frank! Please call me Frank, Chas,' he said excitedly.

With Wolfe on a high and throwing his money around, Charley marched on with the job. Within a few weeks, the new Norfolk reed thatched roof was finished. Wolfe began bending Charley's ear as to when they could move in.

'Just as soon as it's finished, Frank. It won't be much longer now.'

'It looks finished from the outside, Chas,' he said. 'In fact, it looks absolutely stunning in this nice rich autumn sunshine.'

'It may well look finished from the outside, Frank, but we've still got all the ceilings to put up, plastering, second fixings, kitchen and bathrooms, then there's the tiling, and all the decorating to do as well.'

Wolfe gave a sigh. 'The nights are closing in and getting colder, Chas,' he moaned. 'We're all getting anxious. We can't wait to be settled in our new cottage. We've dreamt about sitting around the cozy inglenook, with the fire blazing up the chimney, roasting chestnuts. But knowing our luck, we'll probably get squatters take possession if we don't hurry up and move in…'

'No, you won't, Frank,' Charley reassured him. 'They would have to go through us first, and we're not about to let that happen. Look, I know it's hard, Frank, but be patient. You've come this far. You'll all be moved in, nice and snug, before you know it!'

Chapter 20

Charley was never offered, nor did he expect, Mr Wolfe to pay anything towards the extra cost involved in underpinning and rebuilding the skeletal structure. He was just pleased to know that Wolfe now had sufficient funds in place to pay the agreed fee to finish the entire job.

The big, romantic inglenook that Wolfe could only dream about sitting around, Charley and the boys did it every day during their tea breaks. They may not have had any chestnuts to roast, but they sure did enjoy the hot buttered toast and scrumptious jacket spuds straight from the burning embers each lunchtime.

Charley was normally the first on site each day. While waiting for the others to arrive, he would usually stir up and rekindle the fire. But one gloomy wet day, as he drove over the hill at the top of the lane, he noticed a thin wisp of smoke rising hauntingly from the cottage chimney. Naturally, he assumed that one of the boys had beaten him to it and was rekindling the fire in the old inglenook. He was about to drive onto the property, when he noticed that it was totally empty of vehicles, which gave him cause for concern. To give himself time to think, he continued on past the entrance and parked in the lane, away from the view from any of the cottage windows.

His first thought was that squatters had taken over the property and so he ran back to warn the others and to stop them from driving in. Once they were all gathered in the lane, Charley pointed up to the spiral of smoke. 'There's some bugger in there, boys,' he said, 'and it isn't any of us lot!'

'Oh blimey!' cried Ray. 'What we gonna do?'

'That's my line, Ray. I was rather hoping one of you lot may have the answers…'

'Don't worry, Chas,' said Jake. 'Foul weather like this, it's probably some old tramp dossing down dry for the night. Not that I blame him, mind. I'd do the same meself to get out of this bloody rain.'

'I know what you mean, Jake,' Ray said. 'I'm getting bloody wet standing around out here.'

'Well, whoever it is, they've kept the fire going for us,' said Graham, the new plumber.

'It might not be a tramp,' said Dan, thinking that something far more sinister was going on.

'You've been watching too much television, Dan,' said Charley. 'This is reality, the real world, not some mass murderer scene, or serial killer on the loose. It's only Wolfe's cottage!'

'All right then, Chas. What d'you think's going on in the real world?'

'Well, I hope I'm wrong', he replied, 'but I've got a horrible feeling that it could be Wolfe's worst fear…'

Butch gave a cheeky chuckle. 'What – like Wolfe's mother-in-law moved in to haunt him, you mean?'

Charley laughed. 'You obviously haven't seen her, Butch, have you? Wolfe was all over 'er like a rash the other day when he showed 'er round the job.'

'Yeah, I noticed that, too,' said Graham. 'Wolfe's tongue was dragging along the ground behind 'er.'

'I can't say I blame 'im,' said Ray. 'I wouldn't have minded being the rash.'

'Enough of that dirty talk, Ray,' said Charley, wanting to get on and deal with the situation. 'Until we know for sure what we're dealing with, we'll assume it's the worst case scenario.'

'Which is...?' asked Butch.

'Squatters,' said Charley. 'That was what Wolfe's worst fear was, not his bloody mother-in-law! Squatters! He was only talking about that the other day, and how he feared them getting in and taking possession.'

'I've got some cream for your rash in my van, Ray.'

'What you talking about? I ain't got no rash.'

'You fucking will have in a minute,' said Charley, 'if we don't get on and deal with that squatter before Wolfe finds out!'

'No problem,' said Butch, chafing at the bit. 'Let's all pile in mob-handed and chuck the bastard out, and then we can have a nice cup of tea before we start work.'

'And what if there's more than one?' said Graham, not wishing to get involved in any rough stuff. 'Why don't we just call the police, and let *them* deal with it? That's what they're there for.'

'No, we can't do that, Graham,' Charley replied, "cos if it *is* squatters in there, and they decide to claim squatters' rights in front of the police, we're bollocksed, and so is Wolfe. The time delay it'd cause would be unthinkable, not to mention the cost of actually taking 'em to court.'

'I know this may sound a bit stupid,' said Dan, 'but why don't you just give Wolfe a ring and see if he's got any bright ideas on the matter? It is *his* cottage after all, and he's got plenty of money now to sort it out.'

'No, Dan. I don't want Wolfe knowing anything about this little episode. The stress would be too much for 'im to handle. Besides, he's still trying to come to terms with the mugging he had by the planning system. The thought of a squatter doing the same would just about finish 'im off.'

After a lot of crazy suggestions, Charley decided that, before going into the cottage blind, that they should carry out a little reconnoitre first.

'No! Sod all that bloody bullshit!' said Butch, frowning. 'Reconna bloody what? Why don't we just creep up to the cottage and have a good butcher's through the windows instead? That way, we'll know just what we're dealing with.'

'But a rec— er, yeah, okay. Good idea, Butch. That's what we'll do, mate.'

So, the boys crept up to the cottage like a crack commando unit.

'Look!' cried Dan, in an excited but muffled whisper. He was pointing to a pair of feet sticking out from an old blanket in front of the inglenook fireplace.

'The cheeky bastard!' whispered Butch. 'You were right, Chas. It *is* a bloody squatter!'

Through a series of gasps, gulps, groans and grunts, they all charged into the cottage and pounced on the sleeping squatter. Overpowered within seconds, he didn't stand a chance, though it didn't stop him from struggling. Still tangled up in the blanket, they forcefully dragged him kicking and screaming outside into the pouring rain.

'If you don't shut up,' yelled Butch, 'I'll give you a bash with this lump of 4x2! See how you like that one!'

Fearing for his life, the squatter obeyed Butch's command instantly.

'What we gonna do now?' asked Dan.

Charley was so anxious to get him off the property as quickly as possible, he cried, 'Chuck 'im out in the lane!'

So, the boys manhandled the squatter down the drive, with his feet sticking out of the blanket. But, as they were about to toss him onto the grass verge, a car rounded the bend and stopped about a hundred yards past the gate. The two occupants seemed very concerned and strained their necks to look at the fiasco.

'Who are they looking at?!' said Butch, about to say something to them.

'Don't worry about 'em,' said Charley, 'we've gotta get rid of this one first!'

'Please don't hurt me!' yelped the squatter from the tangle of blanket.

'We're not going to hurt you,' said Charley.

'We bloody will if you come back!' Butch bellowed.

'Look, we've wasted enough time, so just chuck him down there,' said Charley. 'We've got work to do.'

The bundle hit the ground with a mighty thump before rolling over into a muddy ditch.

'Now piss off!' roared Charley. 'And don't come back, 'cos we won't be so friendly next time!'

Turning their attention back to the car, they saw the onlookers take off at speed; their squealing tyres leaving the smell of burning rubber behind.

Looking back to the bundle on the ground, Butch, a keen country music fan said, 'This reminds me of a song…'

'A song?' asked Charley. 'I don't know any songs about squatters on the ground!'

'No! *Blanket on the Ground.*'

'Oh yeah, *Blanket on the Ground*. I know who sang that, Butch,' Charley said. 'It was old thingy … you know … Kenny Rogers.'

'No, it weren't,' said Ray. 'It was Dolly Parton.'

Graham was about to comment on the matter, when a head suddenly broke free from the blanket on the ground.

'Bloody hell!' cried Big Jake.

'Oh shit!' gasped Charley, with a hand over his mouth. 'What have we done?'

'Oops,' whispered Dan.

'Oh dear. What a dilemma,' said Ray, looking over to Charley.

'A bloody dilemma?' raged Wolfe, as he tried to free the rest of his body.

'Er, Mr Wolfe, I wasn't really going to bash you with a lump of 4x2,' said Butch. 'How about I make a nice cup of tea to make up for it?'

'Stuff your bloody tea!' he cried.

'Anyone else?' asked Butch.

'Yeah, all right, go on then. I'll have one,' said Jake.

'Yeah, and me,' said Ray.

'Have you all gone fucking mad?! Tea? Tea?! Is that all you bloody lot think about?!' yelled Wolfe. 'You just scared the bloody shit out of me!'

'Yeah, and I'm sorry about that, Frank,' said Charley. 'We didn't mean to – it just happened...'

'Well, you bloody did. I'd only just got back off to sleep when you lot burst in screaming like a bunch of bloody mercenaries. I thought you were going to kill me at one point!'

'Where's your manners, boys?!' cried Charley. 'Don't just stand there! Give Frank a hand up!'

'I can bloody manage!' Frank shouted, scrambling to his feet. 'Didn't you recognise my voice then?'

'Er, well, no, Frank, we didn't actually, 'cos you wasn't talking a lot of sense at the time. I can only apologise. We really thought you was a squatter, and that you was going to stake a claim to the place. We was only looking after your interests ... that's all. Perhaps if we'd seen your car parked outside, or, if you had just yelled, stop, it's me, Frank, we wouldn't have evicted you in that way.'

'Look, I was bloody disorientated being woken from a dream like that. I didn't know where the bloody hell I was. You see, my missus dropped me over here late last night, and I bedded down with a bottle of brandy to keep the cold out and then, before I knew it, you lot attacked me!'

'Oh, come on, Frank, we didn't exactly attack you,' Charley said. 'It was more the case that we assisted you in leaving the cottage.'

'It's *my* cottage, for goodness sake! How would you feel if a group of thugs pounced on you in the middle of the night and evicted you from your home?'

'Oh, come off it, Frank! How was we to know it was you wrapped up in that blanket? We had to do something! Why didn't you just tell us you were going to sleep here last night? If you'd only kept us informed, none of this would have happened, Frank.'

Still growling like a wounded animal, Frank grabbed Charley's arm and marched him up the drive. 'Okay, perhaps I should have informed you, but I thought I would have been up in plenty of time ready to greet you.'

'A case of the right hand not knowing what the left is doing, eh, Frank?'

'Yeah, I suppose. I also suppose now is a good time to tell you that, finished or not, we are moving into the cottage today. Is that enough notification for you?'

'Yeah, nice one, Frank. You almost had me going then. Look, I'm sorry if we roughed you up a bit, but I'm glad to see you haven't lost your sense of humour.'

'Sense of humour? I'm not bloody joking! Far from it. I'm deadly serious. In fact, the removal van will be here about 10 am, and we're definitely moving in today.'

'No, no, you can't do that, Frank!' Charley pleaded. 'The place is nowhere near habitable yet. There aren't any amenities here. It's still a building site, for goodness sake!'

'It's my property, I can do what I like – and there's nothing in our contract to say that we can't move in.'

'But why, Frank? Why do you want to subject your family to the torture of living on a building site?'

Frank placed both hands on his head, clearly embarrassed. 'Er … you know that … er… legacy I told you about…'

'Yeah, sort of. What about it?'

Frank was about to explain, when they were distracted by the sound of wailing sirens. When they looked, the lane was filled with policemen. Before they had a chance to think, everybody on site was ordered to put their hands on their heads and then herded like cattle – Frank included – into the gateway.

'What's the problem, officer?' Charley asked.

'We are acting on a report of a gang of men disposing of a body in a ditch outside this property.'

'The car…' said Charley, thinking back.

'What car?' asked Wolfe.

'Oh, that's right, Frank, you didn't see it, did you?'

'All right, enough chatter!' cried the officer in charge. 'Perhaps one of you can explain what you're all doing here?'

'That best be me,' said Frank, removing his hands from his head.

'And who are you?' asked the officer.

'My name is Mr Wolfe, Frank Wolfe, and I am the owner of this property. And this raggedy bunch are my builders. There was no body dumped here today, or any other day for that matter. It's all been a big misunderstanding.'

Frank went on to explain what had happened, and after the police had all stopped laughing, they dispersed and left the scene.

As the boys all drifted back to work, Frank broke the worst possible news to Charley. 'What I was about to say before the police came charging in, was … with regard to my legacy…'

'What about it?' Charley asked, hoping he hadn't spent it all.

'Well, it wasn't as large as I first envisaged. I didn't get as much money as I thought I was going to. In fact, most of the money went on the new car. That's why we're having to move in. We've got no other alternative, because we need to conserve whatever funds we have left otherwise I won't be able to pay you.'

'Look, Frank,' said Charley, shaking his head with exasperation. 'While I do sympathise, it would be impossible for you and your family to live in the cottage. It's nowhere near habitable yet.'

'Oh, that's okay, Chas. We'll just have to rough it for a while, that's all. We don't mind doing that.'

'*You* may not mind, Frank, but what about us? How do you think we could work properly with all your furniture and stuff in the way? The job would never get finished and the costs would spiral out of control. I've already absorbed the cost of the underpinning; I can't afford to lose any more money. You'll have me bankrupt!'

'Ah, well, I've been giving that some thought, Chas. What if we store all the packing cases and most of the furniture in the barn? We'd then only have the beds and the bare essentials to worry about inside the cottage. Would it be possible then?' he asked, like a dog trying to please its master.

'I don't know, Frank. I really don't know.'

'Oh, please, please say yes.'

'I'm not happy about it, Frank … but if there really is no other way, then we'd need to have full autonomy, be free to work anywhere unhindered, inside and out, between the hours of 7.30 am and 5.30 pm.'

'Yeah, yeah … anything you say, Chas. We'll put up with anything you say, and we'll do whatever it takes to make the job run smoothly for you.'

'You do realise you won't have any privacy, don't you, Frank?'

'Yeah, we're fully aware of that, Chas. It's not as if it's for the rest of our lives, is it?'

'Well, that just depends on how long you intend to live, Frank.'

'Oh, I'm going to be around for a long time yet, Chas,' he replied, smiling with relief. 'Don't you worry about that, mate.'

Charley was dreading the prospect. He gathered all the boys together and warned them of the impending disaster.

'Tell him to pitch a tent in the garden,' suggested Big Jake.

'There's always room for a caravan,' said Dan.

'No! It was Billie Jo Spears!' Butch recalled.

Charley frowned. 'What was?'

'The *Blanket on the Ground*,' he said. 'She was the one who sung it!'

'Oh yeah, that's right!'

'How about *Wolfe on the Ground* then, Butch? That'll make a good country song, wont it?' said Jake, laughing.

'Yeah. *We Should've Left Him Tied Up in the Blanket on the Ground* – that's got a better ring to it,' Charley joked.

'Yeah, I'd buy it!' said Ray.

Chapter 21

※

Charley didn't sleep easy that night. He couldn't stop thinking about the diabolical consequences of the Wolfe family moving into the cottage. And when he did manage to drift into an unsettled sleep, he dreamt about some of the bizarre building projects that he had cleared up for Doug Langsdale, bitter and twisted people like Mrs Shorefield and deranged clients like the Bainbridges. He eventually awoke in a cold sweat. As he drove to work that day, he knew he was heading straight into another awful nightmare!

Charley and the boys had been working on site for about two hours when an insignificant-looking small white van pulled into the driveway.

'Hey! Look, Chas!' said Butch, laughing. 'It's Wolfe's removal van!'

As the driver's door opened, so too did Butch's mouth. Wearing a tight-fitting top and a very short miniskirt, the driver swung her long, slender legs out from under the steering wheel, giving all the boys a free show. Knowing that all eyes were on her, she walked slowly around the back and opened the doors.

'Bloody hell!' whispered Butch, watching her lean over and reach inside the van. 'She's bloody gorgeous, she is! Is that his missus then, Chas?'

'Reel your tongue in, Butch. It's not his missus. It's our new plasterer. And she's just getting her laying on trowel out before she starts work.'

'Yeah, in your dreams, Chas!'

'All right then, it's Wolfe's mother-in-law. Or, as you would say, Butch, his worst nightmare.'

'Cor, bloody hell, I wouldn't mind having a few nightmares with 'er. How d'you know who she is anyway?'

'I've seen her over here with Wolfe once or twice before.'

'Yeah? What's her name then? Did you speak to 'er?'

'Yeah, I did, as it happens, Butch. Her name's Gertrude.'

'*Gertrude*? What sort of bloody name's that for a gorgeous bird like 'er?'

'I don't know, perhaps her old man had a sense of humour or something.'

'What did she say then ... er, when you spoke to 'er, I mean?'

'I didn't get the chance to say much, 'cos Wolfe was all over her like a rash.'

'I don't care what her name is,' groaned Jake. 'She could take me home any day.'

'I wish I was that rash right now,' said Ray, seeing her again.

'Hey, Graham!' said Charley. 'Give this dirty sod your cream, will you...?'

'Mother-in-law,' Butch repeated. 'I can't believe it. You sure? What's his missus like then?'

'I dunno, mate. I've never seen her before.'

Wolfe then came out and quickly ushered his mother-in-law into the cottage. The boys, still drooling, sat down on a stack of scaffold boards by the gate and started their 10 o'clock tea break.

'What d'you think he's doing in there with 'er?' Butch asked.

'You need some bromide in your tea, Butch,' said Charley.

'Bromide? What's that then?'

'Oh, it's what they gave all the boys during their national service days.'

'That's good then, isn't it?'

'Yeah, you'll love it, Butch, 'cos it stops you from feeling so bloody randy all the time. You dirty sod.'

The banter was interrupted by Frank's new estate car driving onto site.

'Cor, she's a bit of all right!' said Jake, drawing attention to the driver, as she climbed out the car.

Long, platinum blonde hair right down to her waist, dressed in skin-tight jeans and high heels, she walked slowly over towards the cottage, knowing that the boys' eyes were transfixed.

'Hey, look! The young teenage daughter ain't bad either,' said young Dan, his eyes firmly glued on her walking alongside her mother. She occasionally turned back and smiled at him.

'I don't believe this. What's Wolfe got what we ain't?' asked Graham.

'Well, it sure ain't money, Graham,' Charley replied.

'There's only one explanation for it then,' said Jake. 'He must be a big boy. Come to think of it, he does walk a bit lopsided, don't he?'

'More of a limp, I'd say,' said Butch.

'Hmm. This job might not be so bad after all,' said Ray, licking his lips.

'I hate to spoil your fantasies, boys...'

Charley was pointing to Frank's car – to the back of it, in particular.

'Bloody shit! It looks like a grizzly bear,' said Butch.

'A bloody Yeti more like,' said Ray.

The grizzly Yeti was, in actual fact, a ferocious-looking jet-black dog, which, when left unattended, howled like a wolf.

'Bloody hell, I reckon that could be one of Wolfe's kids, don't you?' said Ray, hearing the spinechilling noise it was making.

Alerted to the racket, Frank flung open a window and hollered out, 'Lay down, Satan! Lay down!'

But Frank's voice got the grizzly thing even more excited, till it began scrabbling at the car windows with its sharp claws.

'That blinking dog must weigh a ton,' said Charley. 'Look at the way it's rocking the car on its suspension!'

Concerned for his upholstery, Frank came charging out from the cottage and ran full pelt towards the car. First, he tried to growl commands, but when the dog didn't respond, he opened the tailgate and let the vicious creature leap to freedom. Much like a wild animal trainer, Frank quickly grabbed hold of the long tethering chain as it spilled out from the back of the car. Thinking he could hold the dog, he wrapped the chain twice around his wrist; but once the dog's feet had made contact with the ground, it took off, almost ripping Frank's arm clean from its socket.

'Heel, Satan! Heel!' cried Frank desperately, tugging at the chain as the powerful dog dragged him, like a stumbling circus clown, down the gravel path towards the cottage.

'Hmm. He seems to have that nicely under control,' Charley jested.

'Who – the dog?' Graham whispered.

'Close your ears, young Dan,' said Charley, hearing Frank screaming obscenities at the top of his lungs.

'I've never heard Wolfe use language like that before, Chas!' said Jake, covering his mouth and laughing.

Somewhat embarrassed by the scene, the attractive young lady walked over and introduced herself.

'You must be Charley,' she said, fluttering her long eyelashes and offering her soft delicate hand in greeting. 'My name is Jane, Jane Wolfe, and this is my daughter, Samantha.'

'I am very pleased to meet you both,' Charley replied, by which time Frank's pitiful cries had faded into the distance.

Charley had only just finished introducing the boys to Mrs Wolfe and her daughter when the dog, and Frank, came back into view. Frank was still holding onto the chain and being dragged across the lawn on a collision course with a sturdy concrete bird bath. Mrs Wolfe, attempting to dismiss the episode as normal behaviour, gave an uneasy forced smile and said, 'Look at them two silly fools. Frank can never resist having a little play with Satan.'

'Yeah,' Charley grimaced. 'I can see he's enjoying himself.'

'The dog looks to be liking it as well,' said Jake, grinning.

'Yeah, they have so much fun together,' said Jane, with a nervous laugh. 'I don't know what Frank would ever do without Satan to play with, I really don't.'

'Get a life maybe,' Butch whispered in Charley's ear.

Anxious to avoid a second lap of the cottage, Frank screamed, 'Jane! Jane! Bring the chocolate! For goodness sake, bring the bloody chocolate!'

'Chocolate?' whispered Big Jake. 'Funny time to want to eat chocolate, ain't it?'

Mrs Wolfe rushed inside to get the chocolate.

'I think it's the sustenance he needs to keep up with the dog, Jake,' said Charley.

Captivated by the spectacle, the boys looked on as both the lovely Mrs Wolfe and daughter raced with a huge family-size bar of milk chocolate to Frank's aid. Walking over to join the boys, shaking her head, was the gorgeous mother-in-law. 'I don't know why they don't just shoot that fucking thing and be done with it,' she said, shocking the boys.

'My sentiments exactly, Gertrude,' said Butch. 'I couldn't have put it better meself.'

She frowned. 'Who's *Gertrude*?' she asked, looking around.

Butch turned and scowled at Charley; Charley just raised his eyebrows and grinned at him.

'What *must* you all be thinking? she said.

'What a prat Butch is for getting your name wrong?' said Jake.

Laughing, she said, 'Oh that's all right, Butch. I've been called a lot worse than that in my time. My name is Polly, by the way. Poll to my friends, and so you can all call me Poll. No, when I asked what you were all thinking, I meant about that bloody dog.'

'Oh right. Yeah. Does it eat people?' Charley asked.

'No. At least I don't think so,' she replied. 'The stupid thing's a bloody chicken.'

'A *chicken*? So, you mean it lays eggs then, Poll?' said Butch, brushing his embarrassment aside with a joke.

She smiled. 'No. When I said chicken, I meant it's a bloody coward. It ain't got no bottle. It's even afraid of its own shadow,' she said, trying to put the boys at ease.

'And what a big shadow it's got, Poll,' said Jake grimacing.

Taking no chances, Graham lit his blowlamp.

'What are you going to do with that?' she asked, frowning.

'Oh, I just want to warm my hands up a bit, Poll, cos I feel the cold.'

'Don't you believe him, Poll. It's cos he's allergic to big dogs!' said Butch.

'Allergic? What – you mean he comes out in a rash or something?' she asked, smiling.

'No – he bleeds when they bite him,' said young Dan.

She laughed.

'Ere, funny you should say about rashes, Poll, 'cos Ray wanted to be one not so long ago,' Butch joked.

'What on earth for? You lot are all barking! Mad as that bloody dog you are. All joking aside, though, if that fucking dog were human, it would've been sectioned under the Mental Health Act long ago.'

Despite their banter, the boys were genuinely concerned for their safety with that thing on the loose. However, after toppling the concrete bird bath that had stood for more than 50 years, Mrs Wolfe managed to lure the beast with the chocolate into the narrow open-ended passageway between the cottage and the garage. While it was busy devouring the family-size chocolate bar, Frank chained it to a flimsy black plastic dustbin and tossed it a huge marrowbone to chew on.

'That should keep him quiet for a while,' he said, puffing profusely from his ordeal.

The Wolfe family went back inside, as though nothing had ever happened.

'Don't worry, lads,' Charley said, trying to lift their sprits. 'What just happened can't be real. Think about it. For starters, nobody in their right mind would ever move their family into an uninhabitable building such as this. And creatures like that evil-looking thing, well, they don't exist in real life, do they? It's all just a big bad nightmare. Nothing to worry about – trust me, lads. The alarm clock will be going off any minute.'

'We can't all be dreaming the same thing!' cried Ray, looking at the dog's jaws crunching the marrowbone, like it were a piece of lightly buttered toast. 'It's enough to make your blood run cold, ain't it?'

'Yeah,' whispered Dan. 'Look at the way it looks at us with those big red penetrating eyes.'

'He's right,' said Big Jake. 'I ain't afraid of no man, but that bloody thing is something else. Look at its fangs. They could rip a man's throat out with just one bite.'

Butch grasped hold of a wrecking bar to use in defence, should the dog get nasty. 'Let's just hope you're right, Chas, and that flipping alarm clock hurries up. It's one thing having to put up with the Wolfes gatecrashing the job, but that flipping dog as well – we'll never be able to work properly around here again with that bloody thing lurkin' about biting lumps off us every five minutes.'

As they all began to get back to work, Dan, keeping a nervous eye on the dog, walked past the end of the passageway. Afraid of being cornered, the dog dropped its marrowbone and sprang to its feet ready for a quick getaway; but in doing so, it unwittingly moved the black plastic dustbin that he was tethered to. Thinking it was under attack from the bin, the stupid dog made a dash for it. But, of course, the dustbin followed, making it run even faster. With no time to get out of the way, young Dan jumped high into the air like Superman and somehow managed to stay up there long enough for the dog and the bin to pass under him.

Yowling, the frightened creature tried to escape the clutch of the clattering bin. Hearing the commotion, Frank ran after it in hot pursuit, calling, 'Satan! Satan! I've got another bar of chocolate for you!'

'Still dreaming, are we?' asked Butch, chuckling in amusement.

Jane Wolfe, young Samantha and Polly came outside and stood alongside the boys in disbelief, watching the dog, the bin and Wolfe almost collide with the oncoming removal truck before disappearing over the hill at the top of the lane.

'What a bloody fiasco,' said Polly, walking back inside in disgust.

Jane just shrugged her shoulders and joined her mother, leaving Samantha consoling young Dan over his near miss with the dog.

'I s'pose the dog's nearing Land's End by now,' said Ray, laughing.

'Yeah, and I bet Wolfe's glad he ain't got hold of the chain this time round, otherwise he'll be down there as well!' Butch added.

Graham shook his head. 'What must the neighbours round here be thinking?'

Charley smiled. 'They probably think it's the council's new high-speed refuse collection. Chuck your rubbish in the bin, as the dog and bin pass your house!'

Chapter 22

The following morning, the boys all met up, ready for work. They daren't set foot on site till they knew there was no sign of the dog.

'Go on, Jake, you're the biggest,' said Charley. 'You go in and see if the coast is clear for us to follow.'

'Piss off, Chas! I ain't goin' in there on my own with that bloody thing skulking lying in wait!'

'What we need is a distraction,' said Butch.

'I've got a better idea,' said Ray, producing a large tin of dog food from the back of his van.

'What are you goin' to do with that – chuck it at him in the hope you knock him out?' said Butch.

'I've got a KitKat in my lunch box?' suggested young Dan.

'Dog food! Chocolate!' said Graham, taking the mickey. 'I don't know why you're all so frightened of it. It's only a dog! Just say boo and it'll run a mile. Just like it did yesterday.'

'Yeah, you're right, Graham,' said Charley. 'Dan, go in there and say boo to it.'

'Me? But why me, Chas?' he replied, sheepishly.

'Cos you've got the knack. You got 'im going yesterday.'

'Oh, come on, Chas,' said Ray. 'You're the guv'nor – show a bit of backbone will ya!'

'Backbone!' repeated Charley. 'I ain't showin' it my backbone, thank you very much. You saw what it did to that marrowbone yesterday.'

'What about our autonomy then?' asked Graham.

'Oh, I think the dog's assumed that, Graham. Don't you?'

Although the boys would walk with caution around the site, every day, they never saw hide nor hound ever again. It was as though they had dreamt the whole thing, just like Charley said.

Apart from a few first embarrassing moments, the Wolfe family's early days in the cottage were just about tolerable. They made every effort to be up and out of the way before the boys arrived and started work each morning.

Samantha became infatuated with young Dan, and followed him around the site with lovesick eyes before she left for school each morning, and again when she came home in the evenings; whereas Jane, she began to bring more and more things into the cottage, making the working conditions very difficult for the boys. They spent more and more time climbing over and moving stuff around than actually working.

As the weeks progressed, the strain began to manifest in Jane. The final straw came when she accidentally drove her car into an open trench. Charley naturally went to her rescue, but she refused to accept any help whatsoever.

'Let him bloody well get it out when he comes home!' she cried, climbing out of the car and slamming the door. 'He put us in this bloody mess, so he can bloody well sort it out!'

She then turned and quickly walked back inside, leaving the car sticking out of the ground like a scene from a disaster movie. Soon afterwards, *Mull of Kintyre* was heard booming out around the site. And when it had finished playing, it was heard again. And then again. After approximately an hour of continual playing, Charley pleaded with Ray, 'For goodness sake, do something before I go and kill 'er!'

'Okay, Chas,' he said, before starting to sing along and tap dance at the same time.

'Yeah, yeah, very funny, Ray, but that's not what I had in mind. I was thinking more along the lines of a power cut maybe.'

Ray winked. 'Leave it to me, Chas.'

With no power in the cottage, Jane gave up and went to bed, and the boys were left to plaster the remaining ceilings in peace.

Frank came home from work about 4 pm. He spotted the car nose down in the trench. 'Uh … has there … I mean, is there a problem, Chas?' he asked, pointing nervously to the car.

'Er, yeah, Frank. You could say that. You see, we've finished all the ceilings, with the exception of your bedroom.'

Frank frowned. 'What's my bedroom ceiling got to do with my wife's car in the ditch?'

'Ah, well, I was coming to that one, Frank. You see, it all started with the car. We offered to get it out for Jane, but then she told us to leave it there, saying that you would sort it later, when you came home. She then went to bed. And so that's why we can't finish your bedroom ceiling. We were rather hoping to get them all done today as well.'

Frank's own nervous tension then began to manifest, till he couldn't hold back.

'Sod her!' he snarled. 'I'll soon get her up, the lazy cow! You just get your plaster ready and leave her to me.'

'Don't be too hard on her, Frank. She's had a lot to put up with just lately. It can't be easy for her living here on a building site like this. I know we wanted to get all the ceilings done today, but given the current circumstances, it's not the end of the world if we leave that one until tomorrow.'

Charley thought that would help Frank compose himself and show Jane a bit of compassion. He couldn't have been more wrong. Frank rushed headlong into the cottage and tore up the stairs in fury. There wasn't anybody on site that didn't hear the furore that followed.

'What the bloody hell d'you think you're doing, holding the job up like this?!' Frank raged. 'They're waiting to plaster this bloody ceiling, for goodness sake!'

After a very heated and colourful exchange, Frank returned, shaking with frustration.

'Excuse my French, Chas,' he said, looking powerlessly up at the bedroom window, 'but there are times when Jane makes me fucking angry, and this is one of 'em. I'm sorry to have to tell you this, but she's refusing point blank to get up.'

Frank had hardly finished speaking, when the bedroom window flew open. Charley and the gang looked up to see Jane glaring down at Frank.

'I'm not holding the fucking job up!' she screamed. 'They can do the fucking ceiling anytime they fucking want to, but I'm fucking well staying in bed! All right! So, fuck off, you waste of space!'

The window then slammed shut, giving Frank no time to reply. Whilst the boys all looked at one another in astonishment, Charley whispered quietly into Frank's ear, 'We can't do that while she's in bed, Frank. You'd best go up and console 'er. Tell 'er we'll leave the ceiling until tomorrow. It's no big deal.'

With his head hung low, Frank let out a huge sigh. 'She won't listen to me,' he said, pitifully. 'You heard her – just do the fucking ceiling. It's her own bloody fault if she gets smothered in plaster.'

The window opened once again, only this time, very slowly. Jane's face appeared, all warm and smiling. 'I'm very sorry you all had to witness that, Chas,' she said, politely. 'I would like very much for you, and your nice men, to come up here in my bedroom, while I stay in bed and watch you do my ceiling. Thank you.' She then closed the window and returned to bed.

Charley looked over to Frank for his interpretation of the situation. 'Just do it,' he said.

So, as bizarre as it may sound, Charley and the boys took the boards and trestles up to the bedroom and made a scaffold over the bed. They then covered Jane and the bed with dust sheets and plastered the ceiling.

From that day on, Jane was a very different lady. She took to walking very provocatively around the job in sexy lingerie each morning, and when she finally changed from the lingerie, she would dress very seductively throughout the day while Frank was at work. She knew exactly what to do to get the boys going.

'She's got to be a lap dancer, ain't she?' Ray whispered.

'A pole dancer's my guess,' said Graham.

'Well, we'll soon find out, 'cos I'm gonna fix a scaffold pole in the lounge tomorrow,' said Jake. 'See what she does with that!'

Jane didn't hold back. She seemed to get enormous pleasure from distracting the boys from working. And she was forever giving them tea, along with the odd suggestive remark or two; much like the day she requested a larger than normal bath be fitted.

'It would be much too big for the room, Jane,' Charley said, sticking his pencil behind his ear and slurping his tea.

'I like big baths, Chas,' she said in a sexy, mischievous voice. 'Just think of all the fun one can have in it. *You* can get in as well if you like. I won't mind.'

Charley almost choked on his tea. 'I'd love to oblige, Jane, but I can't swim.'

'Oh, it's ever so easy, Chas. I will teach you, and I'll make sure you enjoy every minute of it. Just put your trust in me.'

With a deep gulp, Charley replied, 'I'm sure I would, Jane, but I must think of my reputation.'

'Well, I won't tell if you don't,' she beckoned, with open arms and a saucy smile.

'As tempting as that sounds, Jane, I can't, cos I'm a good boy.'

'Oh, that's a shame, Chas, because I don't like good boys; I only like naughty ones,' she said, looking him straight in the eye.

'I'm a naughty boy, Jane, and I like big baths!' Big Jake offered.

'I'm naughtier than him!' hollered Butch, with gusto.

'Look, I'm the plumber, so if anyone's gonna test the bath out, it's me!' shouted Graham.

Of course, Frank had no idea about Jane's erotic daytime behaviour. By the time he came home from work each day, she looked very plain and uninteresting.

As the job was nearing completion, Frank was thinking up ways to reduce his final bill, because he knew he didn't have sufficient funds to settle his account with Charley.

'I think, for what we've just been through,' said Frank, trying it on, 'we should be entitled to some freebies and a big discount. What about it, Chas, eh?'

'I beg your pardon, Frank? Freebies and a discount! You're having a laugh, aren't you?'

'No. I'm not laughing; I mean it. I want you to reduce your bill. It's too high.'

'Reduce my bill? That was the agreed price, for goodness sake. You got to think yourself bloody lucky I haven't doubled it, all the extra work we've done here. We didn't just walk away and leave you in the lurch. We saw the job through to the bitter end, even though I was losing money!'

'Well, I'm not paying you a penny unless I get a good big discount,' he said, raising his voice.

'What d'you think I'm running, Frank, a bloody flea market or something? You can't just sign a contract and then at the end of the job renegotiate the price! If you don't pay up in full, I will put the matter into the hands of my solicitors,' Charley growled.

'Oh, I wouldn't be so quick to threaten me, Charles Henry, because I can make life pretty difficult for you if I want.'

'So, what's new there then, Frank? How can you top moving in on us before the job was finished?'

'Because I'm a customs and excise officer,' he replied, sticking out his chest. 'VAT. Books. Get my drift?'

'Oh yeah, I get your bloody drift all right, Wolfe. Loud and clear. Now you fucking get mine! I won't be intimidated by you, your job, or your colleagues, so unless you settle your account forthwith, in full, I will be forced to make a phone call and have a little blow in your boss's ear. See what he thinks about your threats and debts. I'm sure he would love to know just what a bloody liability you've become for them.'

Jane walked over and butted in. 'Just pay Chas what we owe, you tight bastard! All he's done for us, the least you can do is settle his account!'

'Yeah, Frank, man up and do as your wife says. Honour your debts, 'cos if you make any more stupid threats to me, you'll lose your job for certain.'

Frank started to panic, saying how he was only joking about Charley's books. When Charley didn't respond, Frank started to cry like a baby, and begged Charley not to phone his boss. Frank finally admitted, through floods of tears, that he'd become a very desperate man, clutching at any straw to stave off insolvency. Like the sad and broken man he was, he laid his cards on the table and offered Charley all the money he had to settle his outstanding account. Rather than push Frank into total bankruptcy, where he would get nothing at all, Charley agreed to settle for a proportion of the outstanding monies and put the rest down to experience.

After much reflection, Charley found himself at a major mythical crossroads. Straight across was more of the same: other people's building works and their associated problems. Turning left was to get a 9 to 5 job. Turning right was a mighty leap into the uncharted territory of building and selling his own houses.

So, it was at that point in Charley's life, he changed direction and took that mighty leap into the unknown!

This is the end of *A Few Pennies More*, but it's also the beginning of *A Few Quid More*!

To be continued!